RAPID
FALLS

RAPID FALLS

AMBER COWIE

LAKE UNION
PUBLISHING

Published by Lake Union Publishing, Seattle

www.apub.com

Amazon, the Amazon logo, and Lake Union Publishing are trademarks of Amazon.com, Inc., or its affiliates.

ISBN-13: 9781503904743 (hardcover)
ISBN-10: 1503904741 (hardcover)
ISBN-13: 9781503903869 (paperback)
ISBN-10: 1503903869 (paperback)

Cover design by Rex Bonomelli

Printed in the United States of America

First edition

To Ben, my one.
To Morgan, my always.
To Kim, my spirit.

PROLOGUE

June 1992

The night before my seventh-grade field trip to Rapid Falls, the water-fall that our town was named after, my dad came up to my room. He didn't visit my bedroom often, especially to talk about dead girls, so I remember the way he said my name. His voice sounded like a door I was supposed to open.

"Cara? Do you have a minute?"

I nodded as I stepped back to let him in. I climbed back up to the head of my bed, closing my well-worn novel. My dad hesitated for a moment, then sat. His unfamiliar weight made the bed feel odd, almost unbalanced. He cleared his throat.

"I wanted to talk to you about something. It's really important to stay safe tomorrow. No horsing around, okay?"

I nodded, not completely certain what I was agreeing to.

"The year my class went up, there was . . . an accident."

"What happened?" I blurted. My dad looked startled at my eager-ness, and his expression became guarded. I worried that my despera-tion would shut down our talk. Even at thirteen, I knew that the best way to lose something was to want it too much.

"Sorry," I muttered. My dad rubbed his chin before he spoke again. I could see the semipermanent shadow of motor oil in the lines of his knuckles.

"There was no railing back then, on the side of the cliff, and it's not much of one now. If anyone walks too close to the edge tomorrow, if people start pushing or getting wild, I want you to tell your teacher right away. It's important, Cara."

"Okay," I said slowly. This wasn't the talk I was expecting. The outing was an elementary school rite of passage, a moment that marked the end of being a kid. Our town was too small to have a junior high, so the field trip was the last thing seventh graders did before moving on to high school. I thought my dad was going to tell me how proud he was of me, not lecture me about safety.

My dad continued, "When we went up, the teacher wasn't paying attention. I still don't know why not. She was the one who was supposed to protect us." My dad's voice broke on the last word. It made me realize what he had sounded like when he was a teenager.

I nodded.

He went on. "I forgot my water canteen, so I left the group to go back to the bus. That's when I saw her, writing something in her notebook. Probably a poem. She always wrote poems, you know? I don't know why no one noticed she wasn't with the rest of us. She was at the edge, the part of the cliff that the wind gets at from underneath. There was no dirt under the bank she was standing on, but she couldn't tell. I tried to call out to warn her, but my voice was gone. It felt like my throat was filled with sand."

He pressed his hands together, not meeting my eyes.

"She looked up at me, and then the ground just crumbled beneath her."

My dad blinked, and the skin around his eyes wrinkled like a sheet of aluminum foil. When he opened them again, his eyes were glassy but his voice was firm.

"My teacher must have been right behind me. I'll never forget the way she screamed. It was the only sound I heard. The girl didn't yell at all. Maybe she didn't understand what was happening. Maybe she didn't believe she was about to die."

The way my dad said the words made it seem like they had been stuck in his head since it happened. His classmate had been beautiful, my dad said—long red hair and freckles. There was a note in his voice that I had never heard before. Longing, or something like it. I felt a pang of jealousy when he told me what she looked like. I wondered if my dad thought I was as pretty as she had been.

Years later I spent an evening hunting through the online archives of the *Rapid Falls Times*, looking for pictures of her. The records seemed incomplete, but I found one story on the tragedy, accompanied by a grainy photo of a dark-haired girl with clear skin. Memory is odd, the way it let him rewrite things in his mind. My dad was right about the pretty part, though. Even in the grainy photograph, she sparkled. You could tell she was about to turn into the kind of girl who could devastate a person with her smile. A girl like my sister used to be.

The newspaper account confirmed most of the details my dad had told me. She died in 1963 on a sunny June day. The article quoted two chaperones, their words full of sad confusion. A maudlin poem by the girl about a rose and a bee ran as a sidebar. The news piece concluded by calling it an accident that no one could have predicted or avoided. It didn't put forward a theory about why she had been standing so close to the edge. I wondered if my dad ever told anyone what he saw. I never heard anyone else talk about her in Rapid Falls. It seemed like they forgot.

Her name was Josephine—Josie for short. My stomach dropped when I read that. It sounded so much like Jesse, my high school boyfriend, the boy the whole town believed my sister killed. Even though he's been dead for nearly twenty years now, no one has forgotten him. I guess it's different when someone is murdered. People tend to remember that.

CHAPTER ONE

June 2016

In the pediatric emergency ward, they have customized equipment to keep tiny arms and legs from flailing. I look at my three-year-old daughter, restrained like a prisoner on her way to execution. I feel like I'm going to be sick. They allow only one parent into the X-ray room, and for some reason Maggie insisted it be me. If my husband, Rick, were in here, he would be soothing her with endless renditions of "Baby Beluga." I don't sing. I know that nothing will drown out the fear in either of our minds.

I got the call from Rick in the car on my way home from work. Maggie had collapsed abruptly. Conscious, but unable to walk. Rick rushed her to the doctor, who diagnosed possible meningitis and called an ambulance. I changed course and met them at the hospital. Panic sweat still dampens my lower back.

"Mommy. Please come." Her small voice, full of fear, is worse than a scream. I step out from behind the screen. The technician sighs loudly and the buzzing stops.

"We are almost done, ma'am. Please step back." His voice is laced with annoyance. I ignore him and lean toward Maggie. Her warm brown eyes are swimming in tears. She looks so much like my sister when she's frightened. They both seem certain that I can help, but they are wrong. Most of the time, I'm as helpless as they are. I'm just better at hiding it.

"I don't like this, Mommy. Please make them stop."

"I can't, sweetheart. Just a minute more." My throat closes around the sob I'm fighting to keep inside. I try to let go of her hand, but her grip is too tight.

"Don't go. Please don't go," she whispers. I nod and turn back to the technician, quickly wiping a tear away with my free hand.

"Take the X-ray," I say. "It's okay."

"Radiation. It's against hospital policy, ma'am. Step behind the screen."

"I'm not leaving her." My voice shakes with ferocity. We stand in silence until the buzz of the machine once again echoes in the small room.

I realize suddenly that I said the same words before, almost twenty years ago, in a different hospital. The staff told me to let Anna try to walk alone even after she vomited from the pain of standing. Hospitals always remind me of my sister. She's been in so many of them: first, because of the accident, and later, for all the other reasons. I'm grateful that the staff here is taking better care of my daughter than the other hospitals ever have of Anna, even though my sister and daughter often act the same. Both throw wildly careening tantrums, issue sullen responses to questions, and defy direct requests. Maggie is forgiven for this behavior because she is a toddler. My sister is a drunk who has served time for murder. People don't give her the same amount of leeway.

~

Anna's drinking problem started the day she was released from prison sixteen years ago. She stops once in a while, sometimes long enough to make it seem like it will stick, but it never does. There was a hopeful spell about four years ago, after Anna's drinking had escalated to the point where my mother wouldn't take her calls anymore. I understood my mom's decision even though I didn't feel capable of shutting my sister out in the same way. My phone rang often with requests to rescue Anna from awful situations. One Friday night, a guy I had never met called to say that he was leaving her at the hospital. She had cut her head, and they couldn't stop the bleeding without stitches. When I arrived, the guy was gone, and Anna didn't remember what had happened or who he was. Not that it mattered. I was grateful, in a strange way, for the call. I needed to talk to Anna, but I'd been dreading the conversation. I had just found out I was pregnant.

I contemplated trying to talk to her in the car as I drove her home from the hospital. Then she passed out. I turned on the radio so I wouldn't have to hear the hollow thud of her head hitting the window when we went around corners. She was too drunk to hear my big news, and I knew it was better for Rick to be there when I told her. Back then, he was kinder to my sister than I was. He still had hope.

A few days later, we met at a greasy spoon diner around the corner from her house. The server filled Anna's and Rick's cups with steaming coffee. I shook my head when she tried to do the same to mine. Anna turned to me with her eyebrows raised. Her mascara was clumped on her eyelashes like black glue, but the question in her eyes was clear.

"Are you okay?"

Rick squeezed my hand under the table, and I took a deep breath. "Anna, I'm pregnant."

Her face went blank.

"We are both thrilled," Rick said. She turned her gaze to him, then nodded, picking up on his cue.

"Of course! Congratulations." She tilted her coffee cup, as if toasting us. A brown rivulet slopped over the side.

"Thanks, Anna."

She seemed to be struggling to think of something else to say, and the silence between us made me feel like I was sitting across the table from a stranger.

"What a big change for you," she finally blurted.

And you, I thought.

"Yes. It will be." I looked down at my menu so I wouldn't have to meet her eyes.

"Look, Anna, I have a crazy idea." Rick sounded excited. "Being a dad is a big job. I've got nine months—"

"Seven and a half," I interrupted.

"Yeah, seven and a half, to prepare. I need to get back in shape. I want to run a marathon. You used to run, right?"

Anna nodded.

"Want to join me?"

The blank look reappeared on my sister's face. I took a sip of water to hide my discomfort. I expected Anna to roll her eyes or worse. Instead she smiled. It made me remember the look on her face when she used to cross the finish line.

"Okay. Let's do it."

"Yes!" Rick fist-pumped the air.

"Are you going to do it too, Cara?"

Fatigue had been weighing heavily on me for weeks, but I smiled at my husband and sister. I couldn't let the two of them train alone.

"I'll walk while you two run. You can loop back and pick me up on your way home."

We decided that we would have a standing breakfast date together too, every Sunday. Several weeks into training, just as I started feeling sick in the mornings, I began to see a glow in my sister's cheeks that I hadn't seen since her track meets in high school. She ran every day, though Rick's schedule required us to go out only five times a week. She kept going even when Rick's old knee injury and my nausea forced us both to quit. I was relieved when Rick threw in the towel. I had been trying to figure out a way to say it, but the training had been taking a lot of time from our evenings together. Rick and I cheered her on from the sidelines during her first five-mile race. I didn't say it out loud, but I wondered if Anna would celebrate her victory by drinking.

Instead she kept at it. The next month, Anna signed up for a half marathon and finished it. Then she committed to a marathon and finished that too. We invited her for a backyard barbecue to congratulate her. As she settled at the patio table on the back deck, she beamed. I couldn't remember ever seeing her so happy.

"Running has changed my life, you guys."

I was huge by that point and couldn't help casting a look over her lean body. I was glad that Rick didn't seem to be paying attention. He seemed focused on the sizzling meat on the grill.

"That's great," I said.

"When I'm running, I don't want to drink."

I smiled, slightly surprised, and clinked her glass of cranberry and soda water against mine. It seemed like a good sign that Anna was finally acknowledging her dependence on alcohol. She was thirty-two. She still had time to turn things around.

"I knew it!" Rick crowed as he flipped the steak. He had been listening after all. "Endorphins beat booze every day of the week."

I laughed.

"It's kind of true, though," Anna said. "Thank you, Rick. I really don't think I could have done this without you."

I felt something surge through me as my husband grinned at my sister, but I smiled too.

"We almost ready to eat?" I stepped between Rick and Anna to take a look at the grill. Rick turned to me with a proud expression on his face. I could see the triumph that came from rescuing Anna, and I knew how powerful the feeling could be. I hoped he was right, but I felt a little sick. I wasn't sure that anything could save Anna from herself.

In the weeks that followed, she seemed determined to prove me wrong. We went crib shopping together. She bought books with women and moons on the covers to prepare for my baby's birth. I didn't have a lot of close friends, and Anna was sober and ready to help us for the first time in our entire adult lives. I almost felt like I could count on her. Then, days before my due date, Anna mentioned casually during Sunday brunch that she'd had a beer the night before, after she finished her shift at the bar. I pushed back my empty plate as she spoke, feeling Rick's body stiffen beside me.

"Just one. A lot of guys who work there are former alcoholics, but they drink once in a while. They totally keep it together. I think I can too." Anna rolled her shoulders. "It's been hard to sleep lately. The beer really helped."

"Seriously, Anna?" The edge in Rick's voice made a woman at the next table turn in our direction. I signaled for the bill and sighed. I didn't want to see Rick's face when he realized that he couldn't help my sister. No one could.

I turned to Anna, trying to stop Rick from speaking. I knew he was angry, but I was too tired for a scene. "That's a big step for you."

"Do you honestly think you can drink again?" Rick's voice was even louder than it had been.

"Yes. I really think I can." Anna was calm, as if she believed what she was saying. As if she couldn't tell how angry Rick was.

"Be careful, Anna." I touched Rick's arm. "Let's go, sweetheart."

"Cara!" Rick's jaw was tight, but I patted my rounded abdomen pointedly.

"Please, Rick. Let's talk about this another time."

He breathed in sharply, then rose to pay the bill without saying goodbye. I kissed Anna on the cheek.

"Take care, Anna."

"You too! Call me if you feel anything. At this point, any sign could be the real thing!" she said.

I smiled. This was my moment, and I wouldn't let her ruin it. "I will."

As we stepped outside into the sunshine, Rick spoke. "She's making a mistake, you know."

"Maybe."

"Definitely. It's a joke. Why does she want to go back to the way she was living? She was a mess."

"I don't know, Rick. Maybe she can have a drink without losing it all again."

Or maybe she needed to drink to stop herself from remembering all the awful things she had done.

"It's a terrible decision, Cara. She's making the wrong choice."

I heard the betrayal in his voice. Rick hated people with no self-control, and he hated being deceived. It was something we had in common. As it turned out, Rick's prediction about Anna had been correct, disastrously so. Anna's first drink led her right back to where she had started and then dragged her down deeper than I ever thought she would go. A week after her announcement at the diner, Anna showed up at the hospital while I was in labor, so drunk that she tripped and fell onto my bed and nearly pulled out my IV. Security escorted her out. One of the happiest moments of my life was shadowed by shame. When my newborn daughter was placed in my arms, I promised her that she would never feel like trash.

Three weeks after Maggie was born, Anna stumbled into our house, drunk at three o'clock in the afternoon. It was the first time she had met our daughter, and I was glad Rick wasn't there to hear her ask if she could hold her new nephew. The late-night phone calls and requests for money I had been fielding since our daughter's birth were enough to turn Rick's patience for Anna to disgust. Between managing Anna's needs and the demands of our new baby, I was too busy to find a way through his growing contempt for my sister.

He told me that I should cut off contact with her for good when she failed to show up for Maggie's first birthday. I nodded and said that I would think about it, but I knew I could never stop speaking to my sister. Rick thought he understood everything about Anna, but he couldn't. He didn't know what it had been like for us, growing up in Rapid Falls. I made sure of that. Rick was a city kid from a wealthy family and had graduated from a prestigious art school. When we met he was about to start a job at a fast-rising snowboard and skateboard company run by classmates from his private high school. Everything came easy to Rick. I didn't want him to know how different it was for us, given where we'd come from and what we'd been through. I knew that telling him more about Anna would reveal things about myself that I never wanted him to see. Anna's choices brought awful things upon her, but I was someone who had earned a good life. Nobody thought Anna deserved happiness. Not after they found out what happened to Jesse.

I was never sure if the accident was the reason that Anna later became suicidal or if it was just one piece of the puzzle. What changed that tipped her over the edge? Was it Rick's disgust with her? Or my lack of attention? Rick blamed her actions on the alcohol, and my mom backed him up. She sent us articles about how addicts deaden their ability to be happy, changing their serotonin levels with the constant influx of poison. My mother was convinced that after sixteen years alcohol had simply dissolved Anna's willingness to live. It was nobody's fault but her own.

Anna's first attempt was a year ago. Her boyfriend phoned 9-1-1 after he stumbled over her unconscious body on the bathroom floor of her apartment. The boyfriend told me, right before he left me alone with her in the emergency room of the hospital, that it was an accidental overdose—too many antidepressants combined with cheap liquor. I wanted to believe that it was an accident, but I was furious to learn that Anna had been drinking at all. Just days before, she had assured me over the phone that she'd been sober for thirty days, and I had accepted her words without question. I had been too busy to do anything else but pretend she was okay.

While I sat in the uncomfortable vinyl seat by her hospital bed, Anna admitted that she had never really stopped drinking, that what happened was not by accident. Her boyfriend had threatened to leave her, she said. She didn't know what else to do but drink a fifth of vodka and swallow a bottle of painkillers. I was mad that she had lied to me, but I asked her gently why she hadn't called me, why her first instinct had been self-destruction. I must have failed to cloak my anger. She stopped talking. We sat in silence as we waited for the hospital psychiatrist. I bit back words about how futile her actions had been: that despite her dramatic gesture, her boyfriend had left her anyway. I wanted to tell her that maybe the problem wasn't that he was gone but that she had chosen such an awful person to begin with.

First minutes, then hours ticked by. Emergency rooms can't discharge a suicide attempt without an okay from a mental health professional. We needed a psychiatrist to evaluate her and devise a treatment plan before they would let her go. I wanted to leave, but a good sister would never do that. No matter how many times life gets turned upside down.

When the psychiatrist finally walked in, I was surprised to feel a wave of optimism. Maybe this doctor would have the solution for my sister. Surely someone would help her now. My hope faded when the doctor began rushing through his questions.

"So you wanted to die?" he began in a monotone without a greeting. Anna took his blunt tone in stride.

"Yes," she muttered, staring at the grubby drop-ceiling panels above her. He ticked a box on his form.

"History of substance abuse?" he asked, looking down at his clipboard.

"Yes." She plucked at the cheap blanket draping her body.

13

"Drugs? Alcohol?"

"Both."

"Still thinking of suicide?"

Anna paused, then turned her head to look at him. We all knew what the correct answer to his question was. "No," she said clearly.

"Great. I'll draw up the paperwork for discharge." He turned to leave. Anna had made his job simple.

"Is that true?" I asked, loudly, before he was out of earshot.

Anna shrugged and sighed. "It's not like anyone cares."

"I care."

She shrugged and looked down again. I couldn't blame the doctor for wanting Anna gone. I felt the same way about wanting her to stay. If she was in the hospital, I knew she was safe. Contained. Not my responsibility.

I drove her home and then called her every day for the next week, despite her clipped replies when she bothered to answer. I started to think I should heed Rick's advice to leave her alone. Then, back at work one day, I found a gift basket on my desk. It was full of my favorites: chocolate-covered almonds, pistachio biscotti, and a bottle of buttery chardonnay. A handwritten note read:

Thank you for coming to my rescue. Again.

The gift seemed like a turning point. Anna stopped drinking for six months and went back to Alcoholics Anonymous meetings. She started running again. She came by more often, and she was sober when she showed up. Rick taught her how to make sushi one lazy Sunday afternoon with beautiful cuts of salmon and tuna from a local high-end grocery store. When the evening sunset caught her glowing face, I thought we would be able to put it all behind us. Maggie climbed up on her lap and patted her cheeks. I could see that Anna was thinking the same thing: the worst was over. She told us that she wanted to find a place closer to us and move out of her low-income housing unit. I said that I would do anything to help her move. I hated her neighborhood and wanted her close by again. The last time I had dropped off groceries for her, I had nearly stepped on a needle.

Anna hugged Maggie close and told us that she wanted to be a real aunt, finally. Maybe even start giving Rick more time for his freelance design work by babysitting Maggie. Rick and I had smiled brightly, though he caught my eye for a fraction of a second to express his hesitation. We had a long way to go before we'd trust Anna with Maggie. We had never been able to trust her with anything. Still, I felt a swell of hope that this time it was going to be different.

It wasn't. The second time she attempted suicide, I found her. It was a Saturday afternoon in December; we'd had plans to go out for coffee and gift shopping. I had been unable to find space in my schedule so it had been nearly two months since I'd seen her. She didn't answer when I knocked, so I opened the door. I found her sitting alone at the kitchen table in the dim apartment.

"Hi, Anna. Anna? What's going on? Are you ready to go?"

She grinned at me goofily and my stomach sank. Something crunched under my feet as I walked through the cluttered room. When I was only a few steps away from her, my nose picked up the scent of the partially digested alcohol. My sister always drank vodka because she thought that no one could smell it on her breath. She was wrong.

She looked up at me slowly, the clumsy smile still pasted on her face. "Cara, I think I hurt myself." She shifted her body to the left and extended her foot, like a suburbanite gamely trying yoga. I could see a dark stain on her heel.

"Okay," I said, flicking a switch. The overhead fluorescent light made the blood appear redder and blacker, like she had smeared globs of cherry jam or tar onto the sole of her foot. In the light, I could see thick bloody footprints leading from a broken glass on the dirty linoleum floor to where she was sitting. And a vial of empty pills on the table.

"Oh, Anna." I reached for my phone. "What have you done?"

Anna had needed stitches and a stomach pump. That time, the same beleaguered hospital psychiatrist had recommended outpatient rehab. Rick and I offered to pay for it. Rick had been reluctant at first, but I convinced him that it would help. I was wrong. Anna went to one session and then stopped. We had not been able to secure a refund.

The third time was last month. The call came just after I had settled on the couch beside Rick, Maggie safely in bed. Even though it was a holiday weekend, our plans for the night involved little more than a bottle of wine and a movie. Well, my plans involved wine. We were both tired. Work had been busy for me, and Rick was exhausted from full-time Maggie duty. People told me that having a kid changes your life, but they never mentioned how dull it becomes. Of course, if I had a choice, I would never have traded dull for Anna's kind of interesting. I was about halfway through my first glass when the phone rang.

"Who is it?" said Rick as I glanced at the screen.

"Unknown," I said.

"Hello. This is, uh, Bert." An unfamiliar voice, thickened by a strong Eastern European accent.

I struggled to place the name. Probably a constituent who had managed to weave through the layers of electronic switchboards at our office. Working as an assistant to the state representative for the environment meant being available all the time, but I was still surprised to field a call on a long weekend. Most politicians went to cottages or vacation homes on their breaks, too far away to make glaring errors in policy or commit a publicly recorded blunder.

"This is Cara Stanley. What can I do for you?" I used my professional tone.

"Yes, Cara Stanley. I, uh, am calling because of Anna. Anna Piper."

My stomach lurched. Bert. The owner of the house where my sister rented a dingy basement suite. I remembered shaking his hand a few months ago, right after Rick and I had cantilevered her musty box spring into the small space. He seemed like a nice guy, one who shouldn't have to deal with Anna.

"Go ahead." The wariness in my voice was obvious. I reached for my wine, took a sip, and tried to soften my tone. "Is everything okay?"

"She's . . . not doing so well. We heard noises. I go downstairs to check. She's been drinking." The man seemed pained to relay this to me, as if he was betraying some kind of sacred landlord-tenant code. "She's okay, but . . ." He trailed off. He didn't have to say anything else. I knew what my sister was like when she was drunk. "I saw . . . pills. She has pills."

I sighed, then took another gulp as I stood. "I'll be right over."

"Okay. That sounds fine." Relief flooded through his voice. Anna was no longer his problem. She was mine: always mine. I hung up.

"Let me guess. Anna?" Rick asked.

"Her landlord saw pills. She isn't responding to him," I said, feeling a twinge of guilt at my exaggeration. "I need to get over there." I walked to the door, knocking one of Maggie's tiny shoes off the rack as I reached for my own. A small plastic dinosaur flew out, and I smiled despite myself as I remembered her carefully tucking it inside earlier, telling me she was putting it to bed for the night. Rick followed me.

"Are you sure you want to do this again?"

I nodded, forcing myself to meet his eyes. "She's my sister, Rick."

"I know." He looked at me carefully. "Is she okay?"

"I hope so."

"I can't believe this is happening again. I don't know whether to be scared or embarrassed for her. I thought after last time . . ." He sighed. I kissed him on the cheek and spoke before the next question came.

"Maybe she's just drunk." I grabbed my keys and twisted the doorknob. "I'll text you."

I walked into the garage and took a deep breath as I sat in the quiet car, steeling myself for what was to come. Anna was not good at life, but I was. I could do this. Maybe she would see that things couldn't keep going this way. Maybe the third time would end things once and for all. The summer streets were quiet, and I got to Anna's house in less than ten minutes. I pulled over, noting with relief that the main floor was dark. I didn't want to deal with Bert. I walked to the back to my sister's entrance. I opened the unlocked door and let myself in without knocking.

"Anna?" No answer. Maybe she'd gone out. Her boyfriends came and went so quickly that I didn't know if she was dating anyone, which would make tracking her more difficult. A faint orange glow from the streetlight in the alley shone in the window, guiding me to the light switch in the hallway. I clicked it. The place smelled faintly of mold— not overpowering, but enough to make you think it had been a long time since anyone had bothered to open the windows. A furry animal scuttled past my feet. My heart thumped in relief as I realized it was a cat. I didn't know Anna had gotten a pet. I had been too busy to visit since the last crisis six months ago, but we spoke once a week on the phone. I thought it was enough to keep her safe. Wrong again.

"Anna?" I called as I peered in the bedroom. A small lamp glowed in the corner. I could see her shape huddled under a new comforter on the bed: white with a sweet repeating pattern of red cherries. It looked like she was trying to make the place less dingy, but it wasn't working.

"Anna, what's happening? It's Cara."

"Cara?" she said. Even in the low light, she looked terrible. Her eyes were red and bloodshot as she squinted to focus. She looked ten hard years older than thirty-six.

"When did you start drinking again? You told me last weekend that you've been sober since you left rehab."

No response. Her loose features slowly began to rearrange themselves into a coarse, childish frown. I could tell she was trying to come up with a convincing lie, so I kept talking to save us both the trouble.

"How much have you had to drink tonight? Have you taken anything?" I could hear the impatience in my voice and something else too. I was numbed. Her second suicide attempt had been far less severe than the first. She had taken half a bottle of pills and left the rest spilling out on the table, like a prop in a bad play. People who really want to die don't take pills like that; they keep swallowing until they're gone. Anna was calling out for help that she wasn't ready to accept, and I couldn't keep playing along. Rick was right. Something had to change.

"I can't . . . remember." She turned over on her side, letting her arm loll off the bed. My gaze dropped to the floor below her outstretched fingers. A scattering of pills dotted a pile of dirty laundry.

"How much did you take, Anna?" She turned her face into the light. I saw bruises and dried blood. "Oh my God. Did someone hit you?" I rushed to her side as my eyes scanned the room again in sudden panic. Her landlord hadn't said there was anyone else here, but someone could be hiding in the closet. Then I noticed the nightstand. The corner was brown with dried blood. She must have rolled off the bed at some point and hit her head.

"Did you fall?" My words were meant to be neutral, but it sounded like I'd just accused her of losing control of her bowels.

She seized on my scorn with drunken righteousness. "Why are you even here, Cara?" she slurred. "Nobody cares. You don't care." I patted her hand reassuringly as I pulled out my phone. I had to care. Or at least try.

"Hello, 9-1-1. Fire, emergency, or police?"

"Emergency. I need paramedics. My sister just tried to kill herself." *Sort of,* I thought silently. "Again," I said out loud. The paramedics were brusque when they came to collect my sister. They seemed tired of her too. I took the familiar route to the emergency room, following behind

19

the ambulance. Anna looked sweaty and distracted as they wheeled her in under the ugly lights.

"You should have let me die, Cara," she said belligerently. A tired nurse straightened Anna's arm, trying to fit a blood pressure cuff onto her thin limb.

"I can't do that, Anna. I would never let anything hurt you." I squeezed her hand tightly, overearnestly. The nurse gave me a small sympathetic smile. That night, the psychiatrist admitted her for overnight observation. They made up a cot for me, and I slept fitfully beside her. They released her the next day with a piece of paper that listed AA meetings in the area.

~

That was three weeks ago. We haven't spoken since. If I had a regular sister, I would have been able to call her this afternoon when Maggie collapsed. For once, Anna could have supported Rick and me as we waited for the results from Maggie's testing.

As the doctor stares dolefully at the X-rays pinned to the light box, I'm thinking about spending an even more miserable night at the hospital with Maggie. Then the doctor breaks into a smile.

"I'm not seeing anything on these films, which is a fantastic sign. All our tests have come back negative: meningitis, strep bacteria, polio." She speaks brightly, as if she's not rattling off a list of my worst nightmares.

"So what is it?"

"The flu!" the doctor says, and I find myself cautiously returning her smile, though I am confused. "Kids grow so fast that some viruses can actually present in their hips and knees. It's painful, which is why she is having problems moving around, but it's completely normal."

"What is the treatment?"

"Rest, fluids, and good healthy food. Soup, or whatever she will tolerate, and lots of liquids. Keep her on the ibuprofen for now, and it should resolve in the next day or two."

"Okay. Thank you." I take Maggie's small body in my arms and walk back toward the waiting room.

I see relief flood through my husband's eyes as we turn the corner. I go over the doctor's simple instructions with him: let her sleep, prevent dehydration, and never forget that the things you don't suspect can hurt you the most. The doctor didn't tell me the last part. I figured that out for myself a long time ago.

CHAPTER TWO

June 1997

A mechanical hum woke me. I blinked hard, trying to figure out where the noise was coming from and where I was. Pain stabbed my forehead as I turned to the left, where a faint glow of light seeped under a door. A blocky shape beside me beeped, and I realized I was connected to it by a long line clipped to my finger. I turned to the other side, fighting dizziness. A large window was covered with pale green curtains. I was in the hospital. My body ached like I'd been violently tossing and turning all night. I've always been a restless sleeper, but I never felt like this. Both times Jesse and I managed to be away for long enough to fall asleep together after sex, Jesse compared the experience to lying with an oversize, easily startled squirrel.

"But a sexy one," I had said, nuzzling his neck. "After all, squirrels know where to find the best nuts."

"Prove it," he said, shifting his hips toward me as he laughed. That was my favorite laugh: the one that spilled out because of something I said. I could tell he loved me every time I heard it.

The thought of Jesse made me jerk upright in bed, only to find that my other arm was also tethered to a machine by a plastic tube. Jesus. What had happened? Even in the dim light, I could see that my arm was covered in angry bruises. I spotted a call button and reached toward it, straining the cords that bound me. Summoning the nurse never looked this clumsy on TV. Seconds after I pressed it, I heard footsteps and voices out in the hallway.

"She's awake now. I need a minute, and then you can come see her." The door opened and light flooded in from the hallway. I caught a glimpse of my dad outside. He looked terrified. A jolt of fear hit me as I remembered the sound of metal destroying metal. And screams.

"Hi, Cara. I'm just going to take your blood pressure." The middle-aged nurse looked familiar as she smiled kindly. "I'm Sandy's mom. You're going to be okay." Sandy was Anna's best friend. I had seen her at the prom last night. Prom.

"What happened?" I asked her as the band squeezed tighter around my arm. I could hear the fear in my voice. So could she.

Her smile faded. "There was a car accident."

"Is everyone okay?"

She looked down, but I saw the tears fill her eyes. The ripping sound of the Velcro as she loosened the cuff made me wince.

"All done. Blood pressure looks good. I'm going to send your dad in now. And the . . . I think Sergeant Murphy wants to speak with you as well."

I stared at her as she walked out of the room. What was I supposed to say to the police? The whole point of prom night was to avoid them.

～

Last night was supposed to have been the biggest night of my life. Prom began the same way every year. Before the dance, all the graduates draped themselves in overpriced dresses and rented tuxes to march around the hockey rink turned dance floor with nearly the entire town in attendance. Last night the procession had been both exciting and dutiful for me. Jesse and I had seen so many of our older peers go through the ritual that in some ways it felt as if we had already done it ourselves, like we'd seen the photos before our parents even took them. At the same time, I was almost sure he felt the same way as I did, that prom night was our first real step toward the future where he would become my husband. We weren't engaged yet, but his mom had hinted to me a few months ago that he already had a ring. When we walked past Anna, I beamed at my sister, and she smiled back, though a bit slowly. No surprise. Anna was always jealous. I would be the first to graduate, the first to begin a real life.

After we finished our promenade, our parents and relatives filed out. A familiar guitar riff reverberated through the room to kick off the dancing portion of the evening. Anna appeared beside me.

"Want to dance?" She grinned mischievously and I returned the smile. She knew I couldn't resist our favorite song by Meat Loaf. "The DJ didn't want to play it, but I insisted. I'm sorry about earlier."

"It's okay." I brushed off the memory of our argument. It didn't matter. Tonight I just wanted to have a good time.

Anna and I had been doing the same dance to the song since I was in seventh grade, when we won first place in a school talent show. We launched into it instinctively. The students around us stopped and formed a circle, laughing and hooting, even though most of them had seen us perform the same routine at least half a dozen times before. When the song ended, we stood still, panting and laughing, as the crowd cheered. Jesse's best friend, Wade, gave us a long wolf whistle that made me grin.

"One more?" I pulled her into my arms playfully, initiating a stagey waltz to the orchestral chords of Bette Midler.

"Only because you love this one so much." She took my hand, and we moved across the floor. As we slow-danced in and around the people from Rapid Falls we had known all our lives, happiness rose like a bubble in my chest. Anna must have sensed it, because she pulled away so she could look in my eyes.

"You are my hero, Cara. I hope the next year for you is amazing. Everything is going to change so much after tonight." Her eyes welled with tears.

"Thanks, Anna. That means a lot."

Anna was my designated driver so Jesse and I could enjoy the night to the fullest. I promised to come back to do the same for Anna and Sandy the next year. Drinking and driving was a big deal in Rapid Falls. Each year we had an assembly a week before prom to remind us about making good decisions. It was how our parents and teachers assured themselves that they had done what they could to protect us. The afterprom party was held every year at the Field, a big property about thirty minutes out of town up a long dirt road. It had been bought and cleared by some guy from the city. No one in Rapid Falls had heard from the man in years, and nobody asked questions about his whereabouts. It was the best party spot in town. No one wanted to ruin a good thing.

On an average Friday night, if you wanted to get back from the Field, you drove drunk, caught a ride with someone else who was driving drunk, or stayed sober. Very few people chose the last option. On prom night, however, we made sure that our drivers did so. It was important that the graduating class was responsible. In Rapid Falls, prom night was the closest most people came to experiencing celebrity. It wasn't supposed to end in a hospital bed. Something had gone wrong—really wrong.

~

My dad walked in, his face as white as frostbitten fingers. A sickening thud hit my stomach. Was Anna dead?

"Cara." He put a hand on my forearm.

"Where is Anna, Dad?"

"She's . . . she's in pretty rough shape. They had to airlift her to Nicola. Your mom is with her."

Images of icy water. Darkness. Screams. Blood. Jesse.

"Oh my God. Where is Jesse?" My voice tightened around the words, and I had to choke out the last syllable.

My dad bowed his head. I didn't want him to say it aloud.

"He . . ." He shook his head.

"No, Dad." My voice didn't sound like it was coming from my body. Silence filled the room. I saw a windshield with nothing in view but black water. "We went into the river."

My dad shuddered as he nodded.

"This is all my fault," I said.

His grip on my arm felt hard enough to bruise. I gasped.

"Don't you ever, ever say that, Cara. You got Anna out. You pulled her out of the water alone. I don't know how you did it, but you saved her life." His eyes were full of fire and fear.

I nodded, waiting for grief to consume me, but I felt nothing.

"But not Jesse," I said.

"No, not Jesse. There's . . . one more thing, Cara." My dad tried to put on a reassuring smile. "Sergeant Murphy was here. He needs to talk to you. I told him that you'll come by later. After we see Anna."

"Okay," I said dully.

"It's not good, Cara. They think . . . well, they've found alcohol in Anna's blood. Drugs too. It looks like she was drunk, high. I don't know." His voice caught on the words. "She was supposed to be your designated driver. She was supposed to stay sober. What happened, Cara?"

"I don't know," I lied.

CHAPTER THREE

June 2016

The morning after Maggie's hospital visit, I wake at 5:00 a.m. and roll over to look at my phone. There is nothing urgent in my in-box, just the standard requests for meetings and some draft policy to review. Only one message is personal. Debra Black, an old classmate, is trying to put together an organizing committee for our twenty-year reunion at Rapid Falls High. I delete the message immediately. Sometime in between my song-filled oatmeal breakfast with my daughter and my train into work, all hell breaks loose. I have thirty-six new emails and a dozen missed calls on my phone by the time I get into the office.

I piece it together quickly. The *Fraser City Tribune*'s website had published a piece on the new natural gas extraction plant, showing only one-third of the current workers were local. Unfortunately, my boss, Larry, was also quoted, saying, "Above all, natural gas is an economic booster for local communities." His furious emails to me demanded that I figure out where the *Tribune* had gotten the conflicting information. When I was a teenager, I had dreamed of running for office, but my history in Rapid Falls had made that impossible. On days like today, when Larry has to wear mistakes so publicly, I'm glad that Anna made me change course. It's a lot easier to be behind the scenes when things go bad. And I was good at putting out fires.

My assistant, Michelle, rushes in with a coffee and a frown. "Did you see the story this morning?"

"Yes. I've been dealing with it for the last hour. Where have you been?" I'm taking a calculated risk that she was late again, later than I was. It's important in my job to keep up appearances.

She looks down sheepishly. "Transit was slow."

I sigh and reach for the coffee. "Just get Henry on the phone. I need to find his source."

"Sure." She walks out of the office.

My phone buzzes a few minutes later. "Henry is on line one."

I click through. "Henry, we have to stop running into each other like this." I laugh as I take a sip of coffee. I never let anyone see when they have landed a blow.

Henry laughs too. He knows the game. "Of all the natural gas plants in all the world . . ."

I chuckle again and then turn serious. "This might hurt you, my friend. Larry is mad. You need to get a source in the office before you write this stuff."

"What are you talking about, Cara?" Henry sounds surprised, not defensive, which worries me. "You confirmed this piece. I thought you were calling to thank me."

I feel a jolt of tension but keep my voice level. "Me?"

"Yeah, I got an email from you yesterday with a breakdown of the current employee list at the plant. I was going to text you today and ask if I could buy you a drink. You know, to say thanks."

I pivot. "Right, right. I was just hoping you'd follow up before you went to print. I could have given you more context." My brain is racing, trying to remember what I did yesterday.

"Didn't need it. Tight deadline."

"Hey, instead of a drink, how about a follow-up with Larry? I can get you an exclusive this afternoon. I think we have some new data that might round this out a bit."

"You mean dull the edges? Yeah, sure, maybe. Text me later and I'll try to spin something your way." He sounds like he's not really paying attention. I hate that he's not committing to anything, but I need to keep a light touch.

"Okay, great. I'll be in touch later. We'll make it worth your while."

"Sure. Later."

I hang up and breathe in to slow the rising tide of stress. What had happened yesterday? Maggie. Rick's increasingly frantic calls. Had I been distracted enough to send Henry an email without realizing it? I pull up my email and type Henry's address in the search field. My stomach sinks. I find a message with a full breakdown of the employee details from the site, sent to all the senior managers and Larry. All the senior managers except one. Instead of sending it to Harold Graves, our financial manager, I'd typed in Henry's email. A simple mistake, but one for which I could be fired.

Time for damage control. I'm good at this. I never let emotions get the best of me. I will come up with a plan and see it through. Like I always do. I type an email to Larry. He must not have noticed my error yet; otherwise the anger in his emails would have been directed at me. Larry has never been good at details. That's why he has me. I forward the message from me to him with the text *We need to talk about James.* James is the name of my current intern. There is no shortage of eager, ambitious kids available to do the grunt work for a person in a high government position like myself. Kids who can be sacrificed on the altar of self-preservation. I like James and I'll be sorry to see him go, but I can't take the fall for a silly email error. I recite calming words to myself as I wait for Larry to respond. I never did stuff like this before I got pregnant, before I had a kid. As Maggie grew in my body, other parts of me began to disappear. The parts that remembered everything—the parts that were in control.

Larry arrives at my office a few minutes later, looking harassed. He is a good man stuck with a difficult portfolio, and I regret adding more challenges to his day. I've known him for years. He trusts me. He runs his hand through his hair in a weary gesture as he takes a seat beside me. "What happened, Cara? That information was in-house only."

"I'm so sorry. I had James take over my email for a few hours yesterday. I had to leave to take Maggie to the emergency room." Larry has two young children, so I know this information will affect him. His expression immediately changes from frustration to concern.

"Is she okay?"

I sigh deeply. "We think so, but it's still a bit uncertain. She's got transient synovitis." I use the official diagnosis, knowing it sounds much more serious than it actually is. Larry gasps and I keep going. "We were in the emergency room until eleven last night. Maggie is still struggling this morning. It was hard to leave. Rick is handling it . . . but it's been tough."

"Oh my God, Cara. Give my best to both of them."

"I will. Thank you," I say solemnly. "How should I deal with James?"

"It's fine. We can talk about that later. Just take care of your family. Do you need to take the day off, leave early?"

I press on. I need this mistake to be clearly and definitively the fault of someone else. "Sir, all due respect, this is time sensitive. I want to make this right. I've drafted a press release that illustrates that those data are only a snapshot for one month. In the twelve months preceding this, we've had nearly seventy percent employment from the local region. I can send it out this afternoon."

Larry nods and rewards me with a smile. "That sounds perfect. I'm not sure how things would run without you here, Cara."

I laugh self-deprecatingly. "And James . . . ?" I trail off. I need Larry to come to this decision alone.

"It's probably best to send him off with a good recommendation at this point," Larry says, already pulling out his cell phone and scrolling through email.

"That's what I thought too. Thanks, sir."

"No, thank you, Cara. Thanks for being on top of this. Hope Maggie feels better soon. If you need to go early, please do."

"Appreciate it. Oh, and Henry wants to do a follow-up interview with you this afternoon."

Larry grimaces slightly, then smiles. "Of course. Schedule it for after three p.m." I can hear him start to whistle as he turns the corner out of my office. *Success as a bureaucrat can be measured by how good a person is at ducking responsibility,* I think as I walk toward James's desk to deliver the bad news. The best political tacticians know exactly when to throw someone else under the bus. It's the reason I'm so good at my job.

CHAPTER FOUR

June 1997

Jesse was late, as usual. I retouched my lip gloss again even though my mouth already felt thick with the coating of pink, watermelon-scented shine. Jesse told me once that my lips always looked like I was about to tell him a dirty joke. My thick reddish-brown hair was swept up in a French twist, and the hairdresser had used white shadow and liner to make my blue eyes pop. I felt sexy, buoyant with joy and a half tablet of a painkiller left over from six months ago when I got my wisdom teeth out. I'd stopped taking them and doled them out carefully for times when I needed to relax. Tonight I wanted to float. Tension made me look ugly in photos.

I knew my dad would be snapping pictures left and right, over-compensating. Jesse's dad wasn't around. Cindy Foster, Jesse's mom, would occasionally speak of the loser, as she called him, jabbing out her cigarette violently as she described his decision to take up with another woman before Jesse was even born. Jesse was ashamed of his mom's story, but I didn't care. When we were kids, all that mattered was that Jesse liked playing with me way more than he liked being with Anna. Jesse and I were the same age, and I could always keep up with him. We often left Anna behind.

"Did you use my razor?" Anna shouted from the bathroom.

"Yeah," I said absently, pulling a stray hair away from my lips.

"Where is it?" she asked. Her tone was impatient. I knew she hated it when I was the center of attention. Tonight was my prom. It was all about me, and it was driving Anna crazy. I smiled into the mirror, turning my head to make sure my blush was even on both sides.

"Cara!"

"Sorry. Um, I'm not sure? On the shelf in the shower?" I said lightly.

"No. God. Would I be asking you if it was there?" She had come down the hall in her towel and stood glowering in the doorway. I tried not to notice how thin and perfect her body was. Being on the track team gave both Anna and Jesse long, lean muscles. Sometimes I wished I had chosen running instead of volleyball, but I hated the places my mind went when I ran long distances. Running was boring, I told them when they laced up their shoes for weekend runs together. I tried not to take it personally when they ignored my requests to go to the diving rocks instead.

I turned to face her. "Whoa. Take a chill pill. I'm sure it's there somewhere."

"So you took my razor without asking and now you won't even tell me where it is."

I felt a rush of anger, but I squashed it down. "Oh my God, Anna. Just look around."

"Did you take one of those painkillers? You're acting like a total space cadet." She stalked over to my night table and grabbed the bottle.

"Hands off," I said, snatching it from her hands. "Those are for tonight." Not that Anna would ever take one. She glared at me as I smiled sweetly. "I think your razor is in the drawer by the toothpaste."

"It better be." She turned on her heel to leave the room.

"If you are not ready in ten minutes, Jesse and I are leaving without you," I yelled after her.

"You're such a bitch," she called back.

"Whatever," I said to my reflection. No matter what she did, Anna wouldn't ruin my night.

I heard a car engine but no knock. My dad must have heard Jesse and opened the door for him. My parents were excited too. It felt so good to be a central part of the biggest night of the year in Rapid Falls. I had played in big games before on the volleyball team, but even the largest tournament paled in comparison to prom. Tonight everyone in the graduating class would be treated like champions, and Jesse and I were at the top. People looked up to us.

"Hi, son," I heard my dad say.

"Hi, Mr. Piper."

My mom cried with delight, "Oh, Jesse. You look so perfect!"

Her voice made my pulse race. I could tell from her tone that she was starting to understand what all the fuss was about. She wasn't like other Rapids Falls mothers. Normally she didn't care about big dates or school dances. My mom had grown up in Fraser City, and she often said the fever in Rapid Falls around graduation was over the top, but I could tell she was excited now too. Rapid Falls was only three hours away from Fraser City, but it was a different world, especially in June when graduation season came around. I checked my lip gloss one last time and smoothed the front of my deep purple dress. I took a breath, then started down the creaky wooden stairs. Jesse was standing in the kitchen with my parents, his tan skin a golden contrast against the pure white of his tuxedo shirt. He looked amazing, but his eyes seemed strangely sad.

As I caught his glance and smiled hopefully, his expression transformed. I tried not to overthink it. Jesse had been acting odd over the past few weeks, but I knew he didn't handle pressure well. He was probably nervous about everything we needed to do over the summer: packing, saying our goodbyes, deciding whether we wanted to accept spots in the college dorm or try to convince our parents to let us find a place by ourselves. I wondered if some of it was nerves as he worked up the confidence to propose. I knew he felt the same way as I did, that he wanted to be married young.

"Honey, you look beautiful." My mom's eyes shone. My dad cleared his throat as he fumbled for the camera.

Jesse rushed to add, "You really do." I wished he had been the first one to say it. I smiled carefully so lip gloss didn't get on my teeth.

"Pictures!" my mom said. "By the lilac bush? It looks so pretty right now." She herded us outside, and I reached for Jesse's hand. I could hear Anna clunking around upstairs. I tried not to squint in the late afternoon sun as my mom arranged us in pose after pose. It was hot and bright. We pasted smiles on our faces as my dad clicked away.

"Do we have to do this all night?" Jesse whispered as my mom paused to reload her camera with film.

"Not all night," I whispered back, turning toward him to make sure my breath tickled his ear. I knew it drove him crazy. A sly smile crept over Jesse's face right at the moment my dad clicked the shutter.

"That's a keeper," my dad said.

I laughed, glad he couldn't tell what Jesse was really thinking.

Anna burst out of the house.

"Are we done, Mom?" I asked.

"For now, honey."

I turned to Jesse, about to make a joke about how hard models have it, but he was staring at Anna. He looked off again, even though Anna was smiling.

"Jesse?" I whispered. "What's wrong?"

He jerked toward me like he had forgotten I was standing beside him. "Oh, Cara. Nothing. Just . . . it's so hot in this suit."

"Anna! You look wonderful. That dress is perfect," my mom said. Anna was wearing a simple white shift, fitted in all the right places. It set off her brown eyes perfectly. It was the opposite of my dark, structured gown. She looked carefree and elegant at the same time. I touched my stiff hair self-consciously. I had admired it earlier, but now

I worried it was too much. Anna looked effortlessly beautiful. I could feel my makeup drying on my skin.

"Hi, Anna. You look pretty," I echoed as she walked toward us.

"Thanks," she said, without returning the compliment. "Hi, Jesse."

He smiled at her tightly and then busied himself with his corsage. He seemed uncomfortable, probably sensing the tension between us. I narrowed my eyes at her quickly, making sure my parents didn't notice.

"Is it weird to be going to prom without a date?" I asked innocently. Anna's boyfriend, Ross, had broken up with her a few months ago.

"I don't care about Ross Armstrong, Cara." She smiled brightly. "If he can't understand that I want more for my life, it's his loss."

"Oh, good. I'm glad you're not upset."

Anna looked at me. "About what?"

"I heard he was going with Debra."

Her smile slipped.

"Cara." There was a note of warning in Jesse's voice.

"You girls okay?" my mom called. "Can you get together by the lilacs?"

"I just wanted you to know the truth, Anna."

"Yes, honesty is so important. By the way, I have a bit of a headache. Do you have any painkillers?" she said with a thin smile.

I returned the expression with my back teeth clenched, knowing what she was threatening to reveal to my parents.

"Okay, everyone. Stand together," my mom said.

"Mom, we have to go." I shifted restlessly.

"You've got time," my dad said.

"Okay, squeeze in tight!" Anna, Jesse, and I dutifully arranged ourselves while the camera clicked. "Now, one of just Anna and Jesse. You both look so fantastic. Cara, can you move to the side for a second?"

Jesse and my dad spoke at almost the same time. "We do really have to get going, Mrs. Piper," Jesse blurted.

"No, no more pictures," my dad said as he walked into the frame. "It's time to go." He glanced at Jesse with an odd expression.

"What? Just one more. Clay!" my mom said, but Jesse had stepped away.

"We'll get one at the prom, Mom," I heard Anna say as I wobbled slightly in my high heels, trying to keep up with Jesse. I took a deep breath and relaxed my jaw. I couldn't wait to get out of there. It was going to be the best night of my life. I wanted to spend the rest of it without Anna.

CHAPTER FIVE

June 2016

I can hear Maggie's howls of frustration before I open the front door, which makes me all the more grateful that James took his dismissal well this morning. Sounds like I am going to need as much compassion as possible for my daughter tonight, and I'm happy I didn't have to expend it comforting my intern.

"Hello?" I call.

"Did you buy milk?" Rick asks, rounding the corner. He glares when he sees my hands are empty.

"No," I say. I remind myself that his frustration stems from her, not me. Maggie's cries are loud enough to make my chest vibrate. Hearing your own child cry evokes a primitive response. Sometimes it's fear. Sometimes it's anger. That's where Rick is right now. "I'll go out and grab some in a bit."

"I sent you a text to remind you to stop on your way." He's not ready to let it go. The oven timer chimes, and he rushes back to the kitchen. The house fills with the comforting scent of roasted tomatoes. It's a jarring contrast to the screeches coming from the sitting room.

I take a few steps into the kitchen. "I was driving. I couldn't look at my phone until I got here. I'm sorry."

He sets the lasagna onto a trivet on the table as his shoulders slump. "It's been a long day. Maggie's been like this for most of the afternoon. She's still feeling awful." He waves his hand toward the steaming dish. "This needs a minute to cool. Do you want to say hi to her? See if you can get her to calm down? I just need to put together a salad." He looks at me quickly, and I know the fight is over. In his eyes I catch a glimpse of how we used to be. The year before Maggie was born, when he decided to quit his job at the snowboard company and turn to freelance contracts, his creativity had overflowed into our everyday life. Once, I came home from work to a scavenger hunt that led to him naked in our bed, a pair of icy-cold beers sweating on our nightstands for afterward. Now we don't even kiss hello, but I know this is just a phase. Our love is strong despite the battering we take from our daughter and my sister.

I walk into the sitting room. Maggie is systematically ripping pages out of a magazine. Tears stream down her face as she gulps in ragged breaths.

"Hi, Maggie," I say cautiously.

"Duddy won't let me color on the couch!"

I sigh. "Come here, Mags. Let's have a hug."

"No!"

"Just a little one?"

Maggie scowls at me, and then her face changes as she suddenly rushes to my arms. Her small body fills every hollow part of me. Rick and I have chosen to have only one child. We both know it would be impossible to divide our love between two of them; one would always get less. I scoop her up and walk into the kitchen, where Rick is placing a green salad on the table. He looks calmer now.

"Down!" Maggie squirms out of my arms, and I place her onto the hardwood floor beside her booster seat. She picks up where we left off at breakfast and immediately begins singing a rendition of "Twinkle, Twinkle, Little Star." I join in. Both of our voices are off-key, but it still sounds beautiful. To me, at least. Rick's face screws up in mock agony.

"We need to talk about preschool," Rick says over the din. "I think she needs more stimulation during the day."

I stop singing to answer, and Maggie transitions seamlessly into the ABC song. "Okay. Do you have something in mind? Have you spoken with Esther about availability at Sunny Side?" Growing up and going to private school in Fraser City means Rick has lots of helpful connections. I would do anything to make sure Maggie is successful, even though the annual fee for the preschool is more than I paid for my state college tuition.

"She said she might have a spot opening up in the late summer—" Rick's words are cut short by a loud knock at the door. Even Maggie is startled into silence.

"Someone is at the door," she announces.

"We know, sweetie." As I walk to the door, another round of rapid knocking begins. The lack of a polite pause between knocks gives me a good sense of who I'll find on the other side.

"Hi, Anna," I say as I swing open the door. My sister is doing her best to appear sober, but her hooded eyes and weaving stance betray her.

"Hi," she mumbles as she brushes past me. Rick has joined us in the foyer now, with Maggie in his arms.

"Hi, Auntie A!" Maggie says loudly. Rick shifts Maggie on his hip to get her as far away as possible from Anna's alcohol fumes. Anna blinks at Maggie slowly as if she's trying to figure out who she is. Understanding flickers in her eyes.

"Hi, pumpkin. Whatcha doing? I brought you a present." She smiles, but it's as slow and sloppy as her words.

Maggie's expression changes from glee to confusion as she tries to decipher her aunt's words. She opts for the safety of repetition, with slightly more volume.

"*Hi, Auntie A!*"

"Hi, Maggie!" My sister echoes Maggie's volume and gives us all a bleary smile. She's too drunk to realize that she's not being as cute as she thinks she is. She thrusts a plastic grocery bag toward my daughter. "I brought you a present!"

Maggie squeals in delight and snatches it. A multicolored teething ring flies out and skitters across the floor. Maggie pounces on it, then pouts.

"This is for babies," she says sulkily.

"What are you talking about, Mags? You can put it in the freezer. For when you get teeth . . ." Anna trails off slowly, looking at Maggie's mouth.

"I already have teeth!" Maggie begins to cry and runs back to her dad's arms.

Anna looks at me helplessly. Her face crumples. "I didn't think . . ."

I scoop up the plastic ring quickly and shove it back into the bag. "Her adult teeth will be coming in soon. We'll save it for then," I say, trying to rid the room of Rick's disbelief and Anna's embarrassment.

"I don't want to get more teeth!" Maggie hollers, pushing out of Rick's arms again.

"Thanks for the gift, Anna," Rick says politely. "I need to get Maggie to the table. See you soon. Let's go eat dinner, Mags. Noodles!"

Maggie nods gleefully, her oncoming teeth forgotten. Rick casts me a frustrated glance and an unspoken message: *Get her out of here.* Rick hates Anna's drunken, unannounced arrivals, but I don't know how to stop her from showing up, and the truth is, I'd rather she was here than anywhere else when she gets like this. I haven't seen her since her last hospital visit. At least now I know where she is. I kick myself for letting three weeks go by without calling her. Maybe I could have caught this earlier. She smells awful, like stale vodka and unwashed hair.

"Anna, come with me."

She stumbles, misjudging the distance between our bodies and kicking my heels as she trails me to what used to be our home office.

Lately the room has become cluttered with toys and puzzles—evidence of Rick trying to entertain our daughter while finishing a freelance job. It was described as a sunroom by our Realtor; the back wall is built entirely of windows, with a glass door that opens onto the back deck. It's a nice place to work, though I've used it more often to stage interventions with Anna. She and I have had many heart-to-hearts in this room, though I doubt she remembers any of them. She sits on one of the two armchairs in the corner, clumsily propping her elbows onto her knees and burying her face in her hands. I sit down beside her.

"What's going on, Anna?"

"I can't even buy the right present for a little kid. I'm so stupid . . . I'm a waste . . . Why do you even let me into your perfect house?" She chokes on the last words, saliva spraying the air between us. I wait, unspeaking. There's no use engaging—I've learned my lesson many times over. Any words I say will inspire her to new depths of alcohol-induced self-loathing. She needs to get to the reason why she's here without any encouragement from me.

She looks up, her eyes blurred with tears. "I saw someone today."

I struggle to remember the name of her last boyfriend. "Shawn?" I guess.

She twists her face into a theatrical mask of misery. "No. I don't care about Shawn. We're through."

"Okay." I take a deep breath, grateful that she's too drunk to hear my impatience.

"Someone who looked like . . . like him." She looks at me meaningfully, dramatically emphasizing the pronoun.

My hands turn to ice as I meet her gaze and shake my head no. She knows I don't like to talk about Jesse.

"I'm so . . . horrible." She lets out a melancholy moan and covers her eyes again. She's probably trying to force out more tears for effect, but it's hard to cry when you are as drunk as Anna is. "I saw him, and for a second it just seemed like . . . it hadn't happened. I was sixteen again. And he was still . . . alive," Anna continues, her voice muffled.

I am angry that she is talking about him, and it makes me feel cruel, so I play dumb. "Who are you talking about?"

"You know who!" She begins to pull at her hair. The white skin on her scalp rises in painful points.

"Want a drink?"

"Sure." She looks up at me eagerly, her eyes red. I never drink alcohol with Anna. I need to show her a model of good behavior so she can see how her life could be.

"Soda or juice?"

"Coke is fine." I can tell she is disappointed.

I walk to the small bar fridge and grab a can. "Sounds like you've had a hard day, Anna. You have to make your own choices about how to get through . . . everything. Have you thought any more about rehab?"

I split the can between two glasses, one for her and one for me. As I walk over to hand it to her, she stands suddenly and clumsily presses her body against mine for an embrace. I can't hug her back even if I wanted to, because my hands are holding the two glasses. Our foreheads collide as she pulls the back of my head forward with her hand, forcing our faces together. Her breath is awful.

"It's all my fault, Cara. I should be dead. Not him. You're the only person I can talk to. You're the only one who knows what happened."

"Stop, Anna," I say, wiggling out of her embrace.

"I can't. That's the problem." She laughs, a barking sound, and heads for the back door. "Bye."

I can't tell if she slams the door intentionally or out of drunken clumsiness. I walk back toward the kitchen. Later I'll worry about whether she made it home. I'll probably text her frantically, begging her to answer just so I know she's alive. For now, though, I return to my handsome husband and playful daughter, feeling nothing but gratitude that she is no longer here.

CHAPTER SIX

June 1997

Right after he told me about Anna, my dad left the hospital to go home to get me some clothes. When he returned, his face was grim. I realized that he'd had to cross the bridge where Jesse's truck had crashed through the railing. The river cut the town in half: our grocery store, library, and bank were on one side, and the schools, hospital, and church were on the other. About thirty miles upriver was Rapid Falls and then nothing but forest and white water until you hit the largest national park in the state.

He'd picked a pair of jeans that were two inches too short and an ugly T-shirt from when I coached a kids' volleyball camp last summer. I was too tired to ask what happened to the clothes I had been wearing, though I knew I should.

My dad exchanged low murmurs with the head nurse outside the door as I dressed; I had a feeling he was taking me from the hospital without the doctor's permission. Warnings of not allowing me to sleep more than two hours unsupervised rang down the hallway as we walked out the sliding glass doors. I wondered if staff at bigger hospitals, like the one we were heading to in Nicola, were as casual with their treatment plans. People cared more about each other in Rapid Falls than about doing things strictly by the book.

When we got to the car, my dad stopped. He pulled me in for an embrace so tight that tears unexpectedly filled my eyes. My dad never paid this much attention to me. Just the other day, he'd hung up a picture of me in my graduation gown in the upstairs hallway. It hung beneath the framed picture of his parents, who had both died from cancer when I was a baby.

"I wish they could see you now, Cara," he had said. "Next year Anna will be here as well. They would be so proud of both of you."

I had nodded, but frustration knotted my shoulders. My father could never congratulate me without mentioning Anna too. But today, as he held me in his arms, it felt like nothing in the world was more important to him than me.

"Damn. I forgot to get you an extra pillow. Are you going to be okay in the car for this long?" His forehead was creased with concern as he released me.

"I'm okay, Dad." I smiled even though my legs were shaky as I walked to the passenger side. When I reached for the handle of the car door, it felt cold despite the warmth of the summer day. I jerked away, shaking my hands to get rid of the feeling of my fingers grasping for purchase.

"You okay?" my dad asked.

"Fine," I said as I reached out again and forced my hand to unlatch the door. I slid into my seat and stared out the window. The small hospital slipped out of view, changing to trees covered with tiny budding leaves.

I was one of the last babies delivered in Rapid Falls Hospital before state funding dictated that all deliveries take place in Nicola, about an hour and a half away by ambulance. I had spent nearly every day of my life here. I knew Rapid Falls so well that it was difficult to give directions without using landmarks like "turn right past the woodlot the Kinleys used to own" or "keep going straight at the intersection where Mrs. Jones rear-ended the school bus." I sometimes imagined how Rapid Falls must have looked to my mom when her car blew a flat on her way to a camping trip up north, if she had felt confused when directed to the Piper garage.

My grandpa ran the place then, but my dad was on duty when she limped her VW Bug into the service station. She told me once that when he smiled at her, she felt as if she had known him forever.

The paper birch trees would have been whispering to each other in the summer wind, the small field beside the shop dotted with bright flowers. Weeds, mostly, but even dandelions looked pretty on a sunny day. My mom told me that everyone smiled at her in Mr. Johnson's grocery store, where she bought a Coke while my dad fixed the tire. When my dad finished the work, he asked her if she wanted an ice-cream cone. At the small stand about a mile down the road, she marveled at the flavors she hadn't tasted since she was a little girl. My mom never made it to her camping trip that weekend. She spent the next three days with my dad. He taught her to fish and took her up to Rapid Falls. Six months later, they were married. I was born three months after that. My mom chose a flowing wedding dress. In the pictures, you can barely tell she was pregnant, except for the frown on her father's face. Her parents moved to Florida when I was six. They don't visit much. I wondered if my mom would have moved to Rapid Falls if she hadn't gotten pregnant so fast. She was an only child, which was why Anna had been born so quickly after me. My mom said she wanted to give me a brother or a sister because she had always felt so lonely growing up.

Jesse was an only child too. He always wanted to know what it was like to have a sister, but I couldn't answer. It felt like he was asking me to explain what it was like to have two legs instead of one. That's how I felt about Rapid Falls too. I couldn't describe what it was like to live there. I had never known anything else. It was the reason I wanted to leave, to go to a place where no one remembered that Anna beat me at every track meet in elementary school, even though she was a year younger. I wanted to be someone who made decisions: a state representative or a senator. Rapid Falls didn't even have a mayor. City people learned about ideas and art, not the minutiae of their neighbors' lives. The few times I'd visited Fraser City with my mom, the streets vibrated with energy. The only thing in the air in Rapid Falls was the faint odor of cedar when the mill was planking wood. Rapid Falls made me feel like my life was already decided for me. In Fraser City, my choices would be my own. And Jesse's. That's how I'd always imagined it, anyway.

We turned onto the highway and sped past the only hotel in town, the Rapid Falls Inn. Everyone who lived in Rapid Falls knew the road to Nicola well. It was the place where we visited dentists, went back-to-school shopping, and played in sports tournaments. Wealthier families traveled to the Nicola airport to fly even farther away. Not us. I had never been on a plane and neither had Anna. My dad didn't like to travel, and it seemed like my mom had gotten tired of asking. I imagined packing a suitcase and entering a different world with the assistance of a paper ticket that entitled me to a new life, a new place, a new start. Somewhere where my sister wasn't lying in a hospital bed and my boyfriend wasn't dead at the bottom of a river.

About ten miles out of town, I felt the car slow slightly. My dad gripped the steering wheel tightly, but he looked distracted. I knew why. The two white crosses had stood there for nearly a decade, but today they seemed to stand out amid the knapweed and grass. I wondered if anyone would put one up for Jesse. I wondered if people would expect me to be the one to do it.

The white crosses were for Dustin and his mom. Everyone knew him; our elementary school had only two hundred people in it. They were on their way home from a gymnastics tournament. He'd competed in Nicola because no one in Rapid Falls could match his skill. He used to throw his body into the air as if he could control gravity.

Even ten years later, it was hard to believe his blood had stained the road underneath our tires.

The day it happened, a police officer came to our school to deliver the news. I was leaving the bathroom when I saw him talking to the principal, who was wiping tears from his eyes. I returned to my classroom and completed my math quiz, feeling the knot in my stomach twist into a tight cramp. At recess I met Anna on the wooden playground as usual. Anna's friend Sandy approached us with an expression that was almost gleeful.

She announced Dustin's death to us with something close to a smile on her face. I didn't feel sad when she said it—only confused. Even to an eight-year-old, the dissonance between the news and her underlying joy at being the one to deliver it was unsettling. It was my first experience with the malicious delight some bystanders take in other people's horror. I hadn't thought much about Dustin being absent that day. I didn't realize that I'd never see him again.

One of the kids at school, whose dad was a volunteer firefighter, later said that the car had been flattened like a metal pancake. I had nightmares for months as my brain tried to make sense of what happened to bodies inside a car like that.

I turned to my dad as we passed the small town that marked the halfway point to Nicola. His back was straight and his jaw was clenched. Since our conversation in the hospital, he had barely spoken.

"Did Mom go with Anna right away?"

Accompanying her would have been my mom's obvious choice. My mother was a rescuer of broken birds and maimed rabbits. Once, she brought home a kitten she had found, no larger than an apple. She placed it in a shoebox on top of a heated blanket in our kitchen. She and Anna had taken turns spoon-feeding it warm milk. I couldn't do it. I knew the kitten was too small to live. I didn't see the point of prolonging its misery. I still remember the tears in Anna's eyes as she whispered that she'd heard it purr—just once—before it died in its makeshift bed next to a bag of onions. I knew my mom's soft, anxious heart wouldn't allow her to leave Anna alone. That was why she was with my sister and not me. *It didn't mean anything more than that*, I told myself.

"Yes. She went in the helicopter. They weren't sure at first . . . how bad Anna was."

"Did Mom come see me before she left?" I persisted.

"There wasn't time." His face tightened again.

"Is she . . ." I trailed off, not knowing what to say. I wanted to ask if Anna was dying, but the words seemed too cruel to speak. Her body kept slipping out of my arms and plunging back into the freezing water as I dragged her to the shore. The world dimmed to a hollow roar as my ears seemed to fill with ice water again. I think Anna screamed as our car sailed in the air after it broke through the bridge railing. Maybe I did too. It took a moment for the water to engulf us. Just enough time to apologize, but no one had. Jesse's seat belt wasn't on. As our car sank, his body floated up to the windshield. Even in the blurry depths, I could see his eyes were open but empty. It was why I hadn't gone back for his body after I pulled Anna to the surface. I knew it was too late.

"I talked to your mom right before I saw you. Anna's pretty hurt, Cara. Broken ribs, concussion. But she's awake. She's going to pull through." The thought of Anna brought a flicker of a smile to his face, a crack in the hard sadness that encased him. I nodded, keeping my own face blank. Anna would always be their favorite. No matter what the police said she did.

I didn't want to ask my dad what would happen next. I knew that last night was going to undermine everyone's sense of security. Anna, Jesse, and I had not lived up to the promises we had made about drinking and driving. The town was going to want someone to pay for that. Jesse's life would not be enough. They would want more.

For the next thirty minutes, my dad and I sat in silence as we passed by farm pastures and wooded glens. As we got closer to Nicola, the single-lane highway widened and the lanes doubled. Cars, trucks, and buses appeared on the road beside us, streetlights dotted the shoulder, and houses proliferated like mushrooms. Traffic lights and malls entered the view. Usually I felt excited when the city appeared. Today I felt nothing but dread. My hands were numb, as if they had been plunged in frigid water again.

I had never been inside the Royal Nicola Hospital. I was only a baby when Anna was born, and I had been left with my father's parents back in Rapid Falls. The hospital was built on a large hill that buttressed the southern edge of downtown, like a queen on a throne overlooking her lesser subjects. My dad cursed under his breath as he made a wrong turn that resulted in us having to loop back around the entire hospital. Speed bump after speed bump jostled my bruises as he searched for the entrance to short-term parking.

"You okay?" He looked over, concerned, after the car jolted unpleasantly again. I must have whimpered out loud. Usually I would make a joke about country bumpkins and my dad would laugh. He hated driving in the city.

Today I just nodded.

Finally the car came to a stop. Neither of us moved for a moment. The only sounds were the ticks and hisses of the car cooling.

"Ready?" my dad asked, unbuckling his seat belt. Last night I couldn't hear Anna's latch as I unclicked it underwater. I didn't know if I had released her in time as I tugged at the cold metal, my hands barely able to grasp it. I shivered. It was dark in the parking garage, and everything sounded muffled, almost like I was still underwater. I flexed my fingers.

"I'm ready."

He stayed in his seat, and I looked over at him, wondering what he'd forgotten, why he wasn't opening the door. Suddenly he turned and grabbed me tightly. It made me wince, but his arms made me feel safe in a way that I hadn't since I pulled Anna up onto the rocky beach. My lungs had been burning, and the rough ground had felt like sandpaper on my frozen skin. In the darkness of the night and blindness of my panic, it had seemed as if the river were about to surge toward us and suck us back into its black depths. Someone must have seen us and notified the police. I didn't remember calling for help. It was only my father's embrace that let me shake the feeling that something was still coming for me.

"I love you, Cara," he said.

My throat was constricted by the words, but I managed to answer. "I love you too, Dad." I pulled away from his embrace only when his arms started pressing harder than I could bear. It felt like my bruised flesh might split, like the skin on an overripe peach. He looked into my eyes, and I could see his were brimming with tears. I remembered suddenly that this was the place where both his parents died. My mom told me that he had practically lived in the hospital for months. She had been left all alone with two babies, but our neighbors had packed our freezer with lasagnas and sloppy joes. People in Rapid Falls came together in a crisis. I wondered if they would do the same for us now.

"I'm glad you are okay." The words were simple, but the way he said it made it seem like finally he loved me the best.

"Thanks, Dad."

He nodded abruptly, as if he had made a decision, and then jerked on the door handle. "Okay, let's go."

The hospital was shockingly bright compared to the gloom of the concrete garage. My dad led the way confidently down a green-line path to the intensive care unit.

We arrived at the nursing station. My dad asked for Anna's room number, and the nurse murmured a soft response. He turned back to me and motioned the way.

"Anna is awake," he said.

I knew that was a good thing for my family, for me, but all of a sudden, I realized that I didn't want to see my sister. I wanted to run, to never come back to her or my mother or my father. Jesse was dead.

Anna was alive. Everything was wrong, but I had to pretend it was okay. I forced myself to keep moving forward. We approached a partially open door. My mom was inside, slumped in an uncomfortable-looking chair.

"Thank God. Cara!" She half spoke and half sobbed as she caught a glimpse of my face. She rushed toward me, wrapping her arms around my body. I still mattered.

"Suzanne, how is Anna?" my father said, stepping around us into the room. My mother released me.

"She's okay," she whispered. "We're all okay." It sounded like she was convincing herself. *Not all of us,* I thought, as Jesse's wide grin came into my mind. One side of Anna's face looked as shiny and swollen as an eggplant. Her eyes were open. She looked at me. Neither of us spoke.

My father walked toward her; his face crumpled with relief. "I can't believe . . ." His thickened voice clogged the words. He reached for her hand and held it so tightly that I could see Anna's fingers turning white. "We love you so much." He clutched her hand to his chest. I had fooled myself into believing that the accident had changed something, but no, Anna would always be worth more to him than I was. Anna's eyes turned glassy with tears, and my chest swelled with anger. No one here was okay. It was like everyone had forgotten that Jesse was dead because of Anna. Anna looked directly at me. I stared back, hoping she could tell what I was thinking.

My mother touched my dad's arm. "We should . . . let's give them a moment." My dad stood up and tried to wipe tears away without anyone seeing.

He turned to me and nodded. "We'll be right over here." The two of them walked closer to the door, and I could hear them whispering as my mom briefed him on Anna's injuries. It was the most I'd seen them say to each other in months. Maybe years.

I compressed my fury, pushing it deep into my stomach, willing it to be silent and contained as Anna spoke.

"I don't remember anything," she said. An almost overpowering wave of emotion washed over me. Anger, fear, sadness, and relief. I looked into her eyes, seeking something I couldn't explain. They were bloodshot, but she met my gaze dead-on. There was no malice, no deceit. She looked like she was telling the truth. Was she really that messed up? Was she still in shock? Could she have forgotten everything about last night? What about the secret she'd been keeping for months before?

Anna broke the silence. "Mom told me . . ." She swallowed hard. "Mom told me . . . about Jesse." It was not what she said that ignited my pulse of rage. It was the look in her eyes when she whispered his name. I had to stop myself from screaming. I knew the words I said, at that moment, would be the truth we would live by for the rest of our lives.

I took a deep breath. "I forgive you, Anna. I forgive you for killing him."

CHAPTER SEVEN

June 2016

"We need to talk," Rick says as I come down the stairs. His face is serious and my stomach spasms. I just got Maggie to bed. The bedtime routine is one of my only chances to be with her alone, and it gives Rick a break. The moments we share at bedtime are beautiful: her drowsy smiles full of love and the warmth of her soft hand resting on my stomach as I sing her a lullaby. I tell Rick it is the best part of my day, and I want it to be true, but it's a lie. The best part of my day is this moment, when work and childcare are both finished and I am no longer bombarded by relentless demands. I swallow annoyance that Rick wants to launch into a meaningful discussion the second that I have been released from every other obligation. I try to laugh it off.

"Uh-oh," I say. "Is it really important enough to break the Code?"

Rick smiles, slightly chagrined. "Ha. Sorry. Let's chat?"

"Better. Just give me a second." I walk into the kitchen to refill my wineglass from dinner, taking a large swallow before I return to Rick so the pour seems closer to a regular serving. The Code is a guideline for our conversations. When Rick and I first got married, we could not stop fighting: about Anna, about how to handle our finances, about everything. We had been raised so differently. Once our lives began to meld together, I started to hate all the ways that he was better than me.

During our housewarming party, I overheard Rick's mom gently mocking the rugs I had spent hours unearthing at secondhand stores and the antique trim we had salvaged from a construction recycling place.

"It's lovely, for a starter home," she whispered to Rick's dad, sipping champagne that cost more than any pair of shoes I owned at the time. "She's tried so hard."

Suddenly everything that had seemed so chic turned shabby in my eyes. I spent the rest of the party in the bedroom, feigning a migraine.

I told Rick's parents that we wanted to live on the east side of the city to be closer to the art scene, instead of being honest about the fact that our mortgage, nearly twenty times what my parents paid for their home, combined with my student-loan payments left us with very little at the end of every month. The house felt incredibly luxurious to me, but I could never admit that having a garage to park our cars in made me feel like a millionaire. Rick wasn't used to budgeting, and he was annoyed at me for tolerating Anna's drinking. He began taking late meetings, and I stayed over at Anna's a couple of nights a week, which led to even more arguments. One morning he discovered her passed out on our doorstep with her pants covered in urine. That night he told me he wasn't sure we were going to make it, despite the fact that we had been married less than a year. I booked a meeting with a couples therapist. I could not risk losing him. He was the only stable thing I had to hold on to. He was everything I had dreamed of in a partner after Jesse died. I needed us to work.

The session turned out to be worthwhile, despite the therapist's incompetence. The woman kept fumbling our names and was more interested in where I had bought my cardigan than our relationship. She interrupted Rick during his explanation of our issues to suggest we both buy copies of her new book. Ironically her lack of skill brought us together. When she sent us away with "homework," we bolted like kids being released from detention and headed straight to a restaurant where we mocked the therapist's self-serving approach while completing the assignment she had given us: a list of dos and don'ts for our arguments. Our joke became the Code, and to this day we work hard not to break it. Usually.

Rick came up with the first rule: never compare your partner to one of their parents. The second rule was mine: never insinuate that a person's actions or statements are a result of being raised in a small town or as part of the working class. Common sense and respect dictate numbers three and four: do not damage property during an argument, and don't go to bed angry. The last tenet of the Code had been gleefully cemented during our final drink of the night: don't start any conversation with the words "we need to talk." Now, after a grueling day at work, a series of Maggie meltdowns, and a run-in with Anna, Rick is beginning our discussion by breaking the Code. I feel tired before he begins speaking, but I try to hide it as I sit down across from him in a soft gray leather armchair and take a deep drink.

"Okay. Let the chat begin." I try to keep my voice light, but Rick stares at me intensely. He seems to be preparing to say something difficult. I take another gulp of wine as he draws in a breath.

When he exhales, his words spill out. "It's about Anna."

Of course it is, I think. "Yes?" I say. My voice is sharp. I take another sip to try to soften it, but the first few slugs have loosened my movements. I knock the edge of the wineglass against my gums instead of my lips, and I taste blood.

Rick looks at me closely. "Your mother came over earlier this afternoon. She wanted to talk to me."

I raise my eyebrows impatiently. "To you?" I knew my mother had been taking Maggie out to the park once a week or so to give Rick a break. She was nearing retirement from her job as an art teacher at a local college. We are grateful for her help, and I know she loves having a grandchild. It seems highly unlikely that Anna will ever have kids. Even if she did, my mom probably wouldn't see them very often. Anna and my mom have become increasingly estranged despite the fact that they live only thirty minutes apart. Though Anna has never told me directly that she resents how quickly my mom remarried after leaving Rapid Falls, I think it's always bothered her that she didn't meet Ingrid before the wedding.

It must have been odd for Anna to return to the regular world only to find her mother was married to someone she had never met. A woman, no less. It was strange enough for me, and I was the one who introduced them at a fundraising party for Larry when he began his election bid. Ingrid was a well-respected activist for the homeless. I didn't know her well, but my mom hadn't known anyone else at the party, and I was busy with the endless tasks given to the youngest worker on a campaign team. I knew Ingrid would talk my mother's ear off, but it had taken me by surprise when the two of them hit it off, especially when it turned into something deeper. At first Rick and I had assumed it was a phase, something my mom needed to get out of her system after having been married to a difficult man for so many years. But after a decade and a half, the love between my mother and Ingrid was more secure than anything I had seen between her and my father growing up. Ingrid's charity is now one of the leading political causes of the municipal government in Fraser City, and she still works closely with Larry. She spends her days chasing grants and funding to create social enterprises that provide jobs for at-risk youth, women, and men, mostly community gardens with on-site cafés.

I feel lucky that Maggie has one active grandparent in her life. My dad rarely sees her. He almost never leaves Rapid Falls, even though three hours isn't far. Rick's parents see Maggie on her birthday and holidays, but their lives are busy with charities and travel. They don't have much time for a toddler.

"Anna called her last night," Rick continues. "She told Suzanne that she needed to talk to someone."

"Was she drunk?" I feel my stomach cramp again.

Rick nods. "Suzanne said she was out of control. Anna kept talking about how no one could ever understand what she's going through, that there were things that no one knew."

I finish my wine in one swallow. The cold liquid stings the cut in my gums and I wince. "What kind of things?"

"I don't know. She's losing it. It's happening again, Cara. Suzanne sees it too . . ." Rick trails off and looks out the window. The sun has set, and the window's surface has become a blackened mirror. Rick's face is distorted and pale in the reflection. He turns back to me. "I can't do this again, Cara. I can't let this happen again."

I nod.

"She wanted to talk about therapy, Cara. Suzanne is willing to put some money toward a skilled psychiatrist for her," Rick continues. "She wants us to pay for it together. She thinks there's something more than the accident at the root of this behavior."

I try to cool the fire of my irritation with a deep breath. My mom refuses to see Anna unless she is sober, which means they rarely spend time together. I'm surprised she even picked up the phone when Anna called. Usually she sends the call to voice mail.

"Do you agree?"

"In principle, yes."

I shake my head. Rick has brought this up before, but I talked him out of it. Therapy seems like a bad idea for someone like Anna. The last thing she needs is to keep dwelling on the past. I shake my head, annoyed at my mom for bringing this to Rick and not me.

"Anna won't do it."

Rick nods vigorously. "That's exactly what I said to Suzanne. It's a good idea, but it's not going to work until Anna is ready. Your mom's worried that it won't be fast enough."

I'm grateful he agrees with me. "I know."

"So should I tell Suzanne that we can't do it?"

"Let me do it. I'll call her." I need to figure out how to approach this carefully. "Thanks for this, Rick. I don't know what I'd do without you."

"Hopefully Anna figures things out. She's lucky to have you." A yawn distorts his last word and he stands up. "It's early, but I'm exhausted. You coming?"

I nod and follow him up the stairs, wishing for one more glass of wine.

CHAPTER EIGHT

June 1997

I couldn't put off the interview with Sergeant Murphy any longer. My bruises were fading to yellow around the edges, and after a visit to the doctor that gave me an all clear to resume light activities, I had no more excuses. Rapid Falls' limited law enforcement consisted of one sergeant furnished by the county sheriff, and in general, people liked it that way. We all knew each other's secrets, or thought we did, so there were times when things were overlooked to keep the town functioning. Nobody wanted to be arrested if their wife showed up for church with a black eye. Living in a small town meant learning to ignore the truths right in front of your face.

I had known Sergeant Murphy since Anna and I chased bats in exchange for a few dollars and a scoop of ice cream at the end of the local league baseball games. My dad played too and told us that we needed to respect the sergeant even when he got wobbly after a few too many beers in the dugout. We didn't think of him as police: more like a friend who wore a uniform to work. He knew how Rapid Falls operated. After the accident, I was counting on it.

The police station was an inexplicable shade of pink, painted by a team of day laborers. The original hue had been somewhere between Pepto-Bismol and Barbie's dream car, but weather had faded it to the color of a half-healed scab. The station sat kitty-corner to the elementary school. As a kid, that used to make me feel safe. But when I went for my interview after the accident, I felt nothing but dread. I pushed open the double glass doors and entered a small waiting area where the cinderblock walls made the space seem like a cell. To the left of the entrance was a waist-high counter manned by Sheila Black, a heavy-chested woman and my classmate Debra's mom. I'd forgotten that she worked here.

"Hiya, hon." Her eyes were sympathetic under their electric-blue eye shadow but glimmering with the telltale glee of bearing witness to unfolding gossip. As sad as everyone was about Jesse, they knew they were living through the stuff town legends were made of. Sheila Black was no exception. "I'll let him know you're here," she said, even though I hadn't said a word. She gathered up a few sheets of paper. "Take a seat."

As she turned to Sergeant Murphy's office, I saw that the phone on her desk had an intercom function. I guessed that she wanted to deliver the news in person rather than use the phone, probably so she could see the look on the sergeant's face. I pictured her speaking in hushed tones that afternoon with her friends, breaking the code of confidentiality that bound her from releasing all the details about her job. She would swear them to secrecy, of course, knowing that was the Rapid Falls equivalent of throwing a lit cigarette into a field of dry grass. The story about my visit to the station would spread like wildfire. My stomach sank as I sat down on a molded plastic chair. An institutional clock ticked loudly as I willed myself not to fidget. Luckily I didn't have to wait long.

"Come on back, Cara," Sergeant Murphy said. His large body all but blocked the narrow opening to a long hallway. I had to turn sideways to get by. It made me feel uncomfortable right away, which was probably the intended effect. I wasn't sure if the interview was going to happen in an interrogation room—the idea made my stomach twist unpleasantly—so I was relieved when we went into an office. He waved distractedly at a faded leather armchair across from his desk as he sat down. He sighed heavily. The smell of stale coffee drifted across the desk. I could see deep fatigue on his face and something else. It looked like grief. I realized suddenly that he didn't want to conduct the interview any more than I wanted to be questioned. He needed this to be simple. I was happy to oblige.

"Ready?"

I nodded. He reached out to press play on a small tape recorder. My mouth felt dry, as if I had a hangover, even though I had not had a drink since the party at the Field.

He started speaking, enunciating clearly. "This is the official statement of Cara Piper, recorded on June twenty-seventh, 1997. Please state for the record that you realize this statement is being recorded by Sergeant Allen Murphy of the Nicola Sheriff Detachment."

I cleared my throat. I felt cold all over. "I do."

He looked at me leadingly. I stared at him blankly for a second before I clued in. "I do. I mean, I do realize I'm being recorded," I said in a rush of words. I shook my head and took a deep breath. *Get it together, Cara.* I willed myself to focus on him and not the sound of a sickening crunch. My hand clenched into a fist as if I was gripping a gearshift. I gasped and the sergeant grimaced.

"You okay?"

I nodded, and he looked down at a small notepad on his desk covered in scrawling notes. The room became still, and I heard the tapping of Sheila's keyboard. I began to wonder if he was waiting for me to speak again. I cleared my throat at the same time he used two fingers to push a box of tissues toward me.

"Thank you." I hadn't cried since everything had happened, but I could if it would help me get out of this room. I pinched my thigh, hard.

Sergeant Murphy seemed to notice my glassy eyes. "Okay, Cara. This is going to be tough. But I need you to tell me what happened three nights ago, on, uh . . ." He glanced at a wall calendar beside us. "June twenty-fourth, 1997."

I nodded. In my mind, I followed Jesse to his truck in the darkness at the edge of the Field, and he turned to me with a smile. He had never looked so handsome.

"Cara?" The officer's forehead creased, as if he sensed something wrong, as if he had read my mind.

"Sorry, sir. I'm ready." I cleared my throat again, but words failed me. Agonizing seconds passed.

"Let's begin with the prom," the sergeant prompted, his eyebrows raised.

I felt like I was failing. I twisted the flesh on my inner thigh again, and tears sprang to my eyes. The sergeant plucked a tissue out of the box with a shaky hand and waved it at me. I wiped the corner of my eye, and he sighed heavily. I suddenly remembered that Jesse had been on the graduate–police liaison committee. He would have worked closely with Sergeant Murphy and his staff.

Jesse was a good boy. I was a good girl, known to the community for the notable, not notorious, things I had done. My dad worked on the cars of most people in town, and people recognized me. My volleyball team had almost made it to the state tournament last year, and the *Rapid Falls Times* had published our team photo, with me front and center. At least until three nights ago, Jesse and I had been a golden couple. The town had watched us grow up together. I used to look at him and think that if I could land a guy like Jesse, I must be pretty. I had my mom's dark auburn hair, almost red, and her clear blue eyes. Anna was taller, her lips fuller and her eyes lighter, but her hair was mousy brown and her skin was prone to breakouts. My complexion was always clear. I didn't turn heads like her, but I knew I wasn't ugly. I looked like someone who people could trust, not someone who would deceive them with a pretty smile. At least I hoped so.

I began. "Jesse told me he'd stay sober during the prom so he could get us all to the party safely." I let my voice catch on the last word and echo through the room. "He was kind of a stickler about stuff like that." *At least in front of cops,* I thought. The shadow of a smile flickered across the sergeant's mouth. I was on the right track. "We arrived at the party around ten."

"Just you and Jesse in the truck?"

"No, his best friend, Wade, was with us. Wade Turner." I saw the corner of the sergeant's mouth turn down at the name. He made a note in a small blue pad. I had to talk to Wade before the sergeant could.

"Anna wasn't with you?"

"No, she caught a ride with Sandy." I had made sure of it after what she had done at Wade's house, but I didn't volunteer that information.

"So you and Jesse were together at the start of the party?"

I nodded, and all of a sudden my throat swelled closed with the force of my sorrow. I looked out the window at the school, our school, as I tried to force breath back into my lungs. This time, I wasn't pretending. Jesse was gone forever.

"Do you need a minute?" His hand hovered over the recorder.

I shook my head, and words came out before I thought them through. "I loved him so much." The silence in the room felt sympathetic, not condemning, as Sergeant Murphy nodded. I hadn't planned to say that. I was glad Sergeant Murphy understood.

"I know." He paused until I nodded for him to continue. "So you and Jesse were together?"

"Yes, we were together at the beginning of the party."

Sergeant Murphy continued, "Okay. The accident occurred at roughly four thirty a.m. What time did you and Jesse get to the Field?" His voice was gentle, but I knew I already told him the time of our arrival. I swallowed nervously. He was trying to catch me in a lie.

I shrugged. "I wasn't looking at the time. I'm pretty sure it was ten, like I said. We stopped at Wade's for a bit."

"Wade Turner."

"Yes."

"What did you do at his house?"

"We . . ." I trailed off. Wade's parents had always turned a blind eye to underage drinking. They said it was better we did it there than anywhere else. They thought it would keep us safe. So much for that idea, but I still didn't want to get them in trouble. "We watched a movie."

"A movie? On prom night?"

"It was a school project. Kind of a celebration." I remembered Jesse's smile filling the screen, and my stomach flipped.

"So you stayed there for how long?"

"About an hour."

"And you were drinking?"

I stumbled on my words, thrown by my memory. "Yeah."

"A lot?"

"A little."

"Who drove up to the Field?"

"Jesse."

"Was he drunk?"

"No."

He looked at me closely, like he didn't believe me, but then he kept talking. He knew as well as I did that nobody in Rapid Falls wanted to hear that Jesse had been driving drunk. "What happened when you got to the party?"

I shuddered. Silence filled the room again. I needed to get through the next part as quickly as I could.

"Jesse and I talked to Officer Grey at the roadblock. She might know the time we arrived. When we got to the party, everyone was there," I lied. I was gambling that the police officer wouldn't remember if she saw us or not. Jesse had been too drunk to get through the road-block. We had taken the back way to the Field.

"Okay. I'll double-check with her. So what happened when you got to the party?"

I was back on safe ground. I remembered the feeling of leaving the tension of the truck cab and entering the darkness flecked with the light of the huge fire and the laughter and shouts of my friends. In that moment, everything had been perfect again. I knew that Jesse felt it too. It seemed like the beginning of the rest of our lives.

"We walked to the fire," I said.

"Who did you talk to?"

"Mostly Wade and Jesse, I guess. Ross Armstrong. I saw Debra Black."

"Did anything unusual happen at the party?"

"Todd Carter got in a fight." Todd was in his late twenties. He had lived in Rapid Falls all his life. He owned a ramshackle trailer in the crappiest part of town. I'd been there for parties a few times. I'd heard rumors that Todd sold drugs. I was sure Sergeant Murphy had heard them too.

"That doesn't sound so unusual for him." Sergeant Murphy grimaced.

"I guess not."

"I've got a witness saying they saw you and Jesse down by his truck, sometime around two a.m."

A shock of cold hit me. Someone saw us? "Well, yeah. I needed to . . . um . . . pee." I felt like a child using baby words. "I asked him to walk with me. I don't like going into the woods alone." Flickers of fire-light through tree branches. Soft moans and other murmuring sounds. Things Sergeant Murphy didn't need to know.

"Uh-huh," the sergeant said. "Maybe you lost a bit of time back there?" There's a hint of something dirty in his voice that could have been horrible if it weren't a lifeline.

"Yeah, maybe." I looked down at the floor.

"Okay, enough said." He seemed embarrassed too, but satisfied. He made another note in his book.

"Jesse was pretty tired, so he decided to lie down in the truck. It was getting late by then. Most people had left."

He looked at me closely. "Tired?"

"Well, maybe a little drunk by then. It was late," I said, looking up at him with my lids slightly lowered. He nodded and wrote something down.

"Who was left?"

"Anna, of course. Wade. Most of the girls' track team. Some of the hard-cores, like Todd Carter and those guys."

"And how was Anna?"

"What do you mean?" I knew it was the question he had been waiting to ask.

"Was she drinking?"

I paused. I couldn't lie, even if I wanted to. The blood work had already ensured that everyone in town knew the answer to his question.

"Yeah." It was true. Just not in the way he thought.

"Taking pills?"

Careful, Cara. "I'm not sure," I lied again.

He looked at me skeptically before making another note. "So you took the back way down from the Field because you knew she was impaired? Is that how you got past my officers?"

I didn't answer. He motioned to the tape recorder, indicating I needed to speak. It was the first time I saw impatience flash on his face. I knew he was disappointed in my sister's decisions. Maybe even angry.

"Yeah," I whispered. She was my sister. It was still hard to betray her, even after everything she had done.

The sergeant sighed deeply. "So if you and Anna were both drunk, why didn't someone else drive home? Why would you let Anna drive?"

Goose bumps prickled my neck. I could never explain my actions—what I'd done was unforgivable. "I thought she was okay."

The frown on the officer's face felt like a death sentence. I realized suddenly that this was the noose that he'd been trying to tie around my neck. I was complicit, just as guilty as my sister. She was going to drag me down with her. Suddenly something changed in his eyes, and he leaned over and clicked the tape recorder off. I remembered the time he handed me a five-dollar bill as a tip for collecting bats. I never received more than a dollar from anybody else.

"I stopped by the shop yesterday. Needed an oil change."

I nodded, as if I wasn't surprised by the non sequitur about my dad's garage.

"Look, Cara. You were drinking too, right?"

"Yes."

"Maybe Anna hid her drinking from you? Maybe you were just having a good time. Maybe you trusted your sister."

I looked at him incredulously and nodded slowly. He was offering me a way out.

"Me and your dad go back, Cara. He needs one of you to be clean on this. Let's try those questions again." The tape buzzed like an angry wasp as he erased my last answer and absolved me forever.

CHAPTER NINE

July 2016

Maggie wakes up early, stirring around five thirty. Rick is snoring beside me, and for a few moments I listen to Maggie's quiet chatter to the stuffed dog she sleeps with every night. She is an early riser, but she often wakes slowly, gently sliding between dreams and consciousness rather than abruptly jumping awake, like me. Lately I jerk out of sleep before my dreams are finished, gasping as if the bed beneath me is a sheet of ice-cold water, then wait an hour or so for Maggie to wake up. I can never fall asleep again after I dream of the river. When her murmurs turn into a call, I slip out of bed and cross the hallway. In the half light of dawn, I see her sweet smile as I walk into the room.

Rick comes out of the bedroom about an hour later. His hair is tousled, and his eyes look soft with sleep.

"Let's go away tonight."

"What?" I look up from the tower of blocks I am building with Maggie. Only the night before we'd been arguing about my mom's new plan for Anna. "Where would we go?"

"Griffith Hot Springs? I'm sure your mom could stay over. Maggie, do you want to have a sleepover with Grandma?"

"*Yeah!*"

Rick breaks into a grin. "That's settled then. Nice dinner, a little time to ourselves?" He looks at me and raises one eyebrow. Suddenly I notice how his thin, worn T-shirt hugs his chest. A night with just the two of us sounds perfect.

"That is a fantastic idea. I can ask James—" I stop to correct my error. "I'll have someone book it today. Are you okay to call my mom? I'll throw together a bag now so we can leave right after I finish work."

Rick nods. "Perfect. Awesome." He shimmies into a little dance as he wanders into the kitchen. "Coffee?"

I hug Maggie's small body against mine, and she giggles. I love the life that Rick and I have built, the family we've made. Meeting Rick was the best thing that ever happened to me. He proved that I could leave Rapid Falls behind. He gave me so much more than I ever could have had with Jesse. He loved me best.

~

Sometimes I still can't believe how it all worked out for me. One year after the accident, in between my first and second year of college, I lucked into a three-month-long summer internship for Larry. A few people in the office knew about the accident, but I was good at deflecting questions about it after having been asked several times in the first few months of school. I looked down sadly and told them that it was all a terrible mistake. Drinking and driving was no joke. They nodded solemnly when I changed the subject, respecting my need for a new start. I was Cara Piper, the girl with the sad story who had risen above it all and moved on. They didn't see the sweat that coated me at night at the thought of feeling nothing but water beneath me.

For weeks that summer, I ducked invitations to the annual team-building river-rafting trip. I had formulated my excuse not to go while lying sleepless and cold as the dampness dried from my body. I would tell the organizer that I had a severe earache and the doctor had advised me to avoid water.

The day before the trip, it felt like the entire office was chatting about it. Every time I heard a colleague titter about their fear of water, I had to grit my teeth so I wouldn't scream. Then Larry—or Mayor Duncan, as I thought of him then—popped his head into the cubicle I shared with three other student interns. My heart began to pound. He was rarely in the office, and I hadn't had a conversation with just him. I wanted desperately to make a good impression. He was the first person I had ever met who could help me do what I had always wanted to do. This conversation could change my life.

"Cara, will we be seeing you tomorrow? Mrs. Price said you haven't signed up yet. Should be a fun day for everyone."

I stared at him, my mind blank. I was thrilled he knew my name but horrified at the idea of floating on a river so cold that it would send whispers of its depths into the summer air. I panicked, and my excuse came out half-formed.

"I have a . . . I have . . . an earache."

He raised his eyebrows. "That's such a shame. I don't get out much with the team. I had hoped for a chance to get to know the interns. I won't have many opportunities this summer."

"Of course, sir. I'll . . ." My ambition overcame my fear. "I'll be there."

"Wonderful! We'll have the whole office, then. I'll let Mrs. Price know you've confirmed." He strode toward his secretary. I rubbed my arms, worrying my goose bumps as I ran through a list of reassurances. I would have a life jacket. There would be a guide. The sun would shine. Anna would not be there. Nobody would die.

The next morning, I felt gray with lack of sleep as I tugged the resistant rubber of the wetsuit over my clammy feet, trying to keep a pleasant expression on my face in case Larry spotted me in the group.

A couple of people let out yelps of excitement. My throat was too tight to make a sound, even if I wanted to.

"It helps if you get it wet," a man behind me said. I turned, my weak smile shifting so quickly into a real one that I must have looked deranged. The guy was naked from the waist up, a half-zipped wetsuit casually hanging off his muscular abdomen.

"Hi. I'm Rick. You're in my boat."

I realized that my mouth was open and shut it quickly. "Your boat?"

He smiled. His teeth were perfect, white as a child's against his skin. For a second, he reminded me of Jesse, even though they looked nothing alike besides the mischief in their eyes. He was blond and his nose was straight; his pale blue eyes sparkled with the sunshine. Jesse's eyes had been a deep brown, nearly black, and his hair was dark.

He held out his hand. "I'm your guide."

"Okay. Great. Cool . . . I guess I should try to get myself wet, then."

He laughed softly. I walked to the water with cheeks burning, my unintended innuendo echoing through my mind. I thought I couldn't look more foolish than being the last one still fighting with a wetsuit. I was wrong. I stared at the mustard-yellow raft fixedly as Rick gathered everyone for a safety briefing.

Afterward Mayor Duncan called out, "Last one in is a rotten egg!" Everyone laughed and ran dutifully to the rafts except me. I got ankle deep before I froze in place. The wetsuit's thick layer was no insulation from my memory of churning gray water. I urged myself forward, my pride convincing me to grab the ropes near the back of the boat and step over the wide inflated edge. My teeth were chattering as I climbed in, nearly kicking Mrs. Price in my fervor to get out of the river.

"Sorry," I muttered, and she smiled back. I sat down. Rick hopped in easily behind me and pushed off with a big oar. Despite our humiliating first encounter, I felt reassured to be so close to the one person who knew what he was doing. I held on to my oar, concentrating as Rick smoothly issued orders to us on how to row in rhythm. His commands were soothing, and I followed them like a meditation.

The sight of curls of white water reminded me to be scared. Rick's authoritative voice told us to pick up the pace. He sat on the back of the raft, wielding two enormous oars. Despite the currents swirling around us, his movements were smooth and deliberate, as if nobody had anything to fear, and we glided peacefully over the bumps. I took a deep breath. This river was calmer than the one in Rapid Falls. If that current was the worst of it, I would be fine. He smiled when he noticed me looking his way. He was so handsome.

"I'm Cara," I said. My voice sounded higher than normal.

"Nice to meet you, Cara. Glad to see that wetsuit finally learned who's boss." His grin contained no malice. I laughed as I tried to figure out how old he was, hoping I wasn't just a clumsy student to him. I'd kissed a few guys at mixers and class parties, but I didn't have a boyfriend. I didn't have time to date, I told everyone. I needed to study. The truth was more complicated, but I pretended that I wasn't a complicated person when I was at college. I was simple. Easy. Good. Rick made me feel that way for real. I liked it.

"Do you guide here every summer?" A frown crossed his face, and I wondered what I had said to offend him.

The raft bumped suddenly, and a shock of water took my breath away. I gasped as my lungs seemed to flatten when the cold pummeled my face and body. I clawed with my hands, seeking the reassurance of the oar, but I couldn't find its handle. The raft jolted again, and my stomach rose and fell. I was bouncing so much that I felt like I was falling. The water kept hitting me in the face. Rick's voice called something, but I couldn't make out the words. Water slammed into me again, and as the raft lurched I couldn't hold on anymore. My world was suddenly underwater.

Shafts of white light pierced the haze around me. My hands and legs felt leaden. I couldn't escape; I was flailing. The water was colder than I had imagined during those nights in my sleepless bed, colder than I remembered. I could hear the shouts of people on the raft, but the layers of water that engulfed me distorted them so I couldn't tell what direction the surface was. The current pulled me in deeper and my heartbeat stabbed my chest. It was happening again, but this time I was not in control. My hands tore at the water as if I could climb away from drowning. I was about to die.

Then a hand cut through the water. I felt the back of my life jacket lift suddenly, the strap between my legs digging in uncomfortably. In seconds I was back in the boat. I looked up at Rick as he gently released the handle at the back of my jacket. His other arm still held an oar, steering the boat through the heavy rapids. As I gasped and coughed, I felt the waves under the boat stop tossing. Once again the water was calm below us.

"Are you okay? I didn't realize how low the water had gotten back there. That spot was much calmer last week." Rick sounded worried. I wondered if a mistake like that could cost him his job. He had almost killed me.

I still couldn't speak, so I nodded instead. My eyes felt like they were open too wide, and the warm sun was as bright as a harsh light upon waking. I blinked hard. Rick looked at me closely and his lips parted again to speak when Gwen, the intern with the desk beside mine, broke in. I turned toward her and was startled to see that she was also dripping.

"That was crazy, right?" Her voice was loud with unrestrained joy, her eyes shining with excitement. I was confused by her lack of terror.

"You went in the water too?" I said, finding my voice.

"Yeah! Rick pulled me out right before you. He said it happens all the time on this kind of trip. What a rush!" She leaned back and whooped. Everyone else joined in. I realized that no one else thought I had been in danger. I hadn't even been the first to be rescued.

"You're lucky. I'm sweating like crazy. Wouldn't mind a little dunk myself." Mayor Duncan leaned toward us with a laugh. "Need a hand getting back to your seat?"

I realized I was still in the middle of the raft. I shook my head and slid over to my side. "No, I'm great. What a fun trip!"

I tried to smile to make sure no one could tell how scared I really was. Nobody thought that anything had gone wrong. I gripped my oar again, turning to stare at the glassy surface of the river. I hadn't nearly died. I had been fine all along, even if I couldn't convince myself of it yet.

"You were laddering." Rick's voice was low. "I'm sorry I didn't get to you first."

"What?" My lungs felt raw.

"Even the best swimmers do it. People try to climb out of the water, like they are going up a ladder. It's a natural response to shock. We use everything we have to get out. It's so cold, especially when you don't expect it. It must have triggered an instinctual response. I bet you've never felt anything like that before."

I felt his hand on my arm, and I turned back to look into his eyes. They were so kind.

"No, nothing," I lied.

"It's okay to be scared of this river. We need to respect the water. I shouldn't have been so careless. I'm sorry," he said.

"It's okay." I didn't want Rick to feel responsible for me, even as I hoped my reassurances wouldn't make him move his hand off my arm. I liked the feeling of him touching me.

"Maybe I can make it up to you?" A light danced in his eyes, flickering through the worry.

"Maybe." I grinned.

"I get off at five. Can I buy you a drink?"

I felt another rush of shame. He thought I was as old as he was. "I'm only nineteen."

He laughed as if that was no big deal. "How about a picnic dinner, then? I turned twenty-one a month ago. I can buy us a bottle of wine."

"Sounds great." We both laughed like I had told a joke. I turned back to the front of the raft and began rowing slowly. I looked around quickly to see if anyone had noticed our exchange. Everyone was chatting away except the mayor.

He looked at me and winked. "I'm glad you could come today, Cara."

"Me too." I said the words before I realized they were true. I felt purely happy for the first time since Jesse had died. Rick gave me that. It was why I married him.

~

When we pull into the underground parking lot of the resort, I sigh happily. I remember the hot tubs, cedar saunas, and diving pools from our first visit, when we spent hours dipping in and out of the water while servers brought drinks and food at our request.

"When was the last time we got a room alone?" he asks as he unlocks the door of our room. As soon as it closes behind us, he pulls me in for a kiss. He runs his hands down my body and makes a low groan. I press myself against him, peeling off his shirt as he pushes me against the wall. It doesn't take long; we haven't had sex in weeks, and he is ready for me even before I touch him. Afterward his breath is hot and fast on my neck.

"God, Cara. I've missed you."

"Me too. Please, let's not wait so long next time."

"Deal." He pulls away to face me and his eyes are full of love. "This was the best idea I've ever had."

"Last one to the pool has to do dishes for a month!"

He laughs, and we change into our swimsuits quickly.

The sparkling water and the natural granite are gorgeous, but I find my gaze being drawn to my husband's body. His lithe, muscled frame makes me catch my breath as he steps into a huge hot tub. I follow, sighing as the hot water rises above my shoulders. It feels so good to be here alone with no sudden crashes in the other room, no shrieks for attention, no cell phones ringing. We soak for a half hour and then retire to the soft, thick fabric of deck chairs. A waiter brings us a bottle of champagne, and we clink glasses. We needed this: a day for only us. For the first time in months, I feel like Rick and I are thinking the same thing as I look over at him with sex on my mind. I know what just happened was only a taste of our night to come.

"I should check on Maggie," Rick says.

"Great idea. I was just wondering about her too," I lie. I don't usually misread him like that, but the champagne has wrapped me in a pleasant glow. I pour us each another glass. The phone rings in his hand before he can dial.

"It's your mom." There is panic in his voice. "Suzanne? Is Maggie okay?"

His shoulders relax in relief, but then his face crumples into a frown. I can hear my mom's voice, but I can't make out the words. Rick's features grow darker as he raises his eyes to me. They are full of worry and something that looks like anger. He is shaking his head.

"What is it?" I say. He ignores me. My mother is not letting him get a word in edgewise.

"Oh my God, Suzanne. This is crazy," says Rick. He isn't going to let me in on the call until my mother hangs up. Rick's parents were very strict about telephone manners; he never carries on two conversations at the same time. I place my empty champagne flute back on the table but fail to lay it completely flat. It lolls forward like a drunken ballet dancer, but I catch it right before it falls off the edge, then set it back down carefully. Luckily Rick doesn't notice. He is looking off toward the waiter, signaling for the room-charge slip, as my mom's voice hums in his ear.

"Can I talk to her?" I ask, leaning toward him.

"Okay, Suzanne. We'll head back now. I am going to pass you over to Cara."

His eyes are full of disgust as he holds the phone out to me. The look can mean only one thing. This is about Anna.

"I'll go check out," Rick says. "Can you sign for the bill?"

I nod. I can hear my mother talking even before I get the phone to my ear.

"Cara, Cara. You need to get back here." My mother sounds panicked. Something is really wrong. My mom usually talks about Anna with detachment, the same way she treated my dad in the last few years of their marriage, as if his continued presence in her life was puzzling, like a kid at school who wouldn't stop following her around.

"What is going on?" I say, standing up to grab a towel.

"It's Anna. She just called here . . ." A sob interrupts my mom's story. "It was a call from a jail. She called here *from jail*." Her emphasis on the last two words is a dog whistle to me. All my life, my mother taught me that we were better than the other residents of Rapid Falls, especially the ones who lived in the trailers on the banks of the river, who spent their weekdays in welfare lines and their weekends in cells. I know her greatest frustration regarding Anna is the way she pulls us all into places like police stations and rehabs, where people treat you like you are contemptible. It doesn't matter how far you have come or how hard you've worked; your presence in those waiting rooms means you are worthless.

"She called you?" My brain is foggy with anger and alcohol. I can't reason through this.

"I'm at your house, Cara. She called *you*."

"Oh." I should have realized that. I try to shake off my stupor.

"She'll need bail. Or something." My mom sounds bewildered.

I'm shocked too. I didn't think my sister had the ability to surprise me anymore. Going back to prison was one of her greatest fears. She was obsessive about meeting the requests of her parole officer and hadn't missed an appointment.

"Mom. We'll figure this out together. Rick and I will be back in two hours, three at the most. I'll have Rick call his father on the way." I click back into action mode. Rick's father is a semiretired lawyer who briefly served as a public defender. He will be able to walk us through the next steps, maybe even recommend counsel. Rick had talked about the broad strokes of Anna's legal history with him a while after we started dating. I had been upset that Rick had revealed the less savory aspects of my family to his parents. I was even less excited about it now, but we needed information.

"Okay. That sounds . . . Thank you, Cara. You always know what to do." She sounds relieved that she doesn't have to be the one to wade through Anna's mess.

"Okay, good. See you shortly," I say.

"One more thing, Cara. Anna asked if you could call your dad and let him know what is going on." My mother and my father haven't spoken to each other since their separation about a year after the accident, almost twenty years ago.

"Fine," I say after a moment of hesitation. My father and I don't speak all that often either.

My mom sighs. "I don't know what Anna would do without you."

Despite the circumstances, I feel proud to be the responsible one, the one who takes care of it all. It's moments like this when I realize how much my mother loves me. It seems easier for her to do so now that she doesn't have to choose. There is no possible way that Anna could be anyone's favorite.

"Thank you, Mom." I take a step backward and bang my hip against the edge of the patio table. I pick up Rick's glass and swallow the last half as my mom begins to sob.

"Cara, what are we going to do?"

"I don't know, Mom." I realize I have forgotten to ask an important question. "What has Anna been charged with?" The line fills with silence. When my mother answers, her voice is full of humiliation.

"Prostitution." Despite her toneless delivery, the word packs a punch. I clumsily half fall back onto the deck chair. Neither of us speaks. I feel the shame hanging in the air.

"Okay," I say finally. Then the line goes dead between us.

CHAPTER TEN

July 1997

Divers from Nicola searched for Jesse's body for a week before the operation was called off. Jesse's mom, Cindy, didn't wait to schedule the funeral. I felt relief when I heard that Jesse's dead body wouldn't be in the room. Until Jesse, I had never been to a funeral before. Dustin was the only person I had ever known who had died—besides my grandparents, who I didn't remember.

Rapid Falls didn't have a clothing store, unless you counted Stedman's, which stocked sturdy white underwear that was nearly unisex in its stiff, full-coverage design and garish polyester pajamas made of itchy material that smelled like chemicals and felt flammable. Stedman's didn't sell funeral dresses, so I dug out a black crushed-velvet dress that I had worn for a Christmas concert in ninth grade. It still fit and seemed formal enough with the pearls my grandma had given me. My mom's eyes were shining when I walked down the stairs, like they had ten days ago when I came down in my prom dress. This time, though, there was no light dancing behind the tears.

"You look perfect," she said, wiping her eyes quickly. I wonder if she realized that she had said the same thing to Jesse that night. And to Anna.

"Thanks," I answered dully. She reached out for my hand and squeezed it. I wished I had a dress on that didn't make me feel like I was fourteen, but I tried not to think about that. It probably didn't matter much what you looked like at a funeral.

We walked to the car. It would have been easier if my dad was with us, but he had left for Nicola early that morning. Anna was being discharged from the hospital. I had heard my mom and dad whispering heatedly the night before. I couldn't quite tell what they were saying, but I knew Sergeant Murphy had gone to see Anna to take her statement several days before. He had called last night just as I was heading to bed. It didn't sound like it had gone well.

"Mom?" I said as she turned the key in the ignition. She squinted in the jarringly bright sunshine. The layers of makeup were beginning to settle into the lines around her eyes.

"Yes, sweetheart?" she said.

"What's going to happen next?" *To Anna,* I thought, but completing the sentence felt too much like an accusation. My mother let out a long sigh.

"I honestly don't know, Cara. At this point, I'm just trying to get through each day. And when that feels like too much, I start trying to get through each hour." She smiled ruefully, voice trembling with tears. "Right now, I'm taking it minute by minute."

I nodded and looked out the window. "Yeah."

We drove in silence to the church, which was across from the police station and our old elementary school. Anna, Jesse, and I had always passed the church on the walk home to the other side of the river. Even though we did it every day, I always had to will myself not to freak out as the three of us made our way across the big bridge. The rushing current below turned my stomach; it reminded me of the powerful waterfall upstream that could batter a log to pieces in seconds. Even though the river was calmer here, just a few curls of whitewater over rocks, every time my feet touched the road on the other side, I felt like

I had narrowly escaped something. Years later, my high school biology teacher explained vertigo as a sensation caused by an inner-ear vibration, but my ears never felt strange when I walked across the bridge. I didn't think I was going to fall. I was worried I was going to jump.

I looked fixedly at the dashboard as we drove over the bridge on our way to the funeral, willing myself not to imagine Jesse's body scraping against the rocks at the bottom of the river. The churning water looked restless and menacing. I tried to keep my eyes averted but couldn't avoid a glimpse of the police tape over the huge hole in the railing.

The church's parking lot was packed, so my mom pulled over on the road about two hundred yards past it.

"Can you walk a little?" she asked, unbuckling her seat belt. I nodded. I felt stiff, but my bruises had faded to a milky yellow. Soon I would look normal again. My mom opened her black purse; the smell of mint gum and leather was a combination that always reminded me of her. She offered me a piece and I took it.

"I can do it," I said, releasing my seat belt. We both sat immobile for a moment.

"Okay, let's go," she said, moving suddenly, like a diver jumping into a freezing lake. Our hands reached for the door handles simultaneously, like we had rehearsed it. As we walked down the road, familiar faces surrounded us. When we got close to the church, I saw Jesse's best friend, Wade, in the doorway with his parents, greeting people and passing out programs. I wondered who had asked him to do that. I hadn't spoken with anyone since my interview with Sergeant Murphy. My mom had fielded the few phone calls that had come in and brought me food at regular intervals while I sat in front of the TV for hours, endless music videos flickering in front of me.

Wade caught my eye and smiled, then quickly erased the expression. I nodded back solemnly. Neither of us knew how to act.

"Hi, Wade," I said, taking the paper from his hand.

"Hi, Cara."

I noticed his mom staring at me, so I gave her a small smile, moving forward quickly before I could see if she responded in kind. I hadn't been out in Rapid Falls since Anna was charged. I didn't know if Mrs. Turner would forgive Anna for what she had done. Jesse was like a son to her. She might not want Wade to be seen speaking with the drunk girl's sister. My mom led the way through the throng of people gathered in the foyer. The crowd was a blur of old teachers, high school friends, people who knew Jesse, and people who seemed to be there just to say they had been. Rapid Falls didn't have a lot of funerals, let alone funerals for teenagers. Jesse would have laughed at the ghoulishness of the crowd, every gawker and gossip hound in Rapid Falls in attendance. It appeared to be the social event of the season. I smiled at Jesse's old boss, Mr. Johnson from the Food Mart. He hesitated, then responded with a nod and a blank face.

If it wasn't for my mom's hand on my forearm, I might have walked out right then. Jesse, Wade, Anna, and I had played together for years. We were like siblings. Then, one January afternoon when I was thirteen, the sun had caught Jesse's dark hair and turned it the color of milk chocolate. All of a sudden I couldn't look at his mouth without wanting to kiss him. He was the boy I wanted to belong to. And then I did, for a while. Or at least I thought I did.

A few weeks after I realized how I really felt about Jesse, it was Valentine's Day. Every year, the twelfth-grade class sold Candy-Grams: a small bag of cinnamon hearts stapled to a piece of cardboard that you could write a message on. For days I had agonized over the right words to declare my love. I was so desperate that I asked my mom for help. We finally ended up with a quote, something far beyond the sophistication I possessed. It was from a book I had never read, with characters I didn't know. But the words were exactly how I felt.

Whatever souls are made of, his and mine are the same.

—*Emily Brontë*

I handed over my dollar to the older girl with permed hair and painstakingly inscribed the pink-and-red card she gave me. In the high school ecosystem, I was at the bottom of the pecking order, so I was thrilled at her response when I handed it back to her.

"Lucky guy," she said softly, looking at me with what seemed like newfound respect.

I felt heat rise in my cheeks and laughed uncomfortably. I went off to class, but all I could think of was Jesse's reaction. He'd probably get tons of Candy-Grams. It was stupid to think that he felt anything for me. But when I found him after school, his face lit up with a smile as he rushed toward my locker, clutching the cheap card.

"You sent me a Candy-Gram." His voice was full of joy and promise. "I love it," he said.

He gently leaned in and brushed my lips with his.

When I told Anna, she made me recite the story twice. Instead of being enthusiastic about our brand-new love, she was skeptical.

"He said he loved it?" she asked. "It seems kind of dumb. You think your soul is made of the same thing as his? What does that even mean?"

I was too elated to respond to her scorn. "It means we like each other, dummy. We always have. We just didn't know it."

She snorted, then turned back to her Lois Duncan book. "Whatever." *She could never understand,* I thought. What Jesse and I had was one in a million. No one else could ever feel the way we felt.

I must have stopped walking, because I felt my mom steering me toward the last pew. I sat down dutifully on the empty bench. I wondered if he had kept that card and where it was now. I felt like I could cry. For real. I didn't need to pinch myself.

I stretched my neck slightly to look around the room. Cindy was in the front pew, flanked by her barfly best friend and her brother, Dan. Dan was Jesse's favorite uncle. I was glad he was there. There was no coffin at the front, just a lectern and a whole bunch of flowers and wreaths. Anna's best friend, Sandy, was a couple of rows back with her mom and dad. I tried to meet her eyes when she glanced around, but she quickly turned back to the front of the church. Her mom looked pointedly down as well, as if she regretted being so friendly to me at the hospital, before everyone learned what Anna had done.

I took a deep breath. This was the last place I wanted to display my grief. I hoped that the funeral would be cathartic for Cindy and the others who had loved Jesse, a place to mourn a fallen son of the community. But for me, showing emotion here would be like swimming with a flesh wound while waving to a shark. I knew the town needed a scapegoat for Jesse's death. Anna was it. They were still deciding about me.

People slid into the pews around us, but no one entered our row even when space ran out and latecomers stood in the back. Some folks nodded and greeted my mom softly as they passed, extending eye contact to me only occasionally.

There had been only one issue of the *Rapid Falls Times* published since the accident, and the paper had covered the story in an uncharacteristically neutral way, with a brief description of the incident and no mention of alcohol. The sidebar, a recycled list of statistics on the deaths and injuries associated with drinking and driving in our county, was slightly damning, but it could have been worse. The *Times* often served as the court of public opinion in our town, and it rarely took such a measured stance in times of salacious happenings. The paper's editor sat in the front row. The funeral could change things.

A murmur from the back made me think the funeral was about to start; maybe the priest or whatever was walking down the aisle. But instead of a black-suited man of God, a glint of metal caught my eye as I looked back. A wheelchair—probably an older relative coming to pay respects. The hum of voices grew louder as I turned for a better look. It was Anna.

My stomach lurched. My dad pushed her into a spot at the back. I nudged my mom, who turned in her seat and motioned for them to join us. My dad shook his head no. He seemed to be struggling to maintain his composure as he slid the chair between people who had been his friends and neighbors all his life. His jaw was tight. A few people whispered quickly to those beside them as my dad rested his hands on the back of the wheelchair. Anna's face was pale. She smiled quickly when she saw Sandy and then looked down, ashamed, when Sandy turned her head back to the front, face blank. I slunk down in my seat, and my mom squeezed my hand again.

"It's okay," she whispered. Her face was pale, shades lighter than the foundation that now made her look orange. I couldn't tell if she was reassuring me or herself. Then I saw Dan stand up and walk toward the back. I could hear Cindy's sobbing as she stayed in place. Dan met my dad's eyes. The church grew quiet as everyone shifted to watch. Dan shook his head as he looked at Anna.

"No," he said. The word echoed in the silence. I heard my mom suck in her breath. My dad recoiled as if slapped. Anna looked down. She slowly took the wheels in her own hands and clumsily spun the tires backward, running into my dad while trying to turn the chair to face the door. People stepped back to make a path for her.

"I'll go." She looked at my dad. "You stay."

Dan turned and walked down the aisle again. Cindy's cries were still audible. My dad looked helpless as Anna held up her hand, motioning for him to stay.

"It's okay," she said, echoing our mother. Whispers hissed through the church as my dad shook his head and pushed the unfamiliar vehicle back out the door. Each rotation seemed to be defying the laws of physics in its inability to gain momentum. Push, roll. Push, roll.

I had heard the doctors at the hospital tell her that she needed to stay as immobile as possible to ensure her ribs set properly. I knew that I should leave with her. I should walk out and show the town that I would always stand with her, that we were in this together. But I didn't. My mom's body felt tense, as if she was waiting for my decision before she made her move. When I didn't get up, she stayed too. I knew Anna understood why I didn't join her. I also knew that understanding didn't make her feel any less alone. My dad held open the door. Its deep thud echoed as it closed behind them.

CHAPTER ELEVEN

July 2016

As I toss my soggy swimsuit into my overnight bag, I think of Anna and how far she has fallen. When I look through our 1997 yearbook, I can see how pretty she was, prettier than me—her features slightly more refined and symmetrical than mine, her hair shinier, her smile brighter. Maybe that's why my parents favored her. As a kid she could get away with anything, whereas I was always told I should have noticed, should have helped, should have told her not to do it. I was supposed to be the responsible one, the older sister, though now it's hard to tell that she is a year younger. Hard living has visibly aged her, and my jealousy about her appearance has faded away. Anna no longer has the same shy smile she used to reserve for guys she liked and teachers she hated. Her grin, on the rare occasions it appears, is now startling for its yellow teeth pocked with visible cavities.

Last year, at Christmas, I gave her a voucher for $1,500 in treatments at our family dentist. She opened the envelope and turned to me, embarrassed. "I go to the dentist, Cara."

I feigned surprise at her reaction. I knew the gift was a risk, but I thought it would help. "I know, I know. I just thought . . . if there was any big work you wanted to get done. Dentists are expensive." I laughed warmly and prepared to launch into a story about possible braces for Maggie, willing myself not to look at Anna's mouth.

"Thanks for thinking of me," Anna interrupted abruptly before I could begin my story. She covered her mouth every time she laughed that night. She still does, but she's not quick enough to hide the fact that she never used my gift. It's not like she's ugly now, exactly. She still manages to attract a host of men though they rarely stay for more than a couple of months. Like her, they have lost any promise they once had. They are broken by life, angry because they thought they were better than they actually turned out to be. They uniformly curse loudly, make foul jokes, and leer at me when Anna goes to the bathroom. Her last boyfriend stole a laptop from my mom's house during a visit.

Anna used to be able to get anyone she wanted. Anyone, even people she should never have tried to date because other people loved them. It must be hard to lose that—harder still to sink to the point of being for sale. I try to muster up sympathy for her situation, but all I can do is feel annoyed and angry.

As I click my seat belt, Rick offers, "Not the night we planned, huh?"

"Not even close," I say with a tight smile, grateful he's still able and willing to try to make me feel better. At some point, he won't be. Not if Anna keeps up with this. I know that sooner or later her sickening shadow will begin to cast a pall on me as well, and he'll wonder how he ended up with a wife who brings so much ugliness into his life. Rick doesn't have skeletons in his closet. He is perfect and needs his wife to be the same way. The worst thing that Rick has ever done was to spray-paint a statue as a prank in college. He had confessed it in low tones, as if I would be shocked by his immoral act.

The drive back to the city feels much longer. I quickly fill Rick in on the charge against Anna. As we merge onto the highway, Rick dials his father, and the two talk through the car's hands-free system in hurried tones about the next steps. I try to follow the conversation, but my skull feels like a cage that's too small for my brain. My headache builds as the miles pass and the alcohol in my system changes from pleasant to poisonous. I hate letting his upper-crust parents know about my sister's latest disaster. His dad is pleasant, but his tone seems professionally distant, as if he's talking to an objectionable client. It reminds me of the way the prison staff used to treat me.

~

I drove this highway every second Saturday for the three years that Anna was in prison. It took me five hours, round-trip, but I never missed a day. I was the only person who had visited her regularly. My dad had promised to come once a month, but the time between his visits got longer and longer. My mom went a handful of times. The first visit, three months in, was to tell Anna that she had decided to leave my father. Then she moved back to Fraser City and started her master's program in art. Apparently it had been a lifelong dream, but she couldn't realize it in Rapid Falls. After her move, the visits dwindled. When I went, I tried to keep my talk of our parents and the outside world to a minimum. Anna seemed to get duller and sadder every time I saw her. She didn't need me to tell her how wonderful my life had become with Rick by my side.

After she was released, I offered to share my one bedroom with her until she got on her feet. Her parole officer helped her find a job at a fast-food place down the street. The grease from the fryers made her skin break out, and her hair was dry and frizzy. I'd asked if she wanted to try to reapply to film school, but she just shook her head. She seemed far away when I tried to engage her in wedding planning, even though the date was only six months away. I had just finished university, and Rick was three years into his snowboard-design job. I had set the date specifically so Anna could be my maid of honor, but she didn't seem to care.

I was careful about how much I told Rick regarding Anna's crime. He knew that she had served time for drunk driving, that she had killed a boy from our high school. He didn't know that Jesse had been my boyfriend. When we first started dating, I didn't want to scare him away. Later, it felt like telling him would be admitting a sort of a lie since I had kept it from him for so long. When she came to live with me, I swore Anna to secrecy. She agreed. She needed me so badly at that point. I could have asked her for anything.

In our wedding photos, Rick and I are luminous. Anna looks exhausted and sallow, even though I had paid for the most flattering bridesmaid dress I could find. It was the first time in our lives that our father congratulated me without noting one of Anna's achievements. His words were enough to make me feel like I had finally accomplished what I had been trying for all my life. After the ceremony, I asked Anna to come with me to the bathroom, begging her for help to maneuver the beautiful but absurdly wide train of my gown.

Her face brightened at being needed, and she squeezed my crinoline and herself into a small stall. She was holding my gown up around my body as I sat on the toilet when the door opened and a couple of women came in. They chatted to each other about my dress before noting that prison must have made my sister forget that people tried to look pretty at weddings.

Anna's eyes widened like a wounded animal's as their cruel laughter followed them to the door. She looked at me, dropped my gown, then ran her palms from her forehead to her cheeks. It was a nervous habit she'd had all her life. Wiping the slate, my mom used to call it. She did it when she was nervous, uncomfortable, or scared. I knew I should say something, but I felt speechless. Anna dropped her hands and looked at me with tears brimming in her eyes. We stayed in the stall until the girls left. Anna smiled at me when the door closed to let me know that she was okay, even though we both knew she wasn't.

~

The sound of Rick saying goodbye on the phone shatters my reverie.

"What a fucking mess." I swear without meaning to—another remnant of Rapid Falls that I haven't been able to shake, to Rick's chagrin. The more energy I put into Anna, the less I have for Rick and Maggie. Caring for my sister is a zero-sum game.

"Cara. Come on. We need to stay calm."

"I know." I force myself to take a kinder tone.

"So one of us needs to make a call to the station. Probably better if it's you since you are a blood relative. My dad's going to email me the names of several attorneys who specialize in this area."

"Okay," I say. "Should we talk about bail?"

Rick sighs heavily. I can tell he would rather not use our money to save Anna again. I feel the same way, but it doesn't seem like a choice. A good sister would never leave Anna in jail. "We can probably get Anna out tomorrow but not sooner. She'll be arraigned first, and then they'll set bail."

"Okay." I had planned to spend the morning at the gym and then have a leisurely, luxurious breakfast with Rick.

"This is a nightmare," Rick says as he stares out into the dark farmers' fields, lit only by the string of orange lights dotting the highway.

"I know," I say. I worry that soon he's going to realize that he can wake up from it. He could leave it all so easily. I distract myself by thinking about the call I need to make to my dad. I could do it from the car, but I'd rather wait until I'm alone. After Jesse died, my father had been everything I needed for the first week after the accident. Then he had just closed up. Talking to him was like trying to find a station on a radio with a broken antenna. Once in a while, he'd bark at me like a burst of static, but most of the time he was silent. No more conversations, no more hugs. He stared through me when I tried to talk to him, like he was seeing someone there he didn't know. Then his drinking got bad, so bad that I had to make sure to tell him anything important by 11:00 a.m. or he wouldn't remember.

Shortly after their divorce, my mom admitted that my dad's reliance on alcohol was an old pattern. It was how he managed stress when Anna and I were kids; she had to threaten to leave him before he sobered up. Her threat worked, for a while. He didn't drink much when we were growing up: a beer or two after his baseball game or at a party. But after the accident, he started drinking seriously again, and he hasn't stopped since.

Now we barely speak. At first, when I was in college and the silences on the phone stretched to awkward lengths, I attributed it to his loneliness. My mom had moved out, and he was living alone in a house that used to be filled with a family. Eventually I stopped calling and so did he. I thought maybe things would be different when Maggie was born, but nothing changed. Anna's decisions had shattered us all. My mom had moved on; my dad just kept sinking down.

"Maybe it's not as bad as it seems," Rick says. "Maybe this will be what Anna needs to finally stop drinking." He's not a good actor, but I smile to support his efforts.

"Maybe," I say. Neither of us has the energy to say more. The soft hills of the farms harden into used car lots and truck stops as the city rises into view. I turn on a playlist of ambient music, and the soothing electronic sounds fill the car. My headache fades to a dull throbbing, and I feel unexpectedly calm until we pull into the driveway, where I can see my mother frantically pacing in front of the bay window. Her face changes when she sees our car. She looks relieved.

"Thank God you are here." Her eyes are brimming with tears as she closes the distance between us and hugs my arm to her. My mom has a tendency to physically crowd others when she gets upset, as if closing a gap between bodies is the same as closing emotional distance. I smile and move away as I walk to the fridge to pull out a bottle of wine. Rick looks at me with a mixture of sympathy and displeasure. The irony of Anna's alcoholism triggering me to drink more is not lost on my husband.

"Mom, are you okay to stay? Or do you want to go home?"

"No, it's fine. I called Ingrid. She understands. She told me to stay over, if that's okay with you. Help if I can." Somewhere along the way, my mother began talking about herself as someone who could assist me with Anna, as if my sister was my responsibility and her involvement was optional.

"Great. Do you want anything?" I say.

She nods and slides onto a stool. "A glass of wine would be wonderful."

I pour her a glass and discreetly top up the inch or two I've already gulped down from mine.

"Is Maggie still asleep?" I ask.

My mother nods. "She was easy tonight."

"That's great. At least something went well."

"Yeah," my mom says quietly. She stares down at the counter, lost in thought. Rick takes a seat beside her, frowning.

"You okay?" I ask him.

"Yeah." I have a feeling I know what he's thinking about. It's the same thing on all our minds, the elephant in the room. Prostitution. Anna has sunk down to a level that I never thought she would reach, and she's pulling us all down with her.

My mother looks at us both carefully. "She hangs out in pretty bad neighborhoods sometimes. I'm not sure . . . maybe it was about drugs. She's not doing . . . that. I just gave her rent money. She's not a . . ." She drifts off.

I imagine the sweat of a man's body dripping on my sister. I take a deep drink of wine to suppress a gag.

"I still need to call Dad," I say out loud.

My mom winces. "Of course, Cara. Thank you."

"No problem," I say reflexively.

"No, really, Cara. Thank you for all that you do. I don't know how we would get through this without you."

I am warmed by her recognition. Anna's repeated mistakes have brought my mom and me closer. She understands how hard it's been for me, for us. My dad doesn't. He has never acknowledged what I do for my sister or how painful it is for me to have been shunned from his life. I guess it's easy to ignore reality in Rapid Falls.

I trail my hand over the smiling photos of Rick, Maggie, and me in the hallway as I make my way to the office. There is only one picture of Anna on this wall: a group shot of the wedding party. Anna hates having her picture taken, so I don't have any recent shots to include. There is not a single photograph of my father. He and I haven't had our picture taken together since the night of my prom, and it seemed odd to hang it, given what had happened that night. I had asked our wedding photographer for a father-daughter shot, but my dad hadn't showed up for the family shoot. By the time the reception began, he was too drunk. I click on a lamp by the armchairs, sit down, and pull out my phone, willing myself to work up the strength to call my father. I never look forward to hearing his voice, and I know he doesn't enjoy hearing mine.

~

In my third year of college, Rick's father had a cancer scare. I was amazed at the way Rick's family came together during the difficult weeks. The kindness and the worry made me ache for what was left of my family. When his dad's biopsy came back benign, I asked Rick if he wanted to come with me for a trip to Rapid Falls. At that point, weeks would go by without my dad returning my phone calls, and I wanted to check on him. I worried about how Rick would react to seeing where I grew up, whether it might make him think twice about where our relationship was headed. But I knew I had to introduce them at some point, and I wanted to get it over with.

My nerve faltered the moment we passed the sign at the outskirts of Rapid Falls, and I asked Rick to pull over at the inn for a quick lunch. I noticed Sandy sitting at one of the tables in the restaurant, and my mouth went dry with panic.

"Let's sit in the bar instead."

"Lead on."

We slid into a booth with cracked red-leather seats. The table was sticky under my hands.

"Are you sure the food is okay?" Rick whispered. The sound carried through the big empty room, and the waitress's eyes narrowed as she handed us menus. She looked vaguely familiar, the older sister of someone I went to school with, no doubt, but the years on her face and a bad dye job made her difficult to place.

"Thanks," I said. After she left, I answered Rick. "It's not great, but it's the best in town."

In truth I loved the popcorn shrimp, preferred it over the sushi Rick always wanted to eat. Raw fish felt like rubber in my mouth, though I pretended to love it.

"All right. When in Rome . . ."

The waitress returned and we both ordered.

The door swung open again, and a dog ran in.

Rick stared at the animal and then back at me. I knew he was thinking about the numerous health codes that were being broken. I shrugged my shoulders, trying to appear nonchalant, even though my heart was racing. I knew that dog—and who she belonged to. The owner looked around, letting his eyes adjust from the bright sunshine to the shadowed room. His gaze fell on me and a huge smile lit his face.

"Cara Piper." He walked the few steps toward us. Rick looked at me with a question in his eyes.

"Hi, Wade."

"Hi." He held out his thick hand to Rick, who shook it. "Wade Turner."

"Rick Stanley."

I felt my heartbeat thud as my worlds collided.

"Why don't you join us?" Rick asked.

Wade looked at me, and I nodded. "Please." I took a deep swig of beer to try to get rid of the lump in my throat while Wade motioned to the waitress to bring him a drink.

"Thanks. That sounds great. Come on, Skoal. Over here, girl."

"Coal?" Rick asked as he patted the dog's golden fur.

Wade laughed. "Skoal. You know. Like the chew."

Rick probably hadn't ever seen a tin of tobacco in his life, but he nodded knowingly. I looked back and forth between the two men, relieved at the easy exchange between them.

"So. How are you doing, Piper?" Wade turned to me and I felt a rush of love. He looked good, a little older, a little more weather beaten. Wade had the kind of face that had improved with a few lines.

"I'm well. Almost done with my degree. One more year to go," I said.

Wade whistled, and Skoal's ears perked up. "Look at you. It's good to see you, Cara. You look great."

"Thanks, Wade." His kindness made my eyes mist slightly. I thought he hated me. I thought they all did.

"Look, if you guys are around for a few days, I'm sure my mom and dad would love to have a visit." He looked at me, and I could tell we were both thinking about Anna. *Don't ask, don't ask, don't ask,* I thought. He didn't. "Stop by if you can, okay?"

I smiled and nodded. Skoal followed Wade out the door. Our food arrived and we started eating. A few bites in, Rick leaned forward.

"Was he a good friend of yours?"

I thought of Mrs. Turner and the way she had always made sure to bake oatmeal raisin cookies when she knew I was coming over. I remembered Wade's dad showing me how to plant tulips in the fall and how Wade's fierce loyalty meant that he would never have dreamed of ignoring me, the sister of the girl who killed his best friend. Then I looked into the eyes of the man I hoped would become my husband.

"Not really."

"Oh." Rick took the last bite of his burger, then started on his fries. "Why did he invite you over?"

"He was friends with someone I used to—" My face burned as I realized what I was about to admit. I took a sip of beer to drown the thought of Jesse. I didn't want Rick to know anything about what happened on graduation night. It was a mistake to bring him here. "I'm not sure, Rick. Someone told me once in high school that he had a crush on me." I laughed as if Wade was a joke that only the two of us understood.

"All done?" the waitress said as I pushed my plate away.

"Yes." I prayed she hadn't overheard me. It broke my heart to think of my words getting back to Wade.

"Let's go." Rick laid out cash and didn't wait for change.

My stomach was heavy as we walked into the parking lot. Sandy was standing on the steps of the restaurant when we neared our car. I smiled, feeling braver now that Wade had helped dissolve my nerves about being here. Rapid Falls was my home. People would accept me no matter what Anna had done. But Sandy stared right through me, talking to another high school classmate. Her voice was louder than it needed to be.

"Wow. I can't imagine coming back to a place where nobody wants you. Can you?"

The other woman tossed her hair over her shoulder. I recognized her. She had been on the track team with Anna. "No way."

Rick didn't seem to have heard the conversation. He unlocked our doors, and the car emitted a beep. I heard Sandy snort. People didn't lock their cars in Rapid Falls. I opened the door and slid in quickly, ducking my head so Rick wouldn't see my red cheeks.

My chest was aching when we pulled into my father's driveway. The house looked the same as it always had: an A-frame shingled in cedar that had faded from golden brown to nearly silver. The property was beautiful, nestled into a piece of land hugged by the river on two sides due to a slight bend in its course. I went to bed every night listening to the murmur of the water. I used to think I couldn't fall asleep without it. My foot landed in a patch of blackened gravel when I stepped out. My dad had changed the oil of our cars here for years.

Rick turned to me, his face worried. "Do you smell smoke?"

The acrid scent caught in my throat before his question was finished. I ran up the flagstone path that my mom had laid. "Dad?" I called as I tried the handle of the front door. It swung open. I was relieved to see the house was clear of fire, but as I crossed through the kitchen, I caught a glimpse of black smoke outside. The barbecue. I flung open the patio door and then stopped in my tracks, bewildered at the sight of the billowing smoke. Rick didn't hesitate. He crossed the patio and stepped to the back of the propane grill. Its lid was closed, but thick clouds puffed out the side like an angry dragon's breath. Rick covered his mouth with his hand as he turned the valve on the tank, shutting off the fuel source. Almost immediately the smoke lessened.

"This is hot as hell, Cara. Be careful."

I pressed myself against the sliding door, frantically looking for my dad. Where the hell was he? Had he collapsed and had a heart attack? Through the blurred glass, I could make out a large shape on the couch. In our hurry to put out the fire, I hadn't seen him. I slid open the door and walked over to where he was lying prone on the tweed sofa. His eyelids flickered when Rick called, "Close that door or the smoke will get inside too."

My dad heaved himself up slowly as I slid the glass door shut. His voice was thick; it sounded like his tongue was struggling to push the word out of his mouth. "Cara."

"Hi, Dad." I stepped forward as he rose, thinking he would welcome me with an embrace.

"You're early." He stood in place, wobbling slightly.

I didn't respond, still half expecting him to thank us for saving his house from burning down. My gaze returned outside to Rick, who was lifting the grill's lid with the edge of a pair of barbecue tongs. Smoke billowed out and he stepped back, letting it dissipate before plucking the charcoal lump off the metal grate. He caught my eye as he turned to the house and crossed the deck to the door.

"Hello, sir." Rick entered the room and extended his hand. My father looked at it, then reached forward with his. "I'm Rick Stanley. It's a pleasure to meet you."

My father nodded but didn't meet Rick's eyes. I felt a flush of shame but spoke quickly to cover it.

"Were you making lunch for us?"

My dad looked at me blearily.

"The barbecue?" I coaxed.

"Looks like you had a steak on there." Rick's gentle tone flooded me with gratitude.

"Huh." My dad made a sound that I took for an affirmative answer.

"Do you want me to fix us something else? The steak is a bit well done," Rick said, smiling. "Sir?"

My dad sat down heavily. The clock ticked. Suddenly he looked up as if he had just realized we were there. "What do you want, Cara?" He sounded exhausted.

Rick walked over to me and slipped his hand into mine. His touch gave me enough strength to answer.

"We talked last week. I told you we were coming. I wanted you to meet—" My throat became too tight for me to continue. I felt humiliated and ashamed.

"It's not . . . a good time right now." My father reached a hand over to the side table and picked up a tumbler. His Adam's apple bobbed up and down as he tilted back the glass to finish what was left.

I turned to Rick, half-afraid that my father's behavior would be enough to make him leave me forever. "I'm so sorry."

"It's okay, Cara. Maybe we should go."

My father nodded, though his eyes never left the bottom of his empty glass.

"Is that what you want, Dad?"

"It's . . . not a good time," he repeated, slurring. I gripped Rick's hand as he led me back toward the front door.

"Do you want us to leave, Dad?" My heart throbbed when he nodded.

"Not up for a visit."

"Goodbye, sir," Rick said. "Nice to meet you."

I wanted to scream, so I couldn't trust myself to say anything at all. I turned my back and left my father swaying behind me in the afternoon light.

Once we stepped outside, Rick said, "That barbecue is still hot, Cara. Is there anyone we can call to look in on him . . . in case he tries to use it again?"

Let him burn, I thought to myself. "He'll be fine."

We climbed back in the car in silence. As we drove back over the bridge toward the highway, I stared at the water below. Jesse was still down there, somewhere. Whatever was left of him. Anna would be in prison for another year. They were stuck in place, but I wasn't.

"I'm so sorry, Rick."

I'd never seen Rick's eyes look so kind as he touched my cheek. "You have nothing to apologize for, Cara. It's not your fault."

I took a deep breath and gave him a small smile. "Thank you. You have no idea how much that means to me."

~

I stand up from the armchair and cross the room. *I need to treat this call to my father like a business obligation,* I think as I seat myself at the desk. At this point, my father is little more than a troublesome colleague whom I have to deal with occasionally. I have built a life without him in Fraser City. Rick and I haven't been back to Rapid Falls since that visit. Maggie has never seen my hometown. I rarely think of my dad, drinking away his memories and erasing me from his life. Except on nights like tonight, when I have to serve as the bearer of Anna's bad news.

I click on my desk lamp and dial his number. It rings once, twice, three times. *Maybe he's asleep,* I think, glancing at the time. It's only 9:00 p.m.

"Hello?" His voice is gruff with sleep.

"Dad?" As if it could be anyone else. "It's Cara."

"How are you?" he asks flatly.

"I'm . . . fine. How are you?"

"Fine." He's heard something in my voice that makes him wary.

"It's Anna." The words are familiar to both of us.

"Okay." He sounds more comfortable now that we are reading from the well-worn script. "What's going on?"

I can hear rustling in the background. It sounds like he's getting out of bed. I can picture his bedroom so clearly, it's as if I'm there. I'm surprised by the longing I feel, thinking about my childhood home. For the few months after Jesse died, before Anna went to prison, it was the only place where we were safe.

"It's not good, Dad. Anna has been arrested—"

"For what? DUI?" my dad interrupts.

"No, Dad. It was . . . solicitation." I can't bear to say the word *prostitution*.

"Solic—" he begins, then pauses. "Oh."

"Yeah."

Silence.

"Was Ron with her?"

"I don't . . . Who is Ron?"

"Her boyfriend. Her new boyfriend, I guess."

"Oh." I'm surprised. He must talk to Anna more frequently than I realized. I swallow my irritation. He can call Anna but not his own grandchild? I try to keep my voice neutral. "I haven't met Ron yet."

"Anna mentioned him last time we spoke."

"I'm not sure he's around." I fight the urge to ask how often they talk. Silence again. "Okay. Well, I should probably let you get back to—"

"Is she . . . in jail?" His voice sounds achingly sad. It jars me.

"I haven't spoken with her yet. Mom was here at my house when she called. But yeah, she called from the station. We can't get her out until the morning. At the earliest."

"Oh." His voice conveys no emotion.

"Rick and I were away. We rushed back from a hotel. We had to cancel our plans . . . again." I can't resist the dig. My dad doesn't respond. I try to ignore the fact that he doesn't care or understand what I'm going through, what I always have to go through with Anna.

"So I'll know more tomorrow, but I just wanted to keep you in the loop."

"Okay."

"Okay, I'll call if—" I say, trying to finish again when my dad interrupts.

"Does she need me to come down?"

I feel a blaze of anger. All he cares about is her. "No, Dad, it's okay. I'll handle it."

"I know you will, Cara. You always have." His tone is bitter, almost resentful.

"Thanks, Dad." I pretend to take his words at face value.

"Goodbye, Cara."

I'm left holding the phone against my ear, flooded with disquiet.

Rick appears. His face is strained. He looks scared.

"Cara, the police called."

"Have you been able to speak with Anna?"

"No." He looks pale when he steps into the light from the lamp. "She tried to . . ." He takes a deep breath and shakes his head. "They said she started screaming and wouldn't stop. When they finally went to check on her, they realized that she had bit her own wrist so hard that she was bleeding. They had to take her to the psych ward."

I reach for the phone again, wishing it was a glass full of something obliterating.

CHAPTER TWELVE

July 1997

I managed to catch Wade as everyone filed out after the funeral. I asked him to meet me at Rapid Falls the next day. I spoke quickly and quietly so no one else would hear. I didn't fault him for his discomfort. We both knew that people would notice if he spent too much time cozying up to the sister of the girl who killed his best friend. I needed to make sure the story people were telling about me was the one I wanted.

I borrowed my mom's car for the forty-five-minute drive to the waterfall that our town is named after. My parents used to bring Anna and me up here for picnics when we were kids. The last time, Anna and I had fought over the last brownie and my mom had cut the trip short. At first it felt good to be quiet by choice, completely alone. No one had called after the funeral, and each of us had retreated to our own rooms, with the doors closed, for the rest of the day. As I reached the turnoff to the falls, however, my nerves jumped. This wasn't going to be an easy conversation. I had to figure out how much Wade knew.

Wade was a simple guy. He wasn't stupid—but he liked problems that could be solved. It wasn't in him to second-guess or yearn for something more than what life dealt him. Wade was Jesse's best friend and had been since the first day of kindergarten. At Jesse's insistence, he had reluctantly accepted me as the third in their trio. I had won him over a few hours later when I showed him where to find a frog at recess. When we got a little older, Anna tagged along with us too, and I got the feeling that Wade thought of her the same way Jesse and I did: a pesky little sister to be tolerated if necessary and ditched when possible. I always knew where I stood with Wade ever since we were kids. I was counting on that.

As I waited for him at the picnic area, I examined my fingernails closely, trying to find one that had grown long enough to be satisfyingly gnawed off. Jesse used to tease me about the ugly missing skin around my nail beds, often raw to the touch. It was a disgusting habit, but it helped calm me when I was feeling unsettled or out of control. I tore off a small bit of skin and spit it into the dirt below my feet, remembering the last time I was at Rapid Falls was over a month ago.

~

Jesse and I had decided to play hooky from school on an early May afternoon—one of the first warm enough to hint at summer. Rapid Falls High was a squat one-floor building just up the road from the Rapid Falls Inn. The front of the school, where the classrooms were, had a long band of windows that looked onto the highway. Sometimes the view felt like a taunt as I gazed out the windows at the cars heading out of town. There were only three hundred kids in the whole school, so by senior year it seemed like there were no new conversations left to have. During lunch, we would gather in the Cave, a carpeted room at the center of school that served as our drama room. The room would buzz, but it all just seemed like noise to me. I didn't care who kissed whose boyfriend at the Field last weekend or how much money someone had saved to buy their truck. It was May, just weeks away from graduation, and I was tired of the gossip and the mustard-color walls. I was ready for the next part of my life to begin. I was proud of the heavy white leather graduation jacket draping my body as I walked down the hallway. It felt like I was wearing the ticket to the future.

Jesse had shop class after lunch, so he didn't have to worry about leaving early. Our shop teacher, Mr. Crumb, was legendarily lax. He took attendance at the beginning of his class and then retreated into his office, leaving students alone with the engines they were supposed to take apart and put back together. Usually the shop was empty halfway through the period, but Mr. Crumb never reported anyone missing. I, on the other hand, had to fake an illness to get out of history. On my way out the door, the principal stopped me to ask where I was heading.

"Doctor's appointment," I lied. "Women's issues."

He looked at me skeptically, then nodded. I felt wonderful as I walked outside. The air was warm and smelled faintly of flowers. Everything felt perfect. Until I saw her. She was leaning on Jesse's truck, laughing. He was standing close to her, almost touching her. I could hear something in Anna's voice that I'd never heard before. She was tilting her head and talking a little faster than normal. She was flirting. Neither of them saw me coming.

"What are you doing here, Anna?" I said sharply. Just because she had broken up with Ross didn't mean she could flirt with Jesse. She sprang back like she'd been stung. Jesse had a weird look on his face too. Almost like guilt.

"Just . . . talking. Jesse and I were just talking about my . . . film." Anna looked at Jesse, not me, as she spoke. I felt my rage rise at her lack of eye contact, at the way she acted like he was on her side and not mine. For the last few months, Anna had been working on a project to use as part of her application for film school upstate. Jesse was the star. The program accepted students in their last year of high school so they could prepare for a film degree. I hoped that she'd get in because it would mean she would not be able to return to our hometown for Thanksgiving. The program was intensive and didn't allow for long holidays, so Jesse and I would be able to come back to Rapid Falls and celebrate our first months of college without Anna by our side.

Jesse seemed to sense my annoyance and tried to defuse the tension.

"Anna needs to shoot a few more scenes before she sends it off. I told her she could come with us this afternoon." I saw Anna was carrying her backpack. Irritation scratched my throat. I shielded my eyes. Suddenly the sun seemed too bright. It was almost sickening.

"Huh," I said. Anna had been getting on my nerves a lot—always asking to tag along when Jesse and I were hanging out. "It's kind of a full truck." Jesse's pickup truck was ten years old and barely bigger than most people's cars.

"We've squeezed in three people lots of times," Jesse said. "Besides, I'm sure Anna can fit. She's tiny." I felt another wave of annoyance, but Jesse didn't notice. He was too busy looking at Anna.

I was furious. Anna shot me a triumphant smile. *Loser, loser, loser,* I repeated in my head for the entirety of the drive. It didn't make me feel any better, especially since Anna and Jesse were so busy planning the next scene that they didn't notice my silence. The parking lot was empty when we got to the waterfall. The town was trying to redevelop its industry to attract tourism dollars and compensate for the decreasing price of wood on the international market, but so far it hadn't managed to do much more than attract the same bunch of German tourists who came every year to kayak.

The future of Rapid Falls didn't concern me much. I was ready to leave the town for good. My acceptance letter for the political science program at the biggest college in Fraser City had arrived the week before. I was waiting until Jesse got his letter before I told him. My grades were better than his, but he was a good student too, so I had no doubt that if I made it in, he would also. His plan was to become a physical therapist, and I knew the kinesiology program had lower grade requirements than the general arts.

When we arrived at the falls, Anna sprang out of the truck and we both followed. "What a day! I didn't think I'd get light like this until June! Let's get some B-roll."

Jesse rolled his eyes good-naturedly. "You and your B-roll, Anna. Surely you have enough footage of me standing around looking off into the distance."

"This time, I want you to look happy. It's for the opening credits."

Jesse laughed. "I think I can fake happy on a day like today," he said.

She beamed, and I felt something odd shimmer in the air between them.

"Hey," I said softly to him, trying to win back his attention with a sexy tone. Jesse never responded well to my anger, and I was tired of sulking. I would have Jesse all to myself soon. I walked toward him at the back of the truck and bumped him with my hip.

"Hey, yourself," he said with a smile, stepping to the side to pull down the tailgate of the truck. Anna climbed into the back to grab her equipment.

"I had hoped for a little alone time," I murmured. "I've always wondered what it's like to . . . you know . . . by a waterfall." I closed the distance between us and placed my hand high on his thigh. He had never said no to me before. He seemed distracted, but I moved my hand higher up his leg, close to the familiar swelling between his legs. I was surprised to feel softness under my hand, and I pulled away quickly.

He gave me an embarrassed smile and spoke quietly. "Your sister is right there."

I tried not to let my hurt show as I leaned my head toward his, needing his mouth to reassure me. He had never failed to respond to my touch before. A loud bang from the truck bed forced us to break apart.

"Need help?" Jesse asked, turning back toward the truck.

"She's a big girl," I said, my voice tight as I reached for his hand, but he pulled away and hoisted himself over the tailgate. I swallowed my fury. It had been days since Jesse and I had been alone together. This day was supposed to be perfect. I even had a condom in my pocket in case Jesse didn't have one. Anna was ruining everything.

"Okay, fine. If you guys are going to play around, I'm walking to the falls by myself," I said, letting anger bleed into my words.

"Okay," he called over his shoulder, handing Anna a large camera bag.

"We won't be long, Cara!" I could hear the note of victory in Anna's voice. I didn't bother to respond as I stomped down the path. The falls were huge that day—swollen with winter runoff and trees knocked free by the snowmelt. I made it to the viewing platform, then kept walking. Only locals knew about a little path through the trees on the far edge of the platform. There's no guardrail on that side, but the view of the falls and the river below are way better. On a clear day, you can see the water wind almost all the way to town.

Once I pushed through the small pines to the little clearing, I turned my full gaze to the monstrous beauty of the waterfall. The roar quieted my anger. I sat and stared, calming down. It didn't matter that Jesse was paying attention to Anna, I told myself. Anna had always tried to take everything that belonged to me: my dolls, my clothes, my makeup. Every time my dad paid any attention to me, she burst in with a story. When my mom put her book down long enough to listen to how my day went, Anna had to one-up me with something. I was tired of fighting with her about everything. She was trying the same thing with Jesse. But soon he'd be all mine.

After a few minutes, I made my way back down to the parking lot. Anna and Jesse were sitting down together. The camera was about ten feet away from them, mounted on a tripod. They were talking, but I couldn't make out the words, just the lift and fall of their voices. It sounded like a song. Then Jesse leaned toward Anna.

"Anna!" I said, furious. The calmness I'd felt near the water disappeared. Jesse and Anna jerked away from each other. Neither spoke. Anna got up suddenly, brushing off her jeans.

"It's for a scene, Cara. God, you are so ridiculous. Like Jesse and I would kiss for real." She huffed over to the camera to stop recording.

Jesse stood up too and walked toward me, but I couldn't stop looking at Anna. Her eyes glittered, as if she had won a game I didn't even realize we were playing. Rage twisted my stomach.

"What happened to the stupid B-roll? Is this a porn movie?" I spat, this time in Jesse's direction.

Jesse looked at me contritely. "The two main characters are falling in love, Cara." He paused. "We should have told you about this scene. It must have looked so weird . . ." He trailed off with a forced chuckle.

"It's just a movie," Anna said as she shoved the camera back into the bag. I looked at her, forcing myself to swallow the horrible things I wanted to say. I didn't want to show Jesse that I was jealous of my little sister.

"Yeah. Whatever." My eyes were knives I was throwing into Anna. I wanted to kill her.

"Cara, we were just goofing around," said Jesse. "It's a beautiful day. Let it go." His eyes sparkled at me, but it wasn't enough to dissolve the icy churning of my stomach. I fought the urge to tell him to shut up. Anna looked at me smugly, and I wanted to smear the expression off her face.

～

Now Jesse was dead. I wondered if his mom had received his acceptance letter this week, if it had broken her heart to read about the future Jesse would never have. The future that had been denied to us both: Jesse running his own practice in Fraser City while I ran for office, the child I had always dreamed of, the big house and the elegant life. The sound of a truck drowned out the waterfall and brought me back to the task at hand. Wade had arrived.

"Hey, girl," he called as he climbed out of the cab. Wade's dog, Skoal, was a yellow blur as she shot out of the truck toward me. I laughed as she barreled into my legs, then bolted toward the woods. Wade was a big guy, rawboned but solid. Guys like him used to be cowboys. I nodded and smiled. I knew I could count on him. The Turners were solid Rapid Falls residents. His mom was a perpetual volunteer at the school for any activity that involved one of her four children. His dad led the volunteer firefighters' squad and had cooked for its annual fundraising pancake breakfast for over twenty years. I had never seen them turn away a kid who needed help. I hoped I wouldn't be the first. Wade's voice held no trace of the confusion that had marked his mom's face yesterday when she saw me at the funeral.

"Hey," I said. I hoped Wade's honesty and goodness wouldn't make it harder for him to accept what I needed him to do.

"You look like you could use a wine cooler," he said, reaching into a box at the back of the truck.

I smiled. The expression felt unfamiliar. I had been worried that Wade would act as cold as his mother had at the funeral, but I should have known better. He grabbed a beer for himself and headed toward me with the wine cooler outstretched. The bottle felt wet, cold, and welcome in my hand.

"I'm . . . uh, sorry, Cara. Jesse was . . ." His voice broke and he took a long gulp of beer. "I can't believe it." He looked at the waterfall instead of meeting my eyes. In Rapid Falls, we drank when we were happy and when we were sad. Wade would never think it odd to pay tribute to Jesse with a drink, despite the manner of his death.

"Me either." I didn't know what else to say. Wade cleared his throat and took another swig of beer. I looked over and he nodded, swiping his eyes quickly with the back of his hand.

"He was a good friend," Wade said.

"I know." My throat was tight, and the words came out quiet.

"I, uh, got a call from Sergeant Turd a couple of days ago." That was what Wade always called Sergeant Murphy.

"Oh yeah?" I tried to keep my voice casual, hoping to conceal that was the reason I wanted to meet in the first place. About two years ago, Wade and Sergeant Murphy had a run-in when Wade got in trouble with a bunch of farm boys who'd found their dads' stash of high-powered explosives.

The gang, as it were, was talked about in coffee shops all over town. Fathers and mothers scowled as they discussed the booms and bangs that had woken them in the middle of the night and knocked glasses from their shelves. No one issued any formal reports and Sergeant Murphy had turned a blind eye until one Saturday evening when the group had stuffed an abandoned car with so much powder that every horse for miles around knocked down its fence in blind panic. Wade and the rest of the boys had been charged with mischief, which amounted to little more than a meager fine, but the incident had left Wade with a deep grudge against Sergeant Murphy. It gave me hope my plan would work.

"Yeah." Wade crushed his beer can in his hand. "Another one?"

I shook my head no. Wade nodded but headed to the truck to grab another for himself.

"You know what? Grab me one too," I called.

"Sergeant Murphy is a dick," I said when Wade returned. I thought Wade and the other guys were insane for playing with explosives, but I needed him on my side.

Wade nodded and stared at his boots. "He asked me a lot of questions about the ride up to the Field. And about pregaming at my place."

"Really?" I tried to sound unfazed.

"He wanted to know if Anna was drinking."

"What did you say?" There was something frantic and unmasked in my voice. Wade looked at me sideways.

"I asked him why the fuck it mattered. That really got his blood pressure up." His grin was wolfish as he chuckled at his revenge.

"Thanks." I breathed out the word.

"I'm not helping Sergeant Turd." He smiled again, and then a shadow crossed his face as he remembered why the cop was talking to him in the first place.

"He doesn't know that Jesse and I were fighting," I said. My voice caught on the words and I coughed, but it sounded more like a sob. Wade slid his boot across the dirt to knock against my sneaker.

"So you fought with Jesse? So what? He was a little drunk. Don't blame yourself. I didn't tell him what you guys were up to." He nodded to underscore his words. His eyes were blurred with tears. "It's not your fault, Cara."

I took a deep swallow of my wine cooler, pacing myself, trying to sound natural.

"Did you tell him about Jesse passing out?" I asked. In English this year, we had to read a poem about a wheelbarrow. I thought it was stupid, but one line still sticks with me. So much depended on Wade's one small answer.

"Man, I was drunk as hell myself. I don't remember much past punching Todd Carter in the face," he said, shaking his head ruefully. "Anyway. I'm not telling Sergeant Turd any more than he needs to know."

He slung his arm around me, and we sat in silence. All I could hear was the low rumble of the falls, the comforting current of a river completing its inevitable course. I should have known that Wade would come through for me. He would never wonder why I was asking him these questions. Wade was too honest to guess the truth.

CHAPTER THIRTEEN

July 2016

As Rick and I head to the hospital to deal with another crisis wrought by my sister, I am glad that he cannot hear what I'm thinking. On nights like this, driving on streets so empty I don't even recognize them, I imagine terrible things. My life would be a lot easier if Anna died. I would grieve for her; maybe I would be overcome with sadness about the things I didn't say or paralyzed by the ways I didn't help. It is possible that in death she would become a heavier burden for me than she is now. Still, I can't stop thinking about the relief it would bring. If she were dead, I wouldn't have to keep driving to emergency rooms in the middle of the night when I should be in bed beside my husband. I could finally put the past behind me. While she was alive, I would never be released of the obligations that came with being Anna Piper's sister. Or heal the damage she had inflicted on me and everyone else I loved.

"Want a coffee?" Rick asks as we pass a twenty-four-hour Starbucks.

"No thanks," I say. "I'm still hoping we'll get some sleep tonight."

"Ever the optimist."

I smile at him. I'm glad he's here, even though I resisted his initial offer to come to the hospital, telling him I could handle it alone. My mom insisted on staying with Maggie; she said it made her feel better to know that she could take care of at least one person tonight.

I pull into the parking lot and find a spot quickly. The app on my phone recognizes the lot from last time we were here, so it's easy to pay for parking. So much for optimism. I know now that nothing happens fast for a nonemergent suicide, so it is safe to assume that we are going to be here for a while.

"You've got this all figured out." Rick laughs sadly.

"Practice makes perfect," I say.

His mouth twists as he steps out of the car. We thread through a clutch of sick-looking smokers outside the hospital. Rick pointedly puts a hand over his mouth as we step through the sliding glass doors. Once inside I turn right and head past the intake window.

"Don't we have to check in?" Rick asks.

I shake my head. "We'll get more information if we go straight to the nurses' station in Emergency."

Rick raises his eyebrows. "Lead the way," he says. We walk past a congregation of irritated people in the waiting room. A few have large bruises. I see a small girl burrowing her face into her mother's chest. She has an injured arm swaddled against her body.

"God. I don't know how ER nurses do this every day." Rick grimaces. I wonder if he's remembering Maggie's tears during our last trip here.

I take his hand. "Look, if you want to go home at any time, just let me know. You can take the car, and Anna and I will catch a taxi later."

He shakes his head. "I'm fine, Cara."

I'm worried that this episode might finally be bad enough to convince Rick once and for all that we need to cut ties with my sister for good. During my last hospital visit with Anna, we had to listen to harrowing screams from a woman who had attempted suicide by self-immolation. Another time, I heard a guy chatting to his friend that he didn't know why he was in a hospital, but he was pretty sure the hookers had been the ones to call the ambulance. Tonight it feels like Rick's ultimatum is coming soon. I don't know what I will do when he issues it, because I need to keep Anna close.

"I know you are fine. I'm glad you are here. Anna will appreciate it too," I say. Rick looks dubious but squeezes my hand as we stop in front of a circular desk ringed with paramedics. Inside the circle, nurses wearily stare at clipboards and computer screens while sipping cardboard cups of coffee. No one gives us a second look.

"Excuse me?" Rick says. A few people glance at us, then return to their tasks without a word.

"We are here to see Anna Piper," I say. No response.

"I suppose we will just look for her ourselves," Rick says loudly. "Anna? Anna?"

I smile. Rick doesn't like to be ignored. His confidence is enough to get the attention of a young woman with red hair who is sitting about a foot in front of us.

She looks up at us and sighs heavily. "What's the name?" she asks.

"Anna Piper. Admitted by the police." My voice drops on the last few words. Rick looks uncomfortable as well.

"Are you relatives?" she asks.

"Yes, I'm her sister."

Her eyes move to Rick. "Is this the lawyer?" The contempt in her voice sends anger clawing up my spine. The insinuation is clear—an ambulance chaser trying to drum up business by trolling for fallen women.

"No. He's my husband," I snarl. "If you can't help us, maybe I can talk to the shift supervisor?"

She shakes her head and rolls her eyes, heaving an even deeper sigh as she types Anna's name into their system. "Your sister's not here," she says with a hint of a smile on her lips.

"She's here. I know for a fact she was admitted."

"If the police admitted her, it's a criminal matter. She's in the *criminal* psych ward. Not here." She emphasizes the humiliating words. I am furious but cowed. My sister is both crazy and a criminal. Anna is dragging me down with her.

Rick steps in. "And where is the criminal psych ward?" he asks in a level voice.

"Down the hall, to the right," the nurse says without looking up again. She's already turned back to her computer screen. Rick takes my hand, and we walk together in silence. I didn't even know such a criminal component of the emergency room existed. With Anna, I never stop learning new things about depravity. At the end of the gray hall, we reach a set of closed doors with a frosted glass inset at eye level. As we get closer, I can see that the glass is threaded with shatterproof wiring. I reach out and try the handle. A sharp-sounding voice comes out of an intercom on the wall.

"This is a locked ward. No entry for nonrelatives. Who are you here to see, and what's your relation?"

I close my eyes and will myself to be calm as I step toward the speakers to respond. "Cara and Rick Stanley, sister and brother-in-law of Anna Piper. She was admitted by the police a few hours ago."

"Hold your ID up to the camera." A small wall-mounted device swivels toward me. Rick passes me his driver's license, and I quickly pull mine out of my purse. I hold both to the camera and wait.

"Only one visitor a day," the voice admonishes.

Rick turns to me. "Go ahead. I'll wait out here."

"No way," I say, pulling the car keys from my purse. "You don't have to stay. Take the car. Get some sleep. I'll grab a cab later."

Rick hesitates.

"I don't want you to have to wait here. It could be hours." I force a smile. "Go home. Maggie needs you. And my mom."

Rick makes a good effort to return my smile. "Okay. Good luck." He looks into my eyes and kisses me softly before turning. The door finally clicks, and I pull it open. I walk into another long hallway. Everything is white, making the glare of the fluorescent lights seem even bleaker.

Immediately to my left is a small room, also barricaded in wired glass. Three people are huddled around a computer. No one acknowledges my presence. Illness, especially mental illness, strips a person and their family of basic dignity. Hospital staff help to ensure that. Maybe it makes the horrors they see every day bearable, but it also makes the experience more damning for everyone else. I walk past two empty beds lined up headfirst against the wall. I thought privacy was lacking in the regular ward, but this is much worse. The flimsy white curtains that partition the beds from each other stretch only the length of the beds; no curtain is available to block out the staff's gazes from the glassed room that faces them. It feels like a prison. I guess it is.

Anna is in the third bed, lying flat on her back with a thin blanket pulled over her legs. Her face looks waxy. She doesn't open her eyes as I walk closer.

"Hi, Anna," I say. "It's Cara."

"You shouldn't be here," she says flatly, turning away. *No shit,* I want to scream at her. I'm so tired of having the same conversation over and over, the one where I beg her to let me help her. I swallow hard.

"Of course I'm here," I snap, then try to soften my tone. "I'll always be here. I'm your sister, remember?" My feeble joke is enough to make her turn back to me and open her eyes. I see something troubling in them, like she doesn't believe me. Or maybe like she does, but she wishes it wasn't true.

"Is there a chair?" I say.

"No. Probably a dangerous thing to have in a place like this."

"Oh. Right." I remain standing awkwardly beside her. She is still lying flat. I feel like the grim reaper.

"You can sit on the bed, if you want."

"I'm fine to stand." The thought of nestling onto the bed that contains my sister turns my stomach.

Anna breaks the silence. "Cara. I don't remember . . . much about what happened."

The familiar words make me rip a hangnail off with my teeth before I realize I've done it. I feel the exposed flesh stinging and a rush of blood. I clench my fist, hoping to contain the bleeding. "The police haven't told us much either," I lie. The officer told me on the phone that Anna was picked up on a street downtown when she tried to solicit an undercover officer for sex. I don't know if she's telling me the truth about remembering or if it's her way of not taking responsibility. "What do you remember?" I say.

"Nothing. But I think . . . I think I tried to hit on someone . . . I think he misunderstood."

"Okay." I try to keep my tone neutral.

"I think . . ." She stares off into the distance. Her voice is dull and her eyes seem unfocused. "I think he looked like . . ."

"Anna." My voice is cold. My nail bed pulses as I tighten my hand. I know what she is going to say. "You need to stop. What are you on right now?"

"I don't know. They keep coming around with pills. I just take them." She continues, "I think . . . I called him Jesse." She stares at her hands blankly. "I did call him Jesse. The guy looked like Jesse, right?" The whites of her eyes seem huge when she finally meets my gaze. Her pupils are so dilated that she looks like a cartoon character.

"I wasn't there. And he was a police officer," I say firmly, trying to steer the conversation back to safe ground. My heart is beating so quickly that I feel sick.

"No. He. Looked. Like. Jesse." She sounds robotic, like the memory has drained her emotion. Then her face contorts as she begins to shout. *"He looked like Jesse!"*

Out of the corner of my eye, I see movement. A large man in a button-down shirt is coming out of the medical station. My knees wobble in relief.

"You're the sister?" he says. His voice is a less static-filled version of the one I heard on the intercom. "I'm the clinical psychiatrist on the ward. Anna needs to rest now." He turns his attention to my sister. "Anna, it's time for your medication. I need you to take deep breaths."

Anna continues to look frantically toward me. "How was Jesse there, Cara?" Panic rises up in me. This is the worst I've ever seen her.

"I don't know," I say helplessly.

The doctor nods to me coldly. "Why don't you come back tomorrow? This is generally why we don't encourage relatives to visit in the first few days."

Usually I would be affronted by his terseness, but I am grateful for the excuse to leave. I protest slightly to show him that I am a good sister. "I can stay."

"She needs to rest." The doctor eyes me sternly.

"Okay, Anna. Your doctor says I have to go. I'll be back tomorrow." Already I'm dreading it.

"Wait!" Anna says loudly. "Can you check on my cat? Please."

I nod. "Okay. I'll stop by." I walk down the corridor with legs that feel hard to bend. My lungs are tight, as if I'm about to be trapped in the whiteness forever.

"Wait," I hear the doctor call behind me. I fight a nearly overwhelming sense of panic at what he might ask. I have to force myself not to bolt for the door.

"What is it?" I say. My fear makes my voice sharp, almost rude. I try to change my tone. "How long will she be here? It's hard to see her like this."

"I know. But she's where she needs to be. I've done only an initial evaluation, but I suspect Anna's real issues go far beyond substance use."

I nod carefully, trying to remain composed.

"Listen, my name is Dr. Johal. I'll be Anna's primary care physician for the next few days if you can think of anything that might be relevant to her treatment."

"Few days? How long will she be here?"

Dr. Johal hesitates. "It's hard to say at this point, but my thought at this time is that she'll need at least two days to detox. We'll try to get her regulated on her meds. I don't know what kind of charges may be laid. That will directly affect her next steps. But from a medical perspective, I'd like to see her released into some type of rehab program. Do you know if she has the ability to cover that? Is she insured?"

I smile tightly. "It can be taken care of. We have the means." I make a point of looking at my Rolex as I speak.

"I see. That's good to hear." He looks at me closely. "Anna's not been very forthcoming. I'm wondering if there's any information you can give me about her past that might help. Maybe a childhood trauma?"

The lights buzz above me. It sounds like the ticking of a timer. My vision focuses to a pinpoint as my eyes lock on his. "Anna has been through a lot. There was . . . an accident when she was a teenager. A boy was killed. Anna was found at fault."

The doctor nods as if I have confirmed his suspicions. "Does she blame herself?"

"Dr. Johal, I'm not really comfortable with this conversation. I think you need to hear this from my sister."

"Of course, of course. This is entirely in confidence." He looks at me closely. The fluorescent lights bore into my ears again. "Is there anything else you do feel comfortable telling me? Anything else that might help?"

I shake my head. "No." At this point, there's nothing I can say that would help Anna. It could only hurt.

CHAPTER FOURTEEN

July 1997

My mom was in the kitchen preparing dinner when I walked in. The force with which she was handling the vegetables was not a good sign. My parents had been fighting a lot since Jesse's funeral. I hadn't heard them speak to each other this much in years. Usually my mom spent most of her time in her room, reading art books, and my dad worked long hours at the shop, but he had been home more lately. Business had slowed down a lot since Jesse died.

"Hi, Mom," I said.

"Hi," she replied. When she looked up, I saw in her eyes that she wasn't angry—she was sad. Devastated. I felt a cramp of fear in my stomach.

"What's going on?" I said.

She nearly knocked over her glass of wine as she stepped around the corner of the counter. I was relieved to see she had been drinking. It meant she was far less likely to notice I had been as well. The wine coolers that Wade had given me earlier were making my head tingle.

"Anna is going to be arrested tomorrow." Her voice cracked.

I waited, staring at the heap of jumbled items on the countertop: old mail, a fruit bowl with one brown banana, Anna's keys. I wondered if she was sitting in a jail cell at that moment.

"Allen Murphy came a few hours ago. He wouldn't even look at me." Her mouth curled into an expression between fury and disgust. "He is going charge her with drunk driving. Sorry, felony DUI." She looked at a small notepad beside the cutting board with a scrawled phrase on it. I wondered bitterly why she bothered to write down the official charge. No matter what it said on paper, to everyone in Rapid Falls, Anna had been arrested for murder. Jesse's murder.

"Where is she now?" My voice felt raw, like I didn't know how to say words anymore.

"She's here, hon. Allen told us to drop her off at the station first thing in the morning."

"And then we bail her out?" I said, as if the process was familiar to me.

My mom nodded. "After the arraignment. She's a minor. Maybe that will help it go quicker." She turned back to the pile of produce on the counter and stared at the lettuce. I could hear her sniffing.

"Mom. Is Anna going to jail?" I felt my stomach flip-flop in panic and elation. I crossed my arms to try to contain both emotions.

"She was . . . drinking and driving, Cara. It's not a joke. I've told you both, over and over." She trailed off, fresh tears rolling down her cheeks.

"Mom, it was graduation night. It was an accident." I made a case for her because I knew I should, speaking as if I believed the words I was saying.

"Cara. I know. She's your sister, and we all love her . . ."

"Of course." I pressed my tongue against my teeth with anger at my mom's unfailing allegiance to Anna.

"Oh, Cara, we all loved Jesse too," my mom said with sorrow in her eyes in response to the fury in my voice. "I could have come to pick you up . . . I should have . . ."

"Mom, don't. You could never have known . . . what was going to happen. He was my boyfriend. We can all forgive her . . ." I trailed off, incapable of saying what I should. I didn't forgive her, and I couldn't pretend I had.

"Really, Cara? You think we can all forgive her?" My mom looked heartbroken, but I couldn't tell if it was for Anna or Jesse. Or me. I saw bursts of Jesse's blood. Fire. Water. Rocks. I stared off so long that her tears started again.

"It's okay, sweetie." She walked toward me and gathered me in an embrace. She was shorter than me, but she still felt like my mom. I hadn't forgiven Anna. I didn't think I ever would. But maybe I'd get better at hiding it. My mom pulled back to peer into my face. I wondered if she could tell that I hated my sister.

"Look, we need to get through this together. We are a family. Families protect each other." She smiled weakly. "We'll get through this."

I nodded slowly. My mom sounded like she was trying to convince herself too. I wondered if any of us could protect Anna now.

"Your dad is in the family room. Anna is upstairs. We need to eat. Together." She blew air out of her mouth and turned back to the vegetables.

"Okay." I kicked off my shoes and walked down the hallway. I needed to know what had happened with Anna. What she had said. I walked through the living room, past my dad on the couch. He took a long drink of something on ice. His nod to me looked loose enough to indicate it wasn't his first drink.

"Hi, Dad," I said.

"Hello." He stood up, and the ice in his drink hit his glass. His back was rigid. He had barely spoken to me since we saw Anna at the hospital. I couldn't bear to be in the same room as him anymore. He seemed like a different man from the one who had driven me to the hospital and held me in his arms.

"I'm going to go talk to Anna," I said as I turned away.

He made a sound like a choked laugh.

"Are you okay?"

He was acting so strange; I wondered how many drinks he'd had.

"What was Jesse wearing that night?" His eyes were furious. The alcohol had sunk them deep into their sockets, but they still burned at me. Like he knew something.

His eyes forced words from me before I could stop them. "His grad jacket."

I saw a spark of something before his face went blank. It almost looked like hate.

"Why are you asking, Dad?" I said, feigning confusion, even though my hands prickled with fear.

"Cara. What really happened that night? Did you—" He stopped talking, like the words hurt him. He had never said my name that way before, like I was his enemy. We stared at each other without speaking. In the distance, I could hear neighborhood kids playing outside. It sounded far away, like it was coming from a different world.

"I don't know how to save you both," he slurs finally, lifting his drink once again to his lips. The fury left his eyes, replaced by exhaustion. "She was drinking. She was high. The whole town knows that she wasn't the girl they thought she was. Maybe it's too late for her. I should have said something earlier. I saw the way he looked at her. I just didn't want to interfere. Sometimes you try to do right and it ends up worse than you started."

"I don't know what you're talking about, Dad," I said, scrambling to figure out what he knew, how he knew. His words made me feel as if the black water had engulfed me again.

"Do you know what the word *triage* means, Cara?"

I shook my head no.

"You help the one who can be saved. No matter what," he continued. His lips lifted at the corners, but he was not smiling. His eyes were as dark as the river at night. I left the room without saying goodbye, trying to squash down a feeling of panic. It was going to be okay. He was just drunk and confused. Only I knew what really happened; even Anna didn't remember. The truth was down deep, at the bottom of a cold, dark river. With Jesse's body.

I walked by the guest room. The bed was rumpled from my mom. When I asked her why she had taken to sleeping there lately, trying to force her to admit the tension between her and my dad, she told me he snored. As if that was a new development.

Anna's door was closed. I hesitated as I reached for the handle to let myself in. At the last minute, I pulled back and decided to knock.

"Anna? It's me," I said as I cracked the door. The room smelled like stale perfume. Anna was lying on her stomach on the bed, hunched over a book. I could hear the river through her open windows.

"Hi." Her voice was dull.

"What happened? Mom is freaking out."

Anna shrugged. "I'm going to jail." Her lack of emotion made the situation scarier. "What am I going to do, Cara?" Her voice broke like a failing dam releasing a flood of emotion. She put her hands over her face and started to cry.

"Can I sit down?"

Anna nodded and took a gulp of breath. "Where were you?"

"I was with Wade."

"Does he hate me too?"

"Nobody hates you, Anna."

She snorted. "Yeah, right."

I wasn't going to try to make her feel better. It was happening to me too. Rapid Falls was circling its wagons. They wouldn't even serve me at the post office two days ago. The woman who had sold me stamps since I was a kid closed the till as soon as I got to the front of the line, announcing that it was time for her break.

"What did you expect?" I asked her flatly.

"I don't know. It's just so awful. The police treat me like I'm dirt. Sergeant Murphy wouldn't even look me in the eye when he took my statement."

I felt disgusted by her self-pity.

"People loved Jesse."

"Yeah. Everyone loved Jesse." She turned away from me. Her words made me clench my fists, hard. I took a deep breath to will away the anger and regain control. Anna buried her face into a pillow. After a few moments of silence, she said a few garbled words.

"What did you say?"

She lifted her head. "I got in." She gestured toward her nightstand where I saw a folded piece of paper on top of a thick envelope.

"I got into film school. Classes start September fifteenth." She looked at me with a face raw with pain.

"Oh," I said, still thinking of Jesse.

"Yeah. My first day would have been September fifteenth. The same day as the start of my trial."

CHAPTER FIFTEEN

July 2016

If I ignore the lingering odor of cigarettes, I could be in a classroom for troubled kids. The drawings on the walls look childish but desperate. Wobbly letters on one of them command me to LIVE, LOVE, AND LAUGH. Another shows a face with a screaming mouth crammed with a dream catcher. Their raw emotion puts me on edge even before the interview begins. I'm meeting with Anna's counselor at the inpatient rehab center that Rick and I are paying for. After five days in the hospital, Dr. Johal recommended transitioning Anna there. Rick's dad had pulled strings with some of his former colleagues, and the district attorney had agreed to dismiss charges, provided Anna completed the entire program. I roll my shoulders, trying to will away my mortification at involving Rick's father in Anna's sordid story.

The counselor clears her throat loudly. The wet sound makes me wince. "Have you ever been to therapy"—she looks down at her notes—"Cora?"

"It's Cara," I say, trying not to let my disdain for her lack of professionalism change my voice. "And no, I haven't." The couples therapist Rick and I saw is none of her business. I am a stable person. I have never required the kind of help she is asking about. I smooth my hair and look at her with a patient smile. She is overweight but doesn't seem to realize it. Her flesh spills out the top of her too-tight polyester pants.

Anna called the night before, while I was in the middle of giving Maggie a bath, to ask me to come today. It felt like she had waited until the last minute to ask me, as a test. I didn't know how much longer I'd feel obligated to drop everything in my crowded life for her. Maybe it would never end.

"Okay. I'll start slow." The woman winked at me and I smiled back. "I've been trying to help Anna understand the different roles each person in a family can play." She hands me a packet with the title Family Roles. I flip through it quickly. I see descriptions of lost child, enabler, hero, codependent, scapegoat, or mascot.

"So let's begin on page one," she says.

I rush in. "I think I understand. Anna talked to me about this last night," I lie.

"Okay, great," she says. "So what role do you think Anna plays in your family?"

"Um, probably scapegoat." I toss off the word quickly and un-thinkingly. I'm not prepared for the image that springs to mind, of a balled-up piece of paper I found in her room after she went to prison. The words, written in blue ink, were smudged as if she had cried on the page. My stomach clenches at the memory.

Dear Mom and Dad:

I am so, so sorry for what I have done to you. I don't remember anything about that night, but I know in my heart that I made the wrong decision. I was supposed to drive them home and I drove them off a bridge. I'm sorry—

The last sentence had been pressed into the paper so hard that I could feel the outline of the letters. The letter had never been finished.

The counselor is still talking. "So let's read about the scapegoat."

I turn pages robotically and stare at the words without comprehension. Anna was so pale in her black sweater, sitting behind that big oak table for her arraignment in the courtroom so many years ago. Her hair was so shiny it distracted me. I almost didn't hear the judge's words.

"The scapegoat is often blamed for difficult things happening in a family. Others in the family begin to assign blame to the scapegoat and clear themselves of any guilt associated with events. Does that sound like your family pattern?"

An involuntary bark comes out of my mouth, a cross between a laugh and a refusal. It releases something. I shake my head quickly, like a dog trying to dry itself off after an unexpected splash of water.

"I know it's hard to look closely at family roles." She nods knowingly. I am angry at her assumptions about the origin of these feelings—and my weakness in showing them to her.

"This gives me a lot to think about," I manage to say, hoping she finishes. Memories flood my mind. Her body was stiff when I pulled it from the driver's seat. I banged her head hard against the window frame as I clawed her out. Everyone thinks I saved her because I loved her. Not because I couldn't bear to let her sink without her realizing what had happened. What she had done. Anna was no scapegoat. She was responsible for it all.

"What are you feeling right now?" Her voice jerks me back to reality. I need to regain control again. I shut out the questions and instead look at the clock hung in the middle of the juvenile drawings, willing it to move faster.

"I feel . . ."

The sketches distract me before I can reassure her that I've been healed by this session. One piece I hadn't noticed before catches my eye, and I lean forward to see it. She nods, encouraging me to continue, but I can't stop staring at the drawing. It's bleaker than the others, and the thick strokes are mesmerizing. The whole page is filled with black lines, circling each other, like a hellish whirlpool. I know immediately that it's Anna's. Something bubbles out of me before I realize I'm speaking.

"She's not a scapegoat. It was her fault," I say sharply. My face feels fevered with anger, but the woman smiles as if I've had a breakthrough.

"We all feel that way when we are dealing with an addict. Addicts make choices. Our family roles only influence them. Remember, the addiction comes first, always. It's no one's fault."

My unintended words have shaken me, but I nod as if her trite words have reassured me.

She looks up at the clock. "Okay, let's end it there."

I stand and walk at a fast clip through the dingy waiting room. The parking lot is nearly empty, and the darkness makes everything look cleaner than it is. That woman was wrong. It is Anna's fault that she is the way she is, but it is mine too. She's my sister. I knew her better than anyone else in the world; I knew her inside and out. I have seen her in so many different situations; I knew just how she would react. I had to do what I did. For Jesse.

CHAPTER SIXTEEN

March 1997

Jesse draped his graduation jacket around my shoulders, and I smiled gratefully. The wind was blowing hard off the pools at the bottom of the diving rocks, and the chill was no match for the flimsy sweater I was wearing. Ross and Anna were down at the edge of the water, throwing stones. I was glad they were giving us a little space. Jesse passed me a joint, and I took a quick hit before I spoke.

"Did I tell you my parents are going to Anna's meet instead of our graduation lunch?"

"Huh?" Jesse replied.

"Is your mom going? Don't you think it's a bigger deal than a track meet?"

"I don't know," he said, sounding bored.

Jesse's lack of reaction felt like a match scratching on flint.

"Do you not get why I would be mad?"

"Not really, Cara. Who cares? I didn't even know there was a graduation lunch."

"I care, Jesse."

"Cara, the lunch is not a big deal. Anna can qualify for the state championship at this meet."

I let out a breath in frustration. "You don't understand. You're an only child."

"Okay, whatever." His face changed, and I could tell he wasn't thinking about my parents anymore. He slid his leg beside mine and gently rubbed the inside of my thigh. He pressed his mouth to mine, and I breathed him in. His mouth was warm in the cold air. I forgave him for not understanding how unfair it was that my parents had chosen Anna, again, over me.

"Guys!" I heard Wade calling. "I just found a dog."

Jesse and I walked toward the sound of Wade's voice. We found him standing with Anna and Ross. In his arms was a small patch of golden fluff.

"She's just skin and bones. Poor little thing."

"Where did you find it?" Jesse reached out to touch the small pup, and she whimpered.

"Poor little thing," Anna said, moving closer. "Can I hold her, Wade?"

He nodded, and Anna took the small dog in her arms. Wade continued, "Someone must have abandoned her near that casting spot. I thought I heard a little cry, and so I went to look. At first, I thought she was a fox or something."

Anna's eyes looked misty. "Who would abandon a puppy? There are bears out here."

"Probably its mother," I said.

Jesse looked over at me with a comically puzzled face. "Harsh, Cara."

"It's true. Mother animals do it all the time. Maybe she just wasn't able to care for it." I looked directly at Anna.

"Oh my God, Cara. Are you seriously still mad about Mom coming to my track meet?"

"Wait, what's going on?" Ross turned to Jesse for interpretation.

"Don't worry about it, Ross. This is between Anna and me," I said.

"Cara, you're being a cow. Just drop it."

I felt my temper flare at her dismissal. "It just seems really weird to me that you would have Mom and Dad come to your track meet when you won't even be running for Rapid Falls next year after you go to film school."

Anna's mouth dropped. The small puppy squeaked as she tightened her grip.

"Look, Anna, I'm going to take that puppy home and get her warmed up," Wade interrupted.

Anna shook her head as if trying to come to terms with what I had said, but she passed the small bundle back to Wade. "Sure."

Wade opened his jacket and tucked the small dog inside.

"Film school?" Ross crossed his arms on his chest.

"I was going to tell you." Anna glared at me. "I haven't gotten accepted yet or anything. Nothing is for sure."

"Oh my God, Anna. I'm so sorry. You've been working on your application for months. I thought Ross knew."

"I had no idea. When were you going to tell me?" Ross was the captain of the track team, and he and Anna had been dating for the entire school year. They had planned to spend their senior year training together. Or so he thought. I knew Anna had been waiting to tell him until she was accepted, but I was tired of seeing her get away with her dishonesty.

"Jesse, why don't we go see if Wade needs any help?" I said.

"Sure." Jesse edged away from Ross's scowling face.

"Bye, Anna. Bye, Ross." We headed up the trail. I could feel Anna's eyes cutting into me. I knew she was going to get me back for letting Ross know her real plan, but I didn't care. She was taking away my parents when I needed them. It was only fair that I took something from her.

CHAPTER SEVENTEEN

July 2016

Ingrid likes to drink nice wine. Drinking is still relatively new for my mom. She refused to join my father when he brought out his whiskey or beer. Now her face looks pink and joyful, even though she asked me over to discuss Anna and her drinking problem. I agree quickly to her offer of a glass. I am still rattled from the visit with Anna's counselor. I went in the wrong direction as I drove here from the rehab center without even realizing it and was nearly twenty minutes late. I had turned down three different streets to try to change course, and every single one had been a dead end.

I feel happy that my mother has such a beautiful home now. Ingrid bought it before prices skyrocketed in this part of the city; the wide-beamed log house with the water view must be worth millions now. It's just over the bridge from downtown, but it feels quieter here, miles from the rest of the city.

Ingrid rises from the table. We are sitting outside on the deck, and the sunset is lighting the sky in deep orange. "Oh, I almost forgot. I found some of those cookies you like!"

She gently squeezes my mom's arm and then walks back toward the kitchen. Ingrid is like that, making little gestures that remind a person they are loved. I wonder if being with her makes my mother realize all the ways that my dad was absent. Having a partner like Ingrid has made my mother seem more alive than she ever did when she was with my dad.

My mom sets down her glass. "So the place seems okay? Does it really have the resources to help Anna?"

I sigh and lift my shoulders. "I don't know, Mom. I hope so."

"I just really hope the counseling there is effective. Anna seems to be working through some kind of trauma, and she needs skilled people to help her."

"What do you mean?"

My mom takes another sip. "I've been doing a bit of reading lately. This kind of addiction usually comes from somewhere. Childhood, maybe. I suppose it's not that surprising, given what she went through."

The sliding glass door opens before I can remind my mother that I experienced the same accident and I was fine. Ingrid strides over, a plate of softly colored madeleines in her hand.

"Oh, sweetheart. These are my favorite!" My mom lifts a rose cookie and takes a small bite. "We were just talking about Anna."

Ingrid nods. "I so hope that she can get what she needs at EagleWind."

"Do you know the facility?" I ask. Ingrid's clients often battle addiction.

"I know of it. It's a mixed bag, like most of those places. There are some fantastic people working there and others who are not as . . . capable, let's say. Some people have great breakthroughs there. Hopefully Anna is one of them."

"Sure." I hope I sound sincere, even as I'm hoping that's not the case.

My mom sets her half-eaten cookie on the cedar table in front of us, and I am surprised to see tears rolling down her face.

"Mom! What's wrong?"

"I just keep thinking that this is my fault. That it goes back much further than . . . Jesse. I tried so hard for her. I thought if anyone was going to suffer from what happened, it would have been you."

My hands throb like my heart just pumped a double beat. "Me?"

My mom's eyes are glassy as she meets mine. Ingrid pats her arm. Something about the way she touches her makes me realize that this story is the reason I am here. My mom needs to tell me something. Anna's black drawing comes back to me, but I push it away as I drain my glass. Ingrid fills it without asking if I would like more, as if she knows that I'm going to need it.

"I don't know how much you remember about the mill accident in Rapid Falls. When your dad was a volunteer firefighter," my mom begins.

"Very little." Nearly every detail I know about it had come from conversations with my mom in the years that followed. I was five years old when it happened; Anna was four. "Dad was first on the scene, right? It must have been awful."

My mom nods. "It was. Greg McDooley—he worked with your dad at the shop for a few months before he started at the mill. I think your grandpa had been hoping that he would stay on at the shop, but the mill job was just too tempting. Anyway, your dad did the best he could, after the accident, so no one blamed him for what happened."

"It sounds like there was nothing he could have done."

"Maybe." My mom hesitates and wipes tears from both her eyes. "Remember Mr. Johnson? The man that owned the grocery store? Jesse worked for him for a bit."

I nodded. I couldn't think of him without remembering the way he'd looked at me at Jesse's funeral.

"Sure."

"He told me what happened. Your dad would never talk about it. Their training was so minimal, Cara. They learned basic first aid when they volunteered, but your dad wasn't prepared for that kind of accident. They had just gotten the logs off when your dad arrived. Greg was still talking; he seemed fine. No one realized the kind of damage that had been done or how severe shock can be. Your dad left him, Cara. He put a blanket on him, trying to make him more comfortable. There was another guy there who had gotten his hand pinned between two logs, trying to help Greg out. He was bleeding, and I guess it seemed like he needed help more than Greg. Your dad took the other guy up to the office so he could find a splint. He left Greg alone."

"Oh my God."

My mom nods. "It was a spinal cord injury. There was probably nothing anyone could have done. It was ruled an accident. But your dad blamed himself."

I am still piecing it together. "So Greg was alone . . . when he died?"

My mom nods again. "When your dad came home late in the afternoon, he was already drunk. He headed straight to the bar after he left the scene of the accident. I'd never seen him like that before. He was cold, so distant, but angry. I asked him what happened and he exploded. Told me that I had no idea what it was like. I was shocked, and I think I yelled back. I didn't know Greg had died. I didn't know."

My mom starts crying again. "He hit me so hard that I thought I was going to throw up. He had never hit me before. You two must have heard us yelling because you both came downstairs. There was blood everywhere, and Anna started screaming and crying, but not you. You kept looking back and forth between us, like you were trying to figure it out. Even then, you were a problem solver." She gives me a watery smile. "I panicked. I knew I had to get you out of there, but your dad started crying too, and you went to him. You put your arms around him, and it felt like you were on his side. Like you had chosen him, over me."

My stomach flips, but I take another slug of wine to fight the panic. The sound of my parents yelling fills my ears. My face feels frozen. I can only hope I appear calm, as if my mother's words are not opening up something awful inside of me that I can barely contain.

"He told me to go, to leave, that I wasn't welcome there, and you nodded. I grabbed Anna; she was crying so hard that I couldn't leave her. It felt like . . . she was the only person who cared about me."

I was five years old! I want to scream, but I nod instead.

"As I carried her out to the car, you started to follow me, like you realized suddenly what you had agreed to. You were crying, holding on to my leg. I was so angry at you." My mom's chest starts heaving. "Oh God, Cara, I'm so sorry. I know how crazy this all sounds now, but I was hurt and confused. I put Anna in the car and I drove away. I left you there with your dad."

"Where did you go?" My voice is emotionless even though my thoughts are crashing inside my head.

"I went to the Turners. I knew Marlene had a trailer that was empty. She took one look at me and told me I could have it for as long as I wanted. It was awful. We stayed for two weeks and that was as long as I could bear it. No one in town would give me a job. Mr. Johnson told me outright when I applied as a cashier that I should go back to my husband. The trailer was cold and crawling with fleas. Your dad wouldn't let me see you unless I agreed to move back in."

I have a vision of Anna's thin arms covered in angry red bites. The image fills me with rage, but I gulp down half a glass of wine to contain it. I focus on my mother's face, trying to concentrate on her words and not the fact that she left me behind. My head begins to pound as I remember the feeling of sheets plastered to me with sweat. Something happened to me when my mom was away. I had gotten sick. Dangerously sick. And she wasn't there to take care of me. I suddenly feel terrified. Ingrid reaches over to me, and I push the memory aside.

"Are you okay?"

I look at her and nod as I swallow hard. "So you moved back in?"

"Yes. I came back to you."

"Thanks, Mom." My words are barely more than a whisper, but my mom smiles as if I have forgiven her.

"We were never the same after that, your father and I. We stayed together, but we didn't love each other. I hated him for what he had done to me."

"You've all been through so much," Ingrid says.

"It's incredible how resilient you are, Cara. I'm always amazed at how you've been able to weather the blows, while Anna fell apart."

I nod, grateful that I still seem stronger than my sister to her, even though my mind feels as splintered as a frozen puddle trampled by a heavy boot.

"I'm so sorry, Cara." My mother's sentence ends in a sob.

I speak quickly. I know what I need to say, even though none of it is true. "Mom. It was so long ago. I'm okay. Let's put it behind us."

My mother smiles through her tears as she leans over to embrace me, as if she believes all the things I've just said. As if her choosing Anna over me could ever be forgiven.

CHAPTER EIGHTEEN

August 1997

When someone you know is charged with a crime, you spend a lot of time waiting. Cop shows never go into that part. There's a good reason. It's boring.

At first things moved quickly. Two days after Anna was charged, she and my parents met with a lawyer in Nicola. My parents came home tight faced and vehemently opposed to the other's ideas about what to do next. My mom was convinced that the only option was for Anna to plead not guilty and take the case to trial. The idea of Anna spending a single moment in prison was unbearable to her; she couldn't even consider the possibility without breaking into tears. The lawyer thought Anna should plead not guilty as well. Of course the lawyer would say that, my dad said: more money for him if the case goes to trial. My dad kept repeating that she needed to avoid going to court. Anna was going to be found guilty no matter what, he said. Better to make a deal, get a short sentence, and close this chapter. She would be able to move on. She would still be young after a sentence of three to five years.

"How can you say that?" my mom yelled one night over a dinner of scrambled eggs that none of us was eating.

"Suzanne, we can't change what happened. The only thing we can do is get this over with quickly. That way, no one else will get hurt, and we won't have to expose ourselves to the whole town by going to trial. This needs to end now, before it gets worse. We have to make some hard decisions right now. For Anna. But for Cara too."

He stared at me the same way he had when he was drunk, like he was trying to tell me something that he couldn't say out loud. My dad seemed less angry now. More resigned, as if Anna pleading guilty would let us all move on. My mom slammed her wineglass down so hard that the base broke from the stem. She jumped up with the bowl of the glass in her hand, but my dad and I just stared at the thick round piece of glass that was left. The spike at the top looked jagged and dangerous. Anna fled from the table, sobbing. I don't think my mom and dad ever slept in the same bedroom again. They talked like they knew what they were doing, but I could see my parents were scared. Anna could see it too. Late at night, I heard her crying through the wall between our bedrooms.

After a few days, the heated arguments turned sour and silent, and our house felt wrong. None of us met each other's eyes if we happened to cross paths on the way to the bathroom or while grabbing a few stale crackers from the cupboards. It felt like we were all squatters trying to avoid trouble with the other strangers who shared our space. My only escape was Wade, who used to pick me up for drives after dark so no one in town could see us. "What doesn't kill you makes you stronger," Wade muttered in response to me trying to describe what it was like. I realized then that clichés exist only so you didn't have to sit in silence. Silence made you think about the people who weren't coming to visit. Like Sandy. None of us had seen Anna's best friend since the funeral.

Sadness weighed us all down. The TV was on constantly. My dad was usually drunk by 3:00 p.m. Anna rarely left her bedroom. My mom, who used to celebrate her deep, even tan every summer, dismissing skin cancer with a roll of her eyes, was pale as a ghost. We all were.

We stopped going to the grocery store after each of us experienced the damning hush that occurred every time people noticed our presence. For over a month, we survived on canned food and whatever was left in our freezer, until my mother arranged for our old babysitter to begin picking up groceries for us. One night I ate a frozen pizza that was so freezer burned I could hardly tell what it was. It didn't matter. I couldn't taste it anyway. I was grateful when fresh food began coming in from Mrs. Evans and I no longer had to gnaw on eight-month-old fruitcake for breakfast. It wasn't until years later that I realized how humiliating it must have been for my mom to be unable to complete basic tasks.

My mom also kept trying to make me talk to her about Jesse. She said I should go to counseling to "get through it." She wanted me to tell her how much I missed him and how sad I was that he was gone. I knew what she wanted me to say, but I couldn't recite the words. I was too angry to be sad. At Anna. At Jesse. They took away everything.

There was a month left until the scheduled trial when I heard the knock on my bedroom door.

"I'm not hungry," I said.

"It's not Mom." My door opened and my sister walked in. Her hair was greasy, and the pimples on her chin looked deep and sore.

"Hey," I said, shifting my legs to one side of the bed so she could sit down.

"It stinks in here," she said.

"Does it?" I looked over at a pile of unwashed laundry. "Open a window, I guess?" I turned back to my book. I didn't have much to say to Anna. She sat down on my bed instead of walking to the window. I closed my book and absentmindedly looked at my nails. I knew they would bleed if I bit them any more. I could feel my anger rising. All of this was Anna's fault. We both knew it, but neither of us had said it.

"Mom won't leave me alone," Anna said.

"About what?" I tasted blood as I pulled a tiny tag of skin from my finger with my teeth.

"The plea," she said.

"She's pretty obsessed with it. The innocent thing." I sucked on my thumb to try to stop the bleeding.

"Not innocent, Cara. Just not guilty," Anna said.

"I guess." I knew she wasn't innocent. We both did. I could have stopped our silence with my rage, but I swallowed it down. This wasn't the time.

"What . . . do you remember?" she asked me. She sounded scared, as if I was going to tell her something awful. She hadn't asked me about that night since I saw her in the Nicola hospital.

"What do you mean? I remember pulling you out of the car. I remember . . ." I stopped talking to avoid saying too much. I remembered the feeling of mud on my hands that was so warm I had thought it was blood. I remembered things I was going to spend my whole life trying to forget.

"I don't . . . remember anything. Nothing after . . . when we first got to the party. I remember riding up with Sandy. We were listening to the Spice Girls. She hit a huge rock with her car right after we got through the roadblock. I thought we were going to have a flat tire, and I was so glad that we made it up. I remember seeing Jesse."

I turn toward the wall as she keeps talking.

"I don't remember leaving the Field." Her voice fills with panic. "I don't remember drinking, Cara. Or taking pills. I mean, I know I had a wine cooler or two, and I stole one of those painkillers from you before we left for the prom, before Mom took our pictures. But I was staying sober. For you."

Bile rose in my throat, but I pushed it down. Nothing she did that night was for me.

"You stole a painkiller?" I seized on the gift she had unknowingly given me. "Anna, come on. Of course it hit you super hard."

"It was grad night. You seemed like you were having so much fun. I thought . . . I would too."

145

I paused, narrowing my eyes. "How do I know you didn't take a whole bunch?"

"Um, check the bottle?" Anna's sharp tone made my hands clench. She hadn't talked to me like that since the accident, but instead of reassuring me, it made me furious.

"It was in the truck." My tone was as icy as the river. "You know, the one that sank?"

"Oh."

"Do you really expect me to believe that you didn't have more than one drink? The police tested your blood."

"Maybe I was drugged?"

I looked at her with my best doubtful expression. "Seriously? You just told me that you stole a painkiller. Maybe more. Besides, who would drug you?"

"I know. It's stupid. I just don't know . . . Why can't I remember?"

This was dangerous territory. I couldn't let her keep asking these questions.

"Anna, you killed him. You killed Jesse. I have no idea why you can't remember. Maybe your brain is trying to protect you. I don't know."

She flinched as if I had punched her. Her face distorted with the deepest hurt that I had ever seen: pure, unadulterated sorrow. She started to cry. Ragged sobs ripped through the room. I didn't reach out to touch her. She gulped air quickly, trying to stop herself.

"I know. I know what I did. Do you think I don't know?"

I stared at her coldly. "Just stop with the not-remembering stuff."

"It's true, Cara," she said.

"You were at a party, Anna. You drank more than you thought you did. It happens." My voice was frigid, but I didn't feel cold. I felt furious, hot with anger. Even my hands were burning.

"Maybe." She stared off into space, as if trying to convince herself. I needed to turn this around. But first I needed to know if anyone else knew about her gaps in memory.

"Have you talked to the lawyer about not remembering?" I asked.

Anna shook her head. No.

"Mom and Dad?"

"No, Cara. What's the point? Mom will just turn it into another crusade against Dad."

"She's not even sleeping in their room anymore."

"I know."

We were both silent. A few months ago, it would have been our biggest problem. Now it barely even registered.

"So what now?" Anna said. "What am I supposed to do?"

I felt my anger rise again. "About what?" I tried to keep my voice neutral as I dragged another piece of skin from my thumb with my teeth.

"Are you kidding? About what to have for dinner. What do you think I'm talking about?" Anna said.

"How the hell am I supposed to know?" I took a deep breath to keep the blackness from engulfing me. I needed to keep myself focused. I needed control. I kept my voice level. "Anna, it was graduation night. My graduation night. No one is going to believe you stayed sober. If you plead not guilty, you're going to jail. For a long time."

Anna sobbed again, but softly. "Cara . . ." Her voice was pleading.

"I can't lie to you, Anna. I don't believe you. Why would anyone else? I'm trying so hard to make what you did be okay. But it's not."

Anna looked at me with eyes that were full of remorse. I wondered if she was feeling bad for all the things she had done. Even the ones she thought I didn't know about.

"I know. I'm sorry, Cara. I'm so, so sorry."

"Maybe you are, Anna. But it's not enough. Not for Jesse. Not for me. And not for the rest of Rapid Falls."

Neither of us spoke for a while. A dragonfly clicked against my closed window, and we both looked up at the evening light. The sun was setting purple and pink. It was probably a beautiful night.

"You did this, Anna."

She looked at me, and it seemed like her eyes wouldn't ever contain anything but pain.

"You're right," she said. I nodded as she got up from the bed. "Thanks, Cara."

"For what?" I said, unable to keep the scorn from my voice.

"For helping me decide."

I heard her go downstairs and tell my dad she needed to talk to him. My bedroom was right over the kitchen, and I could hear her accept my dad's offer of a drink after she told him what she was going to do. It was the first time I had ever heard my father allow us alcohol.

The next morning, Anna called the lawyer herself to tell him she was pleading guilty.

CHAPTER NINETEEN

August 2016

Rick hasn't spoken since we got in the car twenty minutes ago. His hands are tight on the wheel.

"Are you okay?" My voice is flat. I'm too tired to take care of him today.

"Yeah, I'm fine." He is lying. I muster up the strength to issue a follow-up question. Rick needs attention. Just like everyone else. Maggie was up at 3:00 a.m. last night, crying about monsters. She was inconsolable, and all I could do was hold her, letting her tears warm and then cool my skin as she clung to me with hands that felt like claws. Finally she relaxed into sleep, and her small, soft body melted into my arms. I stayed in her bed all night, listening to her deep, even breaths. My mother's confession kept me from sleeping. I was only a couple of years older than Maggie when my mother had left me all alone with my drunk father. I could never do that to my daughter. Back then, none of them understood what real love was. I have to remember that. Rick and Maggie are what matter now.

"Are you sure?" I reach over to touch his arm, and he puts one of his hands over mine. He is still facing away from me, but we are connected now. I hear a swallow click in his dry throat.

"I just . . . I just don't know what I'm going to say to her," he says.

"You didn't have to come—"

He doesn't let me finish. "I know I didn't have to come. But you do so much. I just want to help."

I don't even know where to begin. Somehow we have to try to halt my sister's self-destruction in the few moments when we are not handling the constant needs of a toddler. We are both so tired. It feels like it's going to overwhelm us.

"Anna's fine. She's safe now. Maybe this time at the center will be what works. We'll get through this." The words feel like a recitation. I wonder if he can tell that I don't mean any of them.

He smiles at me. "I feel like we are parenting two crazy people."

I nod and laugh a little. "I don't even know which one is worse." I am grateful that this elicits a chuckle. It's hard to see Rick like this, to deal with a stressed husband on top of everything else. He's always been so poised, so controlled. It's why I married him. I lived on campus the first year that we were dating, and I was so proud to have a boyfriend who had already finished school. He was clean, stable, unmarked by small-town tragedy and chaos. Marrying him meant I'd succeeded. I wasn't white trash.

"Are you ready?" I ask as he turns the car left into the small parking lot. A handful of people stand outside the building, smoking unhappily. A young girl stares at us as we pull up, and I return her gaze. Despite her youth, her eyes are hard and empty, as if she's reached the end of a harrowing road only to find another more difficult path ahead.

"Yes," Rick says, and he climbs out of the car. Once we've closed our doors, he presses the locking fob, meeting the eyes of the staring girl pointedly as our BMW emits a high-pitched beep-beep. Rick uses his high-class upbringing like armor when he feels intimidated. It looks like snobbery, but for him it's survival. The girl spits deliberately on the sidewalk in front of my husband as we walk past.

"Charming," I say, grabbing Rick's arm as he stiffens in disgust. He wanted to be here to support me, but I need to protect him from the ugliness of Anna's world.

~

"I want to come with you to see Anna tomorrow," he'd said last night in bed. His eyes looked so tired that I was worried he was going to fall asleep before I could answer.

"Really? Why?"

"I've arranged for Maggie to go over to your mom's for the day. I think it's important that I come. For Anna. But mostly for you."

"I'm fine, totally fine," I said. "It's going to be . . . These places can be a bit rough, Rick."

He shifted his body, propping up his pillow so he could lean back. "That's why I don't want you to go alone. You seemed so . . . upset when you got back from your mom's last night. I want to help."

The offer was unexpected, and I was thrown by his kindness but also concerned that I'd been letting myself slip. I didn't realize that I had been visibly disturbed. Maybe I did need his help. I had to talk to Anna, to make sure she wasn't falling apart. Rick could help me do that.

"I appreciate it. Anna could definitely use the support."

"I'm hoping she can finally get through this, you know? Maybe if we are both there, she'll see that she's not alone."

"That would be great, Rick."

"But, Cara?"

"Uh-huh?" I reached for a glass of water.

"We might need to have a conversation soon about what to do if Anna doesn't improve. We can't go on like this forever." He stretched his arms out wide and yawned. He seemed secure that I agreed with him about Anna. I swallowed a gulp of water too quickly, and the glut of liquid moved down my esophagus painfully.

"Definitely," I said, hiding my panic at his hinted ultimatum by leaning over to kiss him. I could not let Anna navigate without me. I had to know what she was thinking, drunk or sober. There was too much at stake for me to cut her out of my life.

"Good night, honey. I love you," he said, his eyelids starting to droop.

"Love you too," I said, but he had already fallen asleep.

~

We walk into a small waiting room. A frizzy-haired woman sitting behind a glassed-in counter glances dismissively at us before turning back to a computer. I lean down to speak in the small hole in the Plexiglas.

"Hello?"

The woman turns slightly, her body still partially angled toward her computer screen. She looks at me impatiently. "Yes?"

"We are here to visit Anna—Anna Piper."

"ID?"

I reach into my purse for my wallet, pressing my driver's license against the glass.

"Slide it through." Her voice is boredom, laced with contempt, at my inability to immediately grasp her system. "His?"

Rick takes his wallet out of his back pocket. The woman looks back and forth between the thumb-size photos and our faces a few times.

"Relationship?"

"Sister." I smile at her, but it's wasted energy. Her brief glance in my direction is only to match the photo with the person standing in front of her.

"Brother-in-law." Rick sounds irritated, and I place a hand on his forearm. It's part comfort and part warning. Women like this are gatekeepers. We need to follow her instructions, or she will make this visit difficult for us. She looks at a crumpled piece of paper on a clipboard in front of her then passes our IDs back through the window.

"Room thirty-two."

"Thank you so much," I say. My supportive sister act is wasted on her.

"Go on through," she says. A harsh buzz sounds from a door to the right of us, and I move quickly to catch the handle before the lock clicks again. I have a feeling she won't wait long.

"You'd think in a place like this, compassionate care would be a priority for the staff," Rick says loudly. I try to get my bearings. There's a common area with a small TV blaring. A couple of people are sitting on uncomfortable-looking sofas, staring vacantly at a soap opera, where overly made-up women on the screen scowl at each other.

"Must be down here," I whisper. Rick doesn't respond. He's methodically scanning room numbers as we walk down the hall. It's institutionally clean, not a speck of dirt in sight, but the air feels filthy. Everything in these places is steeped in misery. I'm not surprised that it rubs off on the staff too.

"Thirty-two." He stops in front of the door, waiting for me to knock. It's closed, but not tightly. When I graze it with my knuckles, it opens.

Anna is lying on a bed with a flimsy light blue cover, the same ones used on hospital beds that never keep you warm, no matter how many you have. She looks better than she did the last time I saw her, but the circles under her eyes are still dark and her skin is patchy with acne. Her corroded beauty makes it seem like she belongs here. I hope I do not appear the same way.

"Hi, Anna," I say, stepping through so Rick can enter.

"Hi, Anna," Rick says.

"Oh, hi. I didn't know you were coming." She smiles at him and he smiles back. After a moment's pause, he takes a step toward her and pulls her in for a hug. Anna looks at me over his shoulder, surprised. So am I. I fight off a flood of jealousy.

"You look good," he says, breaking the hug and looking for a place to sit. He awkwardly pushes a few items to the back of a chair and perches on the edge. It's the only other furnishing besides a small wooden table. The room couldn't hold any more—it's the size of our walk-in closet. Rick settles on the chair, and I lean against the wall. There's nowhere else for me to go, but even if there was, I'd stay standing. I need to keep my distance.

"Liar," she says, blushing slightly. I choke down my anger. Rick is just being polite. Anna looks like shit. There's no way Rick could find her attractive. Silence. They both seem to have exhausted their conversational supply.

"How is everything going here? Feeling good?" My voice sounds overly encouraging, like a primary school teacher readying her star student for a spelling bee. "Has Mom come to visit?" I feel uncharitably happy when Anna shakes her head sadly. I know that my mother hasn't made the trip, but I like making Anna admit it. I don't ask about my dad. I don't want to know. "How are the beds? Comfy?"

Anna looks at me with slightly squinted eyes, trying to figure out if I'm mocking her. She decides to trust my sincerity.

"They're okay. You know, rehab." She laughs a little, and Rick smiles uncomfortably.

"And the food?" I say lamely.

Anna shrugs. "Not bad. Not great. I don't pay much attention. The psychiatrist started me on a new antidepressant. It kind of kills my appetite."

"Huh." This piques my interest, but I try not to let it show. "Is the psychiatrist the person I met? For the family therapy session?"

"No." Anna laughs. "She's just a social worker. Dr. Hinkley is a real doctor." Anna seems oddly proud, as if working with a psychiatrist justifies all her past bad behavior. I try to be supportive.

"That's good. So how is it going?" I ask. I feel awkward discussing Anna's mental health in front of Rick, but I need to know who Anna is talking to and what she's saying. Rick shifts in his chair, but Anna leans forward eagerly. She seems to have no issue revealing these details to Rick. Maybe she thinks of him as family. The thought makes saliva flood to my mouth, as if I'm about to be sick.

"Yeah, it's pretty good, actually. I like her," she says.

"What kind of stuff do you talk about?" I ask.

"Well . . ." Anna looks at Rick carefully. He nods and smiles encouragingly, but I have a feeling Anna can tell he's forcing it. "She's into this idea that addiction always begins with trauma. Like childhood stuff."

Rick pulls out a pack of gum and takes a stick, offering us some. The minty smell reminds me of my mom, back when we were kids and we used to sneak it from her seemingly bottomless purse. I wonder if Anna has the same memory.

"Trauma?" I say. "So, like Mom and Dad and Freud?" I make a joke to diminish what my mom told me last night.

Anna laughs. "Maybe for some people. I don't think that's what's going on with me. Neither does Dr. Hinkley."

"Okay," I say. Rick looks at me sharply. He must detect wariness in my voice. I set my face back to neutral.

"What does Dr. Hinkley think is going on?" Rick asks.

"She . . ." Anna looks at the wall, as if remembering their last session. "She wants to talk about the accident a lot. About life in Rapid Falls when we were young." She turns back to me and looks straight into my eyes. "About . . . everything."

I feel the hair on my arms raise in high alert. Anna knows not to talk about Jesse in front of Rick. She knows I've told him only part of the story.

"How often do you see her? Dr. Hinkley?" My voice sounds level again. Rick looks at me and smiles. Good.

"About once a week. Not a lot. She wants me to find a therapist after I get out. To try to get through more of this stuff."

I nod, trying to figure out a response.

Rick breaks in. "You see her once a week? That doesn't seem like enough."

"Yeah." Anna lifts her mouth into a half smile. "It's not. But you take what you can get here. And there's group sessions. Those happen twice a day. Those are usually led by the woman you met, Cara."

My pulse slows. The groups with a social worker seem safer. Anna needs to speak in a place where no one is going to press her to go further than surface level. Someone like Dr. Hinkley delving into Anna's past is dangerous. It could hurt her. It could hurt us all.

"Maybe we can help?" Rick says kindly. "Those group sessions aren't going to be enough, and you're only in here for a few more weeks. We've talked about finding a good therapist for you, and it sounds like now is the time. I can ask around and find someone to start working with you as soon as you get out. Or maybe Dr. Hinkley can see you as an outpatient." Rick meets my eyes and smiles, as if both of our dreams have finally come true for my sister.

Anna looks at Rick like a dog that was expecting to get whipped but was given a bone instead. "That would be great." The way she says it makes me realize how few people have offered to do things for Anna in her adult life. I think Rick hears it too because his face softens and he looks at her with kindness. I need to think fast.

"You know," I say, as if it's just occurred to me. "I'm almost certain that my boss's wife went to see someone after . . . her miscarriage." The story about the miscarriage is true. I have no idea if she went to therapy. It doesn't matter—I just need to get back in control. "Why don't I ask Larry for that name? It would be a good place to start. You've got so much on your plate right now, Rick." I look at him in a way that's intended to make him feel like we are on the same side, the right side. It's also intended to make Anna feel excluded. It works.

Anna looks slightly ashamed. "Okay, sure. I don't want to be a burden to you, Rick."

Neither of us responds. We both know that she already is, but there is no point in saying it.

I clear my throat to break the awkward silence. "I'll talk to Larry. We can figure something out."

Rick and Anna smile at me. They both seem so happy with the ideas I have presented to them. It is such a nice moment that it's easy to forget that I'm never going to let those things happen.

CHAPTER TWENTY

September 1997

Beaver Creek Correctional Center, the minimum-security prison just outside of Rapid Falls, didn't take juvenile offenders. When the lawyer told Anna that she would be charged as a minor, she was relieved that she would be sent to the prison just outside of Nicola. I wasn't surprised that she hadn't wanted to go to Beaver Creek. I wouldn't want to be guarded by the same guys who used to coach us in Little League either. I was in the kitchen during the call with the lawyer. As her terror lifted, I realized how pretty Anna still was.

My dad and I left Rapid Falls to visit Anna the day after she self-surrendered. The drive to Nicola felt similar to the one my dad and I had taken right after the accident, except back then I felt like my dad wanted to be with me. Now my presence seemed like an irritation. I wondered if he was hungover or if he drank so much that he couldn't even register the effects anymore. I spent the drive looking out the window, trying to get ready to see my only sister behind bars. Anna would be in jail for three years. It was a short sentence, based on her age and clean record, but as we pulled up to the grimy gates of the juvenile detention center, my stomach heaved. Three years suddenly felt like forever.

The visiting room felt more like the waiting room of a doctor's office than a place where you would go to see a convict. Couches and armchairs were grouped in small clusters around the room. My dad and I found a spot where three chairs faced each other around a small wood table.

"This is fine," my dad said as he sat down, as if in response to a question. He seemed nauseated; his forehead looked damp.

"You okay, Dad?" I whispered reflexively, not wanting the guards standing at the front to hear me. His silence made me feel like I was six years old, being punished for something unsaid —something I hadn't even realized he had discovered and, worse, that I wasn't even sure was my fault.

My mom used to tell a story about Anna's first swimming lesson. Anna was terrified to go into the pool and sat on the lip of it for the entire class, watching the other kids. During the second class, she refused to enter the water again, but that time another little girl joined her, and they'd stayed at the edge in silent protest together. Sandy and Anna both used to say it was how they knew they were destined to become best friends. I wondered if Anna was as scared now as she was then. I wondered if Sandy would come to visit her.

There was only one other group of people in the room—an older woman with a scared-looking little girl. Maybe it was their first time here as well. The woman caught me staring. I smiled, but she looked away quickly. A buzzer sounded, and the door at the far end of the room opened. A girl who looked about my age, with dark hair, scowling features, and a khaki-colored jumpsuit, came out. Out of the corner of my eye, I could see the little girl's face light up and the scowling girl smile back with the kind of smile you feel embarrassed seeing on the face of someone you don't know.

"Mommy!" the little girl cried. I would have thought the little girl was her younger sister.

Anna came out next. She saw us right away, and her face broke into a grin, like she had just noticed us on the sidelines of her track meet. The expression quickly changed to sadness. She was wearing a jumpsuit too, but hers looked like it was a few sizes too large. She had to roll the cuffs at the sleeves, like we used to do when we played dress-up with our mom's clothes. Anna looked at the guard standing beside the door and raised her eyebrows, gesturing toward us. The guard nodded and Anna walked forward. Her hesitant approach to the routine made my stomach twist. I squashed down my guilt. After what she did, she should be glad I was visiting her at all.

"Hey," Anna said when she was still ten feet away. Without turning my head, I could see the group beside us had settled in the opposite corner. The little girl was sitting on her mother's knee, and the older woman was setting out containers of food.

"Hey," I said, a second too late. My dad just nodded. His face was hard as stone. Anna slid down into an upholstered chair. We sat in silence for a second.

"Where's Mom?"

My dad didn't respond. At least I was not the only person he ignored.

"She's sick," I lied.

Anna put her hands over her face and wiped the slate, then tried to laugh. "Okay. I hope she feels better soon. What's new?" She seemed nervous.

My dad looked at her closely and finally spoke. "How are you do-ing, Anna?"

Anna's eyes shone and I looked away.

"Well, it takes a little getting used to. It's kind of . . ." She made a choking sound, something between a gulp and a cough. I turned to my dad quickly and saw his eyes were wet too, like an old dog's. I looked away, embarrassed. I was glad the other people weren't looking at us. Prison didn't seem like a place where you would want to get caught crying. Besides, it didn't seem so bad. I could see the family beside us happily munching on sandwiches like they were having a picnic at the park. I realized we should have brought Anna something. Anna looked at me carefully and ran her hands over her face again, trying to compose herself.

"Only three years," she said, smiling as if searching for confirmation.

"Yeah," I said too quickly, eager to find less emotional ground. I didn't have the words to reassure her, and I was not there to make her feel better about what she'd done. I was there to say goodbye. I was leaving for college soon. I was going to get away from Rapid Falls and Anna, forever. My dad sniffed like he was trying not to be heard. I wished I had come alone. Or not come at all.

"What's the food like?" I asked.

Anna blinked hard, then rolled her eyes, making a fake gagging sound. I was glad she was willing to change the subject. "So gross. Like powdered eggs and meat that I can't even identify. It's awful."

I laughed, but Anna didn't. Her eyes had a faraway look again.

"Three years," she said. My dad reached his hand across the table to clutch Anna's, and I looked around quickly again, hoping the other prisoner didn't notice. She was reaching over to brush a strand of hair from her daughter's face.

"You can do it, Anna," my dad said. "You made the right choice to plead guilty." Anna looked at him. There had been no right choice for her to make. Just one that was less wrong. Anna was alone. More alone than my dad or I could ever understand.

"Mom will come next week I'm sure," I said. Anna nodded. She was looking down now, at the table. We were silent again. I struggled to find something to say. Technically our visit was supposed to last forty-five minutes more, but I wondered if we could get away with leaving early.

"So you're all packed up?" Anna forced a smile.

"God, no. Every time I finish a box, Mom comes in and starts giving me more. Dish racks and towels and soap. Like I can't buy any of that stuff there. It's only three hours away, but Mom is acting like I'm moving to Guatemala or something."

"Sounds like Mom," she said distractedly.

"Yeah," I said. "It will be good to finally get on the road."

My awkward statement hung in the air. I looked at the clock again, and this time Anna saw. Her eyes turned frantic, probably at the thought of me cutting the visit short, and she rushed in with another question.

"When do you leave?" Anna said.

"Day after tomorrow," I said. "But I'll be back at Thanksgiving. I'll see you soon." As if November was around the corner, instead of months off. I tried to ignore the tremor in Anna's lip at my answer. I had always imagined leaving Rapid Falls with a celebration thrown by Cindy and my parents. Instead I felt like I was slinking away like an unwanted guest.

"Totally," she said, pasting on a fake smile. "I'll be super fit by then. There's a workout room here."

"Exercise?" my dad asked, seeming lost. I looked over at him quickly, grateful he had decided to enter back into the conversation, even half-heartedly. It was a heavy load to carry alone.

"There's a track and a fitness room. Most people are working on their GED, and they have a bunch of different activities. There's lots to do."

"That's good," he said vaguely, like he had already forgotten what we were talking about.

"Yeah, it's cool," Anna said, her voice shaking like she was trying to convince herself. I gave her an encouraging grin to make up for my dad breaking eye contact. Anna smiled at me. This time, it seemed like she meant it. "Man, I always thought I'd get your room when you left."

"You still can," I said. I would be long gone when Anna got released—nearly finished with my degree and on my way toward a life in politics. "It's all yours."

When Anna spoke, I could tell she was like me. She was never going back to Rapid Falls again. "Right. Thanks."

I didn't know what she was thanking me for, and I didn't care. I came to say goodbye. I didn't owe her anything else. I was finally free.

CHAPTER
TWENTY-ONE

September 2016

Anna's apartment smells awful. When we were growing up, I used to marvel at how disciplined she was about making sure everything was in its place. We always played in her room because mine had too few clear spaces. Now she lives in filth and chaos.

"Jerry?" I call. When I come by, her cat still scuttles away from me like he's feral. It infuriates me that he still treats me like I'm trying to hurt him when I'm the only reason he's survived Anna's stint in rehab. I keep my shoes on and walk to the bathroom where Anna keeps the litterbox. As soon as I walk in, something coppery stings my nose. My shoe sticks to the floor. There are pools of blood on the tile, brown and congealed. My stomach flops at the thought of the animal dying on my watch.

"Jerry? Here, kitty," I call again, walking into the cluttered kitchen. The garbage under the sink is festering. I find a spray bottle of window cleaner with about an inch of liquid left in the bottom. Good enough. A sharp rattle shakes the walls of the small apartment. It makes me jump and scream. Someone is behind me.

I turn into the dark living room and see a white blur clatter across the room. The cat. I laugh at my stupid fear until another shrieking howl fills the space. Jerry is another of Anna's flea-bitten rescue projects, and he sounds like he's come completely unglued. The sound is so awful that I feel close to panic. I find a bag of cat treats on the coffee table and shake it. The cat finally comes crawling over, and I can see he's dragging something on his foot. I spread the treats out on the floor, and as the cat bends down to eat, I see the problem. His paw has been crushed by a mousetrap that is still clamped onto his dark, blood-matted fur. Jerry growls at me, gobbling the treats while shrinking away from my every move. I have to do something. I grab the cat's scruff as he fights and howls. I narrowly avoid his claws as I pull the release of the trap, and Jerry sprints away. I can hear him panting under the couch as I fill his dishes with food and water.

I take the glass cleaner and a musty dishtowel back into the bathroom. The blood from the cat's paw is everywhere. I follow the trail, wiping, spraying, scrubbing. As I'm scraping the dark stains from the cheap linoleum, I gag. I shake my head as my mom's story from last night replays in my mind. *She didn't choose to save me. She left me behind.* I stand up to clear my head, running the rag under water in the sink. The cold water stings my hands, and the sink turns pink with blood. I remember that black whirlpool Anna drew at rehab. I feel like I'm being sucked down to a place that's so deep I can't swim out.

I turn to the litterbox in the corner, which is dotted with fetid lumps. Grabbing a plastic grocery bag and the small scoop, I pull them out, one by one. The simple task gives me something to focus on. When I'm done, my hands aren't shaking anymore. It's a disgusting job, but for once I see the distraction that an animal can provide. The constant stench of a litterbox, the picking up and disposing of warm feces, has never appealed to me. I didn't see the point of putting energy into a cat or dog that could never learn right from wrong. Rick agreed with me about pets. We usually saw the world in the same way, but after we left the rehab facility, he remarked on how happy he was to see something coming to the surface for Anna. He thought it was a good thing. I thought it was terrifying.

As I finish the last of the cleaning, my phone vibrates. It's a text from Larry:

8 a.m. call with mayors' council. Tomorrow.

I look at my calendar app. The entire day is blank, as is the rest of the week. For some reason the calendar isn't syncing. I need to get to a computer to check my schedule. I'm still working to restore Larry's full confidence in me after the whole email fiasco. I need to figure this out quickly. Larry doesn't like to wait.

I walk into Anna's cluttered bedroom to find her computer. The laptop I bought her last year is teetering off the edge of her nightstand. Part of me is surprised to see she hasn't pawned it.

I press Enter and the screen lights up. An internet browser is already open on a social media site. She's still signed in. I tell myself to open a new browser window, but I don't. There are several new notifications. I click on them, already devising an excuse. I'll tell her I thought I had logged into my page, if she even realizes that I've done anything. After all, she'll probably have plenty of new notifications by the time she checks her feed again. She can't be on the internet in the rehab facility.

I see a new message in a thread with our dad. I'm surprised. My dad opened an account years ago, at my pestering, but I haven't received a message from him since his first week on the site. The message to Anna came in yesterday. I raise my eyebrows as I read it.

Hi Anna. I am thinking of you. Sorry I haven't visited. I think I should. Not sure you can see this now. But I wanted to write. I miss you. Dad.

The historical thread between them is long, and I draw a breath as I scroll to read the rest. The previous message was sent about a week before Anna was arrested.

> Hi. I've been thinking about your last message. Sounds like you've got a lot going on, and I'm feeling like maybe I'm not always the best person to talk to. You need to sort through some of this stuff—maybe with a professional? I don't know much about therapy. Think about going to a meeting too. It's not perfect, but sometimes the best thing you can do is be with people who know what you are going through. Love you.
>
> Dad

I can't stop reading. I think the last time my dad told me he loved me was when he visited me in the hospital so many years ago. Something in Anna's last message had stirred him, and I needed to know what it was.

> Hi Dad. Do you ever have dreams about a memory? Or like, a recurring dream over and over? I keep waking up in a panic. Cold sweats and screams. Ron won't even sleep over anymore because he says I scare him. It's been going on for weeks. It always starts with blackness. I'm in a dark place, like really dark, and I don't know where I am or what's going on. But I know something's wrong. Then these streaks of light come in and everything is glowing orange but it's still dark. It's hard to explain, but I can't really see anything except these

weird strands of glowing light, kind of like a fire, but not enough to light anything up. And I get a feeling that I'm in a forest, but there's no sound and I can't really see trees. I just know. And then I know something else. I'm not alone in the trees. There's someone else there, and they can see me but I can't see them. And they are watching me. And they want to hurt me. Then I start to hear them breathe. And it keeps getting louder. I know they are coming to get me. I know it's going to hurt. And I know I can't stop them. Then I'm falling into the coldest water I've ever felt. It feels like glass cutting into my skin. All around me is a roar like a river that's turned into a monster that's trying to devour me. The water feels like teeth, biting me, and then I realize my feet are missing, then my knees. It keeps taking chunks and the water around me turns red, like I'm in the middle of a shark attack. That's when I wake up. But every time it seems to be able to eat more of me. I don't want to go to sleep anymore.

A

My skin is crawling by the time I finish the message. It's the last in the thread. I open a new browser window. I focus on the meeting tomorrow. *Deal with that, then deal with Anna,* I tell myself. I log into my calendar and try to concentrate on my schedule for the next week, but my mind keeps dipping back into the darkness of Anna's dream. She can't talk about this with a psychiatrist. The next time I see her, I need to have a plan. I need to protect her. But most importantly, I need to protect myself.

CHAPTER
TWENTY-TWO

June 1997

When Jesse and I walked into Wade's house after prom, everybody cheered. Anna, Sandy, Wade, and his parents were all gathered around the kitchen table. I could hear Skoal's little tail thump out a welcome even before she bounded toward us to lick our hands in greeting. Out of courtesy to Mr. and Mrs. Turner, Jesse and I went to separate rooms to change out of our prom attire, even though I was dying to see if Jesse looked as good out of his tuxedo as he had looked in it.

As I peeled the pantyhose from my legs, I remembered the feeling of Jesse's body against mine on the dance floor. I was glad I had asked him to match his tie to my dress. I had been able to claim him all night without even saying a word. Everyone knew that Jesse was mine. After the dance, a sudden summer storm had opened up just as we got to Jesse's truck. Both his tux and my dress were soaked, but the rain had stopped just as suddenly as it started, leaving us with nothing but puddles and a chill that I couldn't shake. As I folded my dress and carefully slid it into my backpack, I had realized that the next time I wore anything that fancy, I would be standing at the altar with Jesse. But that was a few years off. We both needed to finish college, maybe travel a bit. Then we'd think about marriage. He hadn't asked me yet, but I knew he would soon, maybe even that night.

I made my way back to the kitchen. Jesse was wearing a T-shirt and jeans with his grad jacket on top. Wade put a beer in Jesse's hand and a wine cooler in mine. I couldn't stop smiling. Prom was fun, but we all knew it was just the preview before the real show began.

"Just one," I said to Jesse as he grabbed the beer from Wade. He was supposed to stay sober until we got to the Field so we wouldn't get hassled going through the roadblock. I was pretending not to know about the flask of whiskey he and Wade had been sipping out of at the prom. Mrs. Turner smiled indulgently at the two guys. She had always let us have a few drinks here before parties. She knew Jesse had a high tolerance. We would be fine. Jesse took the empty seat beside Mrs. Turner.

"You looked so handsome tonight, Jesse," said Mrs. Turner. "And you were stunning, Cara. Just a picture!"

We both grinned happily.

"Thanks. Wish I weren't already taken, Mrs. T. I'm sure you'd make it a night to remember," Jesse said, making Wade's mom scoff and slap his arm playfully.

"Come on, man. That's my mom." Wade's tone was light, but his face shot Jesse a warning.

Mr. Turner hooted and poked him in the ribs. "I'm sure Cara will take care of that for you."

I blushed. I knew I would make this a night he would never forget. I turned to Jesse to smile with a promise of things to come, but he had already turned away. I followed his gaze to Anna, who had arrived just before us with Sandy.

"Drinking game?" Wade suggested.

"We really shouldn't, Wade. We've got to go to the party," Anna said. I felt a little sorry for her. It would be boring to stay sober all night.

Jesse chimed in. "Yeah, let's take a break on Anna. Drinking games are no fun when you have to drive."

Sandy slapped his hand in a high-five. "Thanks, Jesse. We promise we won't make you guys play them next year when you have to drive us around." She slung an arm around Anna. "Besides, Anna has something better to do than play a boring drinking game."

"Yes," Anna said, switching to a terrible British accent. "I'm ready to screen my masterpiece."

Wade groaned louder and Sandy kicked him.

"Come on! She's been working on this for ages," Sandy said, trying to herd us toward the living room. "It's so good!"

"Wonderful!" Mrs. Turner said. "Does anyone want snacks?" Jesse and Wade cheered in response.

"I just sent it off to film school today," Anna said.

"If only Ross could be here to see it," I added. Something about the pride on Anna's face made me feel petty. Anna shot me a glare. I would rather play drinking games, but I was curious to see what Anna had done. I still hadn't shaken the weird feeling she and Jesse had given me that afternoon at Rapid Falls. We crowded into the living room. Wade passed around more drinks. Everyone was happy on prom night in Rapid Falls. I could be gracious, even if my little sister was trying to make this about her.

As Anna fiddled with the camcorder, I thought back on the night so far. Right after my dad had snapped the final photograph, he asked me to join him in the house.

"What's going on, Dad?" He looked so serious it made me wonder if something bad had happened.

"I have something for you, Cara. It's not much." He reached into the breast pocket of his suit and pulled out a faded velvet case. "It was your grandmother's." My dad stretched his arm out, and I took the box from his hand. It was warm from being pressed against his chest.

"Dad. Thank you."

He nodded and looked right into my eyes. His were shining with tears. I opened the box and a golden oval caught a ray of sunshine from the window. A locket.

"I, uh, had it inscribed," he said shyly. I turned it over, fighting against tears that would run my mascara. I read the date on the back: June 24, 1997. My graduation day.

"There's room at the bottom. I told the engraver to make sure. For your daughter."

I breathed deeply as I turned so he could clasp it around my neck.

"Thanks," I said again. I wished I could be more eloquent, but I hoped he knew how much it meant to me. I couldn't wait to show Anna.

"Be safe tonight. Your mom and I love you."

"I know. Me too. Thanks again."

My dad reached over to hug me. It made me feel like an adult, but also like a kid.

"Take care of Jesse," he called as I turned. "And your sister too."

"I promise," I said with a grin. After my dance with Anna, the prom had passed in a swarm of well-wishers and friends seeking one last dance with me to special songs. I wanted more time dancing with Jesse, but I wasn't worried. I knew we had the whole night at the Field ahead of us and our whole lives ahead of us after that. Close to the end of the night, I heard "More Than Words" begin to play. It was our song.

"Can I have this dance?" he said as he approached. I gave him my hand, and he twirled me onto the floor. We swayed to the familiar guitar strumming. I looked over his shoulder and saw Anna on the side of the dance floor, staring at us. When I caught her eye, her expression changed, and she smiled. I fought to forget the look that had been on her face. I leaned into Jesse's body and tightened my hold on his back.

"It's over," he whispered. His voice sounded wistful. "High school, everything."

"Not everything. This is just the beginning of what we are going to do together," I said. I looked into his eyes to savor the moment, but he was looking down. The song ended, and he moved away quickly.

"I need to go to the bathroom," he said. I tried not to take it personally that he didn't kiss me. Everyone was fidgety. It was hard to focus when there was so much happening.

The sound of Anna clicking the VCR on and off brought me back to the present.

"Hurry up, Little Piper. Some of us have partying to do!" Wade lifted his beer bottle in the air. Jesse clinked his bottle against his friend's, and I lifted mine up as well.

"Jesse?" I said quietly.

"Yeah?" he said.

"I love you."

"I love you too."

My chest thrummed with warmth. Everything was fine between us.

"Snacks are here!" Mrs. Turner said as she walked in with a bowl of chips and some popcorn.

"Shhh!" Anna shushed our chattering as the TV came alive with an image of Jesse, sitting by the river. The sun was shining on his hair, making it look like brown silk. He was smiling at the camera as if looking at someone he loved. I pushed down a feeling of dread with a generous gulp of my cooler.

The film was about two young lovers, played by Jesse and Anna. I finished my drink, and Wade passed me another. It was mostly flowing images: their hands touching, a close-up of his lips, his hands in her hair. As the screen faded to black, I swigged my drink, feeling dizzy and disoriented.

Mrs. Turner broke the awkward silence. "Great job, Anna. It was so . . . beautiful."

"Yeah," echoed Jesse. I tried to catch his eye, but he was still staring at the screen.

"What did you think, Cara?" Anna asked.

"It was good," I forced out. It must have sounded genuine because Anna's face looked relieved. "Though weird to see you and Jesse like that," I admitted.

"It's just a film, Cara," Jesse said quickly.

"I know," I said, catching a fingernail in my teeth.

"I thought the river looked amazing," said Sandy slowly.

Wade stood up from the couch impatiently. "Okay, enough TV! Enough talking!" he cried. I wasn't sure he'd paid attention to any part of Anna's film.

Everyone got up quickly, and Jesse reached for my hand to pull me off the couch.

"I'll be there in a second." I sat immobile. Jesse raised his eyebrows. "I just need to fix my lipstick." As he walked out of the room, I realized Mr. Turner hadn't left either.

"Quite a show," he said, looking my direction. I nodded, wondering if anyone else had seen what I thought I had seen. "But just a show, Cara. She's always wanted to be like you. She wanted to walk in your shoes."

I smiled and nodded again, letting the words sink in. Anna had always wanted the same toys I had, the same clothes I wore. I hoped he was right and this was just another example of her imitating me. It didn't mean she wanted Jesse. The look between them at Rapid Falls came to my mind, but I drowned it with peach-flavored liquor.

"You okay?" said Mr. Turner.

"I'm fine."

He smiled. "Better get going, then."

"Yeah," I said. "Thanks for the, uh, talk."

"Anytime, Cara," he said as he stood. "I had a younger brother too. They're all the same. Have a great night. And drive safe."

"Always," I replied with a smile. It fell from my face the second he left the room.

CHAPTER
TWENTY-THREE

September 2016

At 3:00 p.m. the office is empty, but the feeling of celebration still lingers in the air. The meeting that Larry had scheduled over the weekend had been a success. After months of local protest and bureaucratic negotiations, the opening of several natural gas extraction plants had been approved, so Larry invited everyone out for afternoon drinks. I told them I would join them after I wrapped up a few things. I like how it looks when I'm the last person at work after everyone else knocks off early.

As I walk outside, the warmth of the day is welcome after the artificial air conditioning. I turn the corner toward the restaurant and see a few familiar faces on the patio who smile at me. Despite the success we are celebrating, I can't shake Anna's haunting description of her nightmare, as if I had dreamed it instead of her. I see Larry holding court with a couple of people I know vaguely. One is a new guy, a tall, good-looking senior manager. Brian or Cameron—something generic. The other is a plain woman pulling nervously at her blouse. About twenty people I recognize from the office are standing around the tables beside them. I walk over, and someone hands me a glass of wine.

"Well, it's the woman of the hour. Hi, Cara." Larry is exuberant as he welcomes me into the circle. He doesn't usually drink, let alone in the afternoon, so his spirited greeting makes me smile. I've always admired his public persona. Friendly and charming but distant, as if slightly removed from each interaction. He knows how to be inviting and professional at the same time: the perfect politician.

"Hello. Congratulations to you. I was just there to hold your coat." I smile at him self-deprecatingly, then turn to the others.

"Hello, Cara," says the tall man, stretching out his hand confidently. "We met last week."

"Of course. Brian?"

He grins. My gamble in guessing his name pays off. I see Larry nod in approval out of the corner of my eye.

"Yeah, Brian Campbell. And this is Sara."

I nod in her direction.

"Cheers!" I say, lifting my glass to clink against hers.

"Cara, I wanted to thank you for your work with the mayors this morning. I hope you'll let Rick know how much I appreciate your dedication. Cara has a young daughter at home. Maggie's three now, right?"

"That's right," I say with a smile. "It's been a while since I've been out for a drink, unless a smoothie at my daughter's swimming lesson counts." Both men laugh and I take a large sip, surprised to find the glass now less than half-full.

"I have a daughter as well," says Sara. I see a wedding band on her finger. She looks too young to have children.

"How old is your daughter?"

"She's two."

"That's great," I say flatly, grateful for the sudden buzz of my phone. I demonstratively fish it out of my pocket. It looks good to be in demand.

It's a text from Rick:

Anna's acting strange. Talking a lot about Rapid Falls. Can you call me?

My hands go cold and my shoulders tighten.

"Sorry, I need to take this," I say, and Larry nods as I take a step back. I raise my glass to the waiter and nod for another. I text Rick quickly.

Let me handle it. I'll contact her now.

I don't want Rick involved. I start a text to Anna, but before I've typed two words, another message from Rick comes in.

Don't think she's got her phone, they only let her use the landline there. She said she'd try to call again tomorrow. She was asking about that boy who was killed, kept asking me if you still had his graduation jacket? Why would you have that?

I swear, unintentionally. Larry looks up and steps over to me.

"Everything okay, Cara?" He sounds genuinely concerned, but his presence registers as admonishment. I shouldn't swear in public, especially in front of my boss. My phone buzzes again and I jump slightly, forcing myself to look at Larry, not at the screen.

"Fine. Actually, not really. My sister . . . she's hurt," I blurt out. Larry knows nothing about Anna. I've made sure of it. I've never told anyone at work about Anna's downward spiral. I don't want to let on that I've got a sister who is a few bad decisions away from living on the street.

"Cara, that's terrible. Is it serious?" Now he's sympathetic.

"She's okay, I think. Car accident. Fender bender. Not her fault." My words won't stop.

"Feel free to leave. I'll be ducking out shortly for a dinner engagement." Larry pats my shoulder. "Run of bad luck for you. Hope it gets better."

"What do you mean?" I snap quickly. Had he found out about Anna's arrest?

"Maggie's illness." He looks at me closely.

"Oh, right. Thanks." I try my best to sound sad but calm. In control. He gives me one last pat before he steps away and begins to circle the crowd, making his exit. My second glass of wine arrives, and I take a deep gulp. "Can you come back with a double gin and tonic?" I ask the waiter. He nods, and I take another generous sip. I need to talk to Rick, but I'm not even sure which way to go to head Anna off. She's falling apart. How could she ask Rick something so stupid? I finish my glass and dial Rick, nodding to Larry as he waves goodbye.

"Hi, sweetheart." He sounds distracted. As I begin to speak, he interrupts me with a shout.

"Are you okay, Rick?"

"Maggie is pouncing on me like a little kitty!"

His breath sounds short, and I hear her giggles in the background. I speak quickly. "Rick, about Anna?"

"Yeah, I'm not really sure what's going on with her." Maggie begins meowing in the background and Rick responds, "Is the little kitty hungry?"

"*Yes!*" Maggie cries.

I take a breath. "Do we need to discuss it?"

"No, Cara, it's okay. It can wait until tonight," Rick says.

Relief floods me. I can hear the laughter in his voice. I won't let Anna ruin this beautiful moment.

"Sure. I'll talk to you later."

"Bye."

I hear a clunk in the background before Rick hangs up. He won't be thinking too much about Anna's disordered questions until he can get Maggie to bed. I'm safe for now. I walk back over to Brian and Sara. I feel angst leaving with each step, and I smile at the waiter as he comes forward to place the cool, sweating highball in my hand.

"Sorry about that. Family emergency," I say.

"Is everything okay?" Sara looks relieved at my return.

"Yes, thank you." My eyes are on Brian, who is looking at me intently. "My sister was hurt," I say, trying to keep his attention without seeming like I'm doing so.

"Serious?" he says.

"A fender bender. She'll be fine." My tongue feels thick. One more drink and then I'll go home. It's nice to be out in the sunshine, talking to a handsome man. But I have obligations. Rick needs my help. I am never free of people in my life who need my help.

"We were just talking about James. What a disaster." Brian laughs. There's a mean edge to his voice, which catches me.

"I enjoyed working with James. He did his best." The thought of Jesse is still with me, stirring something deep. I am suddenly angry on James's behalf. He had been a good employee. Brian is actually talking about my mistake.

"Really? He seemed pretty . . . slow." Brian laughs again cruelly. His laugh sounds like Sandy's the day she told us Dustin was dead, and my head spins. Brian sees the scowl on my face, and his mocking expression falters. He turns to Sara for corroboration, but she's staring at her phone.

"My husband is pulling up to get me. I'll see you tomorrow," she says brightly, oblivious to the conversation around her. I smile as she gathers her bag and waves awkwardly.

"Take care," I say, a bit too slowly.

Brian smiles goodbye and waits until she's out of earshot. "I hear James really fucked up."

"James left for a job with the United Nations at the Hague. It was an appointment, not an open call," I lie, smugly noting the flicker of envy in Brian's eyes.

"Really? He . . . I didn't realize."

"That's politics. Everyone you know can become an ally. Or an enemy."

His eyes narrow and his expression is no longer flirtatious.

"Well, I guess I learned a lesson today." His sarcasm is obnoxious. I am grateful he is acting like a jerk. I shouldn't be flirting with anyone. I take another deep drink.

"You can never have too many friends, Jesse," I say, raising my glass as if to toast. My words cause a slight dissonance, but I can't place the reason.

"It's Brian." His tone is cold.

"Sorry," I mumble. "I, um, met a lot of people last week." I realize suddenly that the crowd is thinning. I should leave too.

"Yeah, me too." He nods at another senior manager, who I know is his boss. "Did you meet him?"

"Melvin? I've known him for years," I say. "He owes me a couple favors, actually." I am hearing words before I realize I am saying them. The sun is pounding on my head, making my scalp sweat. *I need to get out of here,* I think. I can't remember where I set down my purse. I take another drink as I look around for it.

"Really?" He smiles, warm again. "How's your drink?" he says quickly. I am about to reply that it's fine when the waiter appears by my side.

"Can I get eight Sambuca shots?" Brian says.

I quickly count the remaining staff on the patio. "None for me."

"I'll do yours," he says with a grin. Brian takes a step toward the larger group and I follow. Maybe my bag is over there. We join the rest of the staff. They nod and smile at me, including me in their circle of small talk. I am filled with euphoria as I accept their kindness and the shot glass that Brian is holding out to me. *I'll have one more drink.* I need to forget about Anna and Jesse and Rick and Maggie. We down the shots. Moments later, another is pressed into my hands. The syrupy burn of Sambuca is still in my mouth, so I drink the second shot to get rid of the taste of the first. It's something milky and sweet.

I need a glass of water, I think as I finish my gin and tonic. I need to find my bag. I need to pee. I carefully walk to the bathroom. When I look in the mirror, I look happy. Not the downcast, tired-looking woman I've been seeing lately. I look like the girl Jesse asked to the prom. The one who worked her way up the political ladder with no connections. The woman whom other women want to be. I put on lipstick confidently, wiping away a smear at the corner of my mouth. It's nice to be out again. I rejoin the group and hear people saying goodbye because it's a Wednesday, they have children, too many shots, all the excuses. Only a handful of people remain.

"Still here?" I say to Brian. My tongue feels too big for my mouth.

"I'm always the last one at the party," he says, running his fingers through his hair in a rueful, practiced way. It looks scripted yet somehow sexy at the same time. "Unless I have something else to do, of course," he continues with a laugh and a meaningful look in my direction. I feel my phone buzz in my pocket. I ignore it. Another shot appears in front of me.

"What the hell?" I clink glasses with Brian, and we smile before we pour the liquor into our mouths. As I lower the shot glass, the world doubles for a moment and I blink hard.

I'm drunk, I think. Brian grins again. I must have said it out loud. It's still light outside. It's been a long time since I've been drunk in the daytime.

"Me too." Brian smiles slowly.

"Cheers," I say. Somehow I have another fresh drink in my hand. *I'll finish this and then go,* I think.

Brian puts his hand on my leg. "Congratulations on today. It's a big win for us." He is leaning forward. He is really close. *If I wanted to kiss him, I could,* I think suddenly. For a moment, it seems that I've lost control, that my body is just going to do it. It's the same feeling I used to have on the bridge in Rapid Falls. I always wanted to jump. But I never did.

"Brian," I say. "I need to get home. It's been a pleasure." I slur slightly on the word *pleasure.* I slide off the edge of my chair. It tips a little, and I feel cold liquid on my hand and my shirt. I scan the patio again and am relieved to finally spot my purse. I wobble toward it, open my wallet, and turn back to the table to throw out a few bills. Far too much money for what I drank, but they're the only bills I have, and I can't trust myself to wait for the change. I get up and say my goodbyes to the others. I walk back to the bathroom and look in the mirror again. My eyes are bloodshot with dark circles forming underneath them. I look drunk. And sad. At least I haven't made any big mistakes tonight. I nod to congratulate the drunk, tired woman in front of me for avoiding disaster. As I walk out of the restaurant, I eye the street for taxis, but there are none in sight. I spin slightly on my heel and scan down the street when a body bumps mine.

"Brian?"

He leans in and smiles, slowly. "I wanted to say goodbye properly."

"I'm leaving," I say, stepping back and ignoring the invitation in his smile.

"I figured." He steps even closer. "I had a really good time with you, Cara." He reaches for my hand and mock solemnly shakes it.

I laugh. The closeness of his body is making my heart beat faster, and I feel a flow of unprocessed alcohol rise up in my throat. "Me too."

He leans in again and presses his lips against mine. I kiss him back. This man is not my husband. I pull away. People can see me. They can see what I just did.

"I need to get home now." I overemphasize the last word and stumble a step backward.

"Cara?" He sounds confused.

I turn and walk away.

CHAPTER
TWENTY-FOUR

June 1997

I didn't even realize how angry I was until Anna tried to climb in the truck with me and Jesse and Wade to head up to the Field.

"Graduates only, Anna. Go with Sandy," I said. "This truck is too small for four people."

She looked at me with a hurt expression. "I just thought it would be fun for us all to be together tonight."

"Just go." Something in my voice made her turn quickly. Jesse heard it too. Out of the corner of my eye, I could see him looking at me, like he was testing me, but I kept staring straight ahead. I needed to snap out of it. This was our night. I wasn't going to let Anna's stupid film project ruin it.

It's just like at the diving rocks, I told myself. Jesse always climbed to the highest point before he jumped. That's all it was. Just him pushing me, trying to figure out where the edge of the cliff might be.

"Are you okay?" Jesse asked.

"I'm fine. Just cold." The air was warm, but my hands felt frozen.

"Here." Jesse reached into the space behind the seats and pulled out his graduation jacket. "Put this on."

"This is it! We did it!" Wade let out a chesty war whoop, and the call was returned from another house down the block. Everyone in Rapid Falls was either out, getting ready to go out, or preparing themselves to sleep through squealing tires and hollering guys like Wade.

"Finally free," I said in agreement, forcing myself to sound happy. Wade waved his beer around in time with the bass of the stereo. Jesse started the truck and revved it. The engine roared.

"You're still in neutral, numb-nuts," Wade said as he cracked open another beer.

"Dude," Jesse cautioned. "There'll be police at the bottom of the hill."

"Don't matter. We're heading up the back way. Want one, Cara?"

I shook my head. Wade took a deep draw of his beer and started a sentence, but Jesse cut him off.

"I can't go the back way, Wade. I helped organize the dry graduation, remember? Officer Grey from Nicola likes me." He winked. "She'll be expecting me." I knew he was joking to lighten my mood, but I felt irritation rise.

"She's not going to notice, Jesse. The back way is a lot safer. How many drinks have you had tonight?" I said.

"Cara, calm down. I'm fine."

"Are you?" I said testily.

"I'm better than fine, babe. I'm great." He faked a swerve to the shoulder.

"Whoa!" Wade laughed and started whooping out the window again.

"Yeah. You're the greatest. You were really great in Anna's film," I said sarcastically as I looked angrily out the windshield. Jesse's body tensed with my words. Wade leaned over to turn up the music. I quickly glanced at Jesse. He seemed panicked, not self-righteous. He looked like he had done something wrong. My stomach lurched as he denied my accusation a moment too late.

"Are you serious? It's . . . an art project. It's for her school."

"Am I serious? How could you let her show that in front of Mr. and Mrs. Turner? It was embarrassing."

Wade rolled his window down. "Mind if I smoke?"

"Yes," said Jesse at the same time I asked Wade to give me one.

"Gross. You're going to smoke?" Jesse said. I was looking at the road, but I could tell he was rolling his eyes.

"Tonight, I just might do anything." I meant it as a joke, but my anger made the words seem threatening.

"Great," he muttered.

"Like you have any right to be mad at me right now," I said, deliberately blowing smoke in his direction.

"Oh really?" He laughed coldly. "You practically just accused me of screwing your sister because I helped her with a couple of scenes so she could get into film school."

"No, Jesse, I accused you of flirting with her. You're the one who said screwing." Even though we were still fighting, I felt better. Deep down, I knew Jesse wasn't really interested in Anna. He just liked attention. He would never have said it out loud if it were true.

"Goddamn it, Cara. Stop being such a bitch." He pulled sharply onto the gravel road that led to the back side of the Field, too fast. We fishtailed, veering hard to the left, then back to the right.

"Jesse!" The truck righted itself. My heart pounded, and I took a deep drag of the cigarette. Jesse spoke again. He seemed humbled by his error.

"Cara," he said softly. The music came to an abrupt stop. In the quiet truck, I could hear the hiss and pop of Wade opening another beer.

"I can't believe you sometimes." I didn't look in his direction. I decided I wouldn't until he begged my forgiveness, and then the fight would be over. We did this all the time. Jesse knew how to end it. We lurched up the bumpy road. The only sound was the truck jerking over potholes.

"Should I put on another tape?" Wade asked. I almost laughed. Wade didn't notice much when he was set on having a good time.

"Sure," Jesse said.

CHAPTER TWENTY-FIVE

September 2016

My stomach sinks as the house comes into view. The lights are on. I was hoping Rick would be in bed. Small waves of gin have been washing over me for the last twenty minutes, blurring the course of the train ride home. I was hoping the short walk from the station would clear my head. It hasn't. I can't tell how much drunker I will become, but my stomach is still sloshing with undigested alcohol. I straighten my shoulders as I walk through the door, trying not to squint too much as I step into the light. I have to stay sober enough to hide my secrets from my husband. Rick is watching TV in the living room. Maybe he has forgotten all about Anna's phone call.

"Hi," I call as I slip off my shoes, leaning against the wall for support. My head spins and my body rolls forward. I recover and right myself. I hope Rick hasn't heard me stumble. I hope I don't vomit.

"Hi." His voice sounds inviting, not as tired as I want him to be.

"How did bedtime go?" I walk two steps from the foyer to the main room, pleased at how steady I appear.

"Pretty good. Congratulations on the natural gas plants. I just heard it on the evening news." Rick's eyes look distant.

I fake a yawn that quickly becomes real. "Thanks."

"Let's talk." He gestures at the empty space on the couch beside him.

"You know, it's been a long day. I was planning on heading straight to bed."

"Cara, we need to talk."

He always breaks the rules when it's about Anna. "Rick, I'm really tired. Can it wait?"

He sits up straight and sets down his glass of water with more force than necessary. "Until when, Cara? Maybe I can book five seconds tomorrow evening before you start snoring? I barely saw you yesterday."

I sigh. I'd been on Anna's computer for hours at her place. I told Rick that her cat had darted out as soon as I arrived, and I had been forced to search the neighborhood for it rather than admit that I had gone over every conversation she's had in the last year. Besides the back-and-forth with my dad, there was nothing important, except for one heart-stopping message to my mother, asking about Jesse's graduation jacket. Luckily my mother rarely checks her social media accounts, so there was no reply. It made me furious that Anna was asking everyone for something that she shouldn't have. That she had no right to.

"Okay." As I walk toward the couch, I knock my knee against a side table and bite my lip to stop myself from cursing at the pain.

Rick looks at me. "Are you drunk?"

"Larry was quite generous with the bar tab tonight." I smile, hoping I'm looking at the right version of him in my doubled vision. "Mostly just tired." I rub my hand over my face as I sit on the edge of the couch, as far away from him as possible. I realize that the gesture is almost identical to the way that Anna wipes the slate. I straighten my posture and look at Rick with exaggerated poise. Another rush of alcohol hits me. The room tilts.

"Cara! I can smell the liquor coming off you." He doesn't sound friendly anymore.

"It was just a few drinks, Rick." I smile as calmly as I can.

"I've been waiting up for you. I would have gone to bed an hour ago if I knew you were going to come home wasted."

I get up, willing myself not to grab on to the couch for stability. "Okay. I should just go to bed then." I can't lift my eyelids above half mast.

"Cara, while I was waiting for you, I found this." He's waving his tablet at me. Even if I wasn't drunk, I wouldn't have been able to read the small type. Unfortunately I don't need to read the fine print to see what page he has open. I recognize the header. The *Rapid Falls Times*. It's the same website where I found the story of Josie, the girl who died at Rapid Falls.

I grab it clumsily. "Why are you looking at this?" My tongue blends the words together. I'm surprised Rick can understand me.

"I can't believe you've kept this from me for so long." He trails off. He sounds worried. I look him full in the face and decide it's safer to go on the attack.

"Fine, Rick. Anna killed my boyfriend. Happy?" I am too drunk to feel the way I usually do when I say that sentence.

"Of course I'm not happy. We've been together for years, and you never once thought to mention this?"

"I don't exactly advertise it," I say dismissively.

Rick's face contorts as if I've slapped him. "Are you serious? I'm not some random person. I'm your husband. The boy Anna killed wasn't just a guy from your high school. He was your boyfriend. Don't you think that matters? To us all?"

"Rick, stop."

"I'm trying to help. You're just too drunk to see it right now."

I scoff. "You sound like your father." Rule two. I can tell he notices because his neck goes blotchy, like it always does when he's about to lose his temper.

"Cara, you can't even see that you are falling apart. You're breaking your own rules."

"Our rules."

"I don't care about that stupid code, Cara."

"It's not stupid, Rick. Jesus. We have rules so we can keep everything straight."

"Do you seriously need rules to tell you how to live with me? Okay, here's some. Stop lying to your husband. Don't drink every day."

I feel like he has punched me in the stomach. "I am under a lot of pressure right now, Rick."

"Yeah, it must be hard to lie to everyone you know all the time." The accusation unleashes a dark fear that he is finally seeing me clearly.

"I am not a liar, Rick." I remember Brian's lips on mine. "You have no idea. You will never be able to understand. Just leave me alone." I say the last words through clenched teeth.

"Maybe I don't understand about back then. But I know what it's like tonight and all the nights before. What is it with the Piper girls? Why are you both such drunks?"

Pure rage overcomes me, and I reach for the nearest thing I can find. Rick's glass of water explodes against the wall. Shards fly into Maggie's toy box. I am panting with anger. I am not like Anna. I will never be like Anna.

"Cara!" Rick looks horrified but I hear his fury. "What the hell is wrong with you?"

I try to calm down. "Nothing is wrong with me, Rick. Anna and I survived a horrible accident. I moved on. She did not."

"Ha." His laugh is sarcastic. The sound makes me want to throw another glass. "I'm not sure that getting wasted every day qualifies as moving on. You need therapy, Cara."

He thinks that I'm like Anna. My anger swells again.

"What would therapy do? I loved Jesse more than I've ever loved you. And he's dead. Anna killed him." I throw the words at him as hard as I hurled the glass.

"Maybe you should have married someone like him. Then you could be back where you belong, and I wouldn't have to worry that my alcoholic wife was going to smash things like we live in a trailer park." He vengefully breaks the rule about bringing up our past. Just like me, he's doing it on purpose now. The Code was designed for kindness, not cruelty.

"Yeah, sure, maybe I should have found someone with a heart. Someone like Jesse." I spit out the words even though they aren't true. Jesse was heartless too. Rick is really angry now. He yells at a low volume, trying not to wake up Maggie.

"My God, Cara. I feel like I don't even know you. You're drunk half the time. Generously speaking." Cold spite enters his voice. "I'm just here to clean up the messes that you and Anna make."

The anger at being compared to Anna again brings out the worst part of me. "You're right," I say coldly. Rick's face screws up, perplexed at my admission. I can't stop myself. "You don't know me. Not at all."

"What?"

"Only Jesse knew me."

Rick shakes his head and looks down, but it's not enough. I don't want him to be sad. I want him to be punished. "I guess there's always hope, though. I met someone tonight who reminded me a lot of Jesse. He was kind."

"Cara, what are you talking about?" Rick looks confused.

I narrow my eyes before I deliver the fatal blow. "And such a good kisser. So much better than you." I speak slowly so I can emphasize every word while looking straight into his eyes. He looks stunned.

"Cara . . ." He chokes out my name.

I cut him off. "I can't be here right now. I need to think. I'm not sure I can do this anymore." I walk to our room, anger lending me an unearned sobriety. I don't feel drunk anymore. I feel alive. I won't let a man hurt me again. I'll get a hotel room tonight. My suitcase is half-full before I even register what I'm doing.

I am leaving Rick. Leaving Maggie. Reality fights through the fog of anger and alcohol in my mind. This has all gone wrong. Anna is destroying my life, again. This is not supposed to be happening; I have clawed through hell to be everything Anna is not. Beautiful. Successful. Happily married. Free.

Rick looms in the doorway.

"What is it?" I say. My tone is neutral. I could forgive him right now, if he's sorry enough.

"You are acting crazy. How can you even think of doing this? What is wrong with you?"

His words make me hate him. I turn away, snapping the suitcase closed. Something bad is going to happen if I stay in this room. I can't trust myself when I get this angry. I weave around him and rush down the stairs.

"Goodbye, Rick," I say over my shoulder, nearly out the door. Rick follows me.

"Anna's rehab ends tomorrow. She's heading to Rapid Falls. To stay with your dad. He asked her to come back. To get better."

"What?" The words sting, as he wants them to. He knows my dad hasn't invited me there since I was in college.

"You should go too, Cara. You need to deal with this. With her. With that town. With yourself." He sounds disgusted, not angry. As if my past has already rotted my core. "Figure this out, Cara. Because until you do, you're not setting a foot back in this house."

"It's not your decision where I go, Rick."

"No, it's not. But it's my decision whether or not you return here." He stands in front of the door and plants his feet in front of me as if staking a claim. "Go home, Cara," he says. Until tonight, he has never called Rapid Falls my home.

"Get out of my way."

He steps aside and I grab the handle.

"How could you do this to us?" he says to my back as I open the door.

I turn and look at him blankly. I've done so many things wrong that I can't tell which one he's talking about. I close the door without a word and walk down the street. I'll stay at Anna's tonight. It is the least she can do for me since this is all her fault.

CHAPTER
TWENTY-SIX

June 1997

Jesse slammed the door as he got out of the truck. I waited for Wade to slide out, and then I got out too, stepping around the edge of a huge puddle. Wade slapped his arm across Jesse's back.

"Let's do this!" Jesse said. His voice was loud with excitement. It was contagious, and I felt my anger start to fade as I stared at the fire about two hundred yards away from us. Our graduation night at the Field had begun. We stood on the uneven, muddy ground, just steps from Jesse's truck, to take it all in. The Field was crammed with cars and trucks; Jesse had parked so far away that we were practically in the forest. It was a good sign. It was only 10:00 p.m., and it already looked like this might be the biggest graduation party that Rapid Falls had ever seen.

"Looks like everyone in town is here," Wade said, handing me a can before grabbing the case of beer for himself and Jesse. "This is it, guys. Graduation night."

"Yeah. *Our* graduation night, Wade. We made it," Jesse said reverently. The enormity of his words swept me up in a wave of adrenaline. My grin felt almost maniacal. Tonight was going to be amazing. Jesse would apologize, and we would have make-up sex in the woods. Soon we would leave Anna and her pathetic flirtation. Everything would be fine once we moved away from Rapid Falls. This was our night. Nothing would spoil it.

"Ready?" I said. "Cheers, boys!"

Without hesitation, Jesse and Wade both punctured their unopened beers and gulped from the ragged holes. I did the same. Wade whooped and Jesse joined in; their voices sounded almost beautiful.

Wade popped another can as we walked together, avoiding a few small puddles along the way to the bonfire. I wondered if this was the last time we would ever come to the Field together. I wasn't sure how often Jesse and I would get back to Rapid Falls after we moved. A few guys passed us on their way to the fire.

"Hey, Wade! Jesse! Cara! Right on!" Ross said. I wondered if Anna had seen him.

"Hi," I said.

"This is your night! It's awesome," Ross said.

"Whiskey for all!" Wade shot a smile at me as he pulled a bottle out of his back pocket. It was the Rapid Falls equivalent of champagne. Wade was planning to share it with anyone who congratulated him.

"Sure! Let's start the night right," Jesse said, looking straight at me.

I allowed him a smile as I took his jacket off my shoulders. I could tell his words were the beginning of the apology he would give me later. "Do you want your jacket back?"

Jesse hesitated. It was a tradition in Rapid Falls for the guys in the graduating class to wear their jackets at the Field, but I could tell he was worried about upsetting me.

"Aren't you cold?"

"I'm fine, Jesse. You should have it."

"Okay, sure." He nodded and smiled as he slid the white leather back over his shoulders.

"Big party this year," Ross said. He was right: it was bigger than any I had seen before. All around us, vehicles heaved over the bumpy road, searching for parking in the jumble of wandering people and haphazardly stopped cars and trucks. Wade lifted the bottle of whiskey in a toast to a truck whose occupants screamed wildly at us as it passed. He thumped on the tailgate a few times.

"Who was that?" Wade muttered to me.

"No idea," I said. It was pitch-black, save for the light from the roaring fire. We walked closer. I could see dozens, maybe even a hundred people, as the light got stronger. Cheers rang out as people noticed our arrival. Wade was engulfed by his farmer buddies and pulled over to a tailgate. Jesse and I followed.

"Shots!" Wade cried. Someone must have wished him well. The three of us took turns passing around the bottle before we gave it to the farm boys. I winced slightly at the burn, hoping I wouldn't be asked to drink any more of it. I nudged my way toward the fire. I wanted to check out the rest of the party. Whiskey made my mind dance with the idea of finding Anna and telling her what I really thought of her film-school application. People grabbed my shoulders and squealed as I walked through the crowd.

Someone called, "Congratulations, Cara! We graduated. Can you believe it?"

"I know! It's amazing!" I kept walking closer to the fire, smiling at people as I moved past them. I wanted Rapid Falls to remember this night forever, and when people spoke about it, I wanted them to say my name. A couple of young girls eyed me as I squeezed by them.

"That's Cara Piper," one said.

"I know. She's so pretty."

I smiled at them smugly. I finally got close enough to the fire to feel its warmth. The inner circle was mostly graduates, but there were a few guys in their thirties and forties who attended nearly every party at the Field. Someone had pulled up their truck and was blasting AC/

DC. The tailgate was packed with people. I noticed Debra, the student council president, standing by the fire.

"Hi, Debra!" I walked over.

"Cara! You looked so beautiful tonight."

"Thanks. I loved your dress too," I lied. I didn't remember seeing her.

"Thanks. My mom had it specially made."

"So pretty."

Voices swelled around us. Through the crowd, I could see Wade and Jesse were now standing on a tailgate. Wade was pouring a beer into a funnel attached to a hose that Jesse was holding. I couldn't believe he managed to look sexy even while gulping from a rubber tube. I realized that it didn't matter that Anna thought Jesse was hot. He was hot. And he was all mine. We had the rest of our lives to be together. Jesse was the only guy I had ever loved. When he looked into my eyes, I knew he could see the real me. I didn't have to be near him to know what he was thinking. Right now, he felt sorry for being such a jerk to me. Our fight earlier was just a game we were both playing. He loved me and would always love me. I didn't need to be impatient for him to ask me to marry him. Tonight was the beginning of the rest of our lives. We had all the time in the world.

"So, Cara." Debra caught my attention. "What's next for you? What are you going to do after graduation?"

"I'll be here for the summer. Then college in September for both of us." I didn't have to say Jesse's name. Debra knew.

"Awesome."

"Yeah, I'm so excited. You?"

"Not sure yet. I got accepted to a couple schools. But there's the horse camp as well. I might stay on to help my mom."

"Oh, cool." I was always surprised when a person wanted to stay in Rapid Falls. I couldn't understand why anyone would choose a life of safety. I wanted possibility. I wanted to live like everything could change in a moment.

Wade stumbled over, the whiskey bottle in his hand nearly empty.

"Come on, Cara. This is all yours, girl." He waved the remaining half inch at me.

"Oh God," I said, grabbing for the bottle and raising it high. "To the class of '97. *To us!*" The crowd erupted in cheers, and I tilted the bottle to the sky, draining the last of it. I looked around to see if Jesse had joined in the toast. I couldn't see him. Every time the conversation faltered, someone shoved another drink in my hand. Wade put his arm around my shoulders, swaying and belting "Don't Stop Believing." People pulled me aside to reminisce even though I'd probably see them at the grocery store the next day. The music was loud, and there seemed to be more alcohol at the Field than could be consumed by the hundreds of people here. It felt like the best night ever.

I stepped away to pee. I walked about thirty feet from the fire and pulled down my jeans to squat. Then I saw Jesse. I was about to call for him when I realized he wasn't alone. He was holding someone's hand, walking to the edge of the woods. Anna's hand. I finished, zipping up my jeans quickly as I followed them. I tripped on a bottle and tumbled hard enough to rattle the teeth in my head. I tasted blood from my tongue. I was about ten feet behind them, two black shadows slipping into the trees together.

I hid. The cries and yells and music from the party faded to a dull hum. I could hear their low voices whispering, but I couldn't make out the words. Then he bent his head to hers. My boyfriend was kissing my sister. Anna was kissing Jesse. They broke apart and Jesse chuckled. His laugh made me lurch forward, snapping a branch. They didn't even notice through the strains of Led Zeppelin. It was like I wasn't there. Anna giggled too. It sounded like they were laughing at a joke only they knew. The joke wasn't on me. It was me. Then their laughter stopped. They kissed again, and I saw his hand brush her chest. He was unbuttoning her top, kissing her neck. Her hand reached down and I heard his zipper. His gasp as she touched him made my stomach turn.

"Oh, Anna," he said. The words felt like they were being sliced into my skin. She bent down in front of him.

I turned and slowly walked out of the woods. Just before I stepped out of the ring of trees, my stomach seized, and I fell to my knees as it emptied violently. I wiped my mouth with the back of my hand and returned to the fire. Wade was there, and I let him sweep me up in an unbalanced hug. He let out another howl. This time I joined in. Rage had made me sober, but I could still act drunk. In fact, I needed to. I had convinced myself that I was wrong about Anna and Jesse. I had ignored what I knew to be true. But I was right, the whole time. Jesse knew me better than anyone else in the world, but he had chosen her. She had won. Again.

Wade had another bottle of whiskey, and I pretended to take a big swig when he passed it to me. We made our way back to the music, and I hopped up on the tailgate, letting Wade's drunken conversation wash over me. Images flickered through my mind like Polaroid pictures. The almost kiss between them at Rapid Falls. The way he looked at her when she came out of the house this afternoon. Her video. Then the pictures sharpened. A fight. A puddle. A tire. A river. I smiled and laughed along with Wade and the others, but I was far away. About twenty minutes later, I saw Jesse standing by the fire, alone. Anna must have gone in a different direction to make sure I didn't see her. I wondered how many other times they had done the same thing. I was glad she wasn't there. I couldn't bear to see her face. It was hard enough for me to see Jesse.

His cheeks were flushed and his hair was messy. He looked so happy. He seemed like someone else. He was not the guy I had trusted and counted on and given everything to. He was not Jesse because Jesse was loyal to me and only me. He was not the man I loved. The man I loved was mine and could never be with anyone else. The man I loved always loved me. Unconditionally and unrelentingly and unquestioningly. The man I loved was faithful. Jesse was no longer the man I loved. I turned away from him and interrupted the guy talking loudly beside me.

"Todd Carter! I didn't see you. Good party?" Todd had always had a soft spot for me.

"Cara Piper. How you doing?" He looked at me with a smile. Wade swerved toward us to join the conversation, moving too fast for how drunk he was. He hip-checked Todd, who turned to him with a snarl. Perfect.

"Watch it, Wade," Todd said.

"Todd," I cooed, "Wade's just drunk. Wade, why don't you sit down for a second?" I hopped off the tailgate to make room for Wade and moved closer to Todd. I looked at him wide-eyed, suggestively. It was important that I appeared just as drunk as Wade and, even more important, that Todd noticed.

"Todd, did you bring any wood?" I said, touching his leg. My hand was high enough on his thigh that it seemed impossible for him to miss my double meaning. I shifted my body slightly so Wade couldn't see. Todd's mouth hung open as he looked down at my hand, and then he grinned.

"You know it." He reached toward the back of his truck and threw a round of wood into the fire, a little too hard. Sparks showered on a few people, who stepped back.

"You're crazy," I squealed. The group around the fire laughed, and Todd looked at me, proud of himself.

"Plenty more where that came from," he said. Jesse looked in our direction as Todd threw another piece of wood and sparks rose again. I looked across the red glow and caught his eye. He smiled at me like my sister's lips hadn't just been all over his body.

I mouthed the word *hi*.

"Hi," he mouthed back. "I'm sorry."

I smiled at him. He had no idea how sorry he was going to be.

"I'll be right back, Todd. Wait for me." I leaned forward, blocking Jesse's view as I whispered into Todd's ear. "I'll make it worth your while."

He turned to me, surprised. "I'll wait." He touched my arm, and I pulled back suddenly.

"Stop it, Todd," I said forcefully and loudly. Wade looked up from his drunken nodding on the tailgate. Todd took a step back, confused.

I spoke softly so only he could hear. "I have a burn on my arm. Sorry, you just touched it. It's sensitive."

He nodded. "I'm going to take a piss," he said.

"Wade?" I said after Todd left. I arranged my expression into one of hurt as I whispered, "Can you come meet me and Jesse in, like, five minutes? We'll be over there." I gestured toward Jesse.

Wade blinked at me slowly, then nodded. "Are you okay, Cara?"

"Not really," I said sadly. "I'll tell you in a second. I just need to talk to Jesse first."

Wade nodded, and I could see the gears in his mind beginning to grind. Wade liked to fight when he got drunk. I just needed to give him a reason. I walked over to Jesse, willing my eyes to be as hurt as they should be, pushing my hair from my face in a way he once said he liked.

"Hey, Jesse," I said.

"Hey back." He grabbed me by the waist. He always grabbed me there. I wondered if he did the same thing to Anna. I tasted bile.

"Am I forgiven?" I said as playfully as I could.

"For what?"

"God, Jesse. Can't I just apologize?" My tone was too sharp, but I couldn't stop my real feelings from bleeding through. I needed to curb my temper. "I mean, I don't want to fight anymore. Let's make up."

He smiled widely, like it had all been a joke. "Okay, okay. I forgive you. It's graduation night after all."

"Okay. That's better." I leaned in and kissed him. He tasted like beer and strawberry wine coolers. I tried not to gag as I kissed him again. When I pulled away, there were tears in my eyes, but I hoped it was too dark for him to see. I looked down. "I'm so glad I found you. This party is getting . . . kind of weird."

Wade walked up. At least I could still count on someone.

"What's going on?" Wade stood shoulder to shoulder with Jesse, and they looked like an unbeatable force. Just what I needed.

I pressed my lips together, like I couldn't bear to speak. "It's . . . Todd Carter. He grabbed me and tried to kiss me. He said . . . he said I was asking for it."

Wade swore loudly. Jesse grabbed my shoulders. "When did he do this?"

I looked at him hard. "About twenty minutes ago," I said, just to see his face when he realized that was when he was in the bushes with Anna, but it was too dark to see if his expression changed.

Wade said loudly, "I hate that guy. Let's go get him, Jesse."

I made an innocent expression. "I wasn't flirting with him, Jesse. You know I'd never do that to you."

"Of course. That guy is a dirtbag."

"Come on, Jesse." Wade pulled on his arm, and they left me behind in their blood rage. I stayed at the edge of the crowd to watch them bump and jostle people out of their way on their path to Todd.

"Hey, you fuck!" I heard Wade yell and then the sound of a fist hitting a face. Cheers roiled up like they always did at the Field when there was a fight. I waited a couple of minutes before I broke through the crowd, calling Jesse's name.

"Let's go, let's get out of here." I struggled to hold on to his flailing arm.

"No way!" he yelled, his nose pouring with two streams of blood. He had a lump beginning on his forehead. I finally got a solid grip on his jacket and jerked him out of the furor, far enough away that the spectators crowded us out, eager for a glimpse of Wade landing another blow. I pulled his panting body back across the Field to his truck near the edge of the woods. We could barely hear the fight from there.

"Cara, Wade is on his own. I need to help him."

"Jesse, please don't fight anymore. You're all beat up!" I said through fake tears.

"I'm okay, I'm okay." He stumbled, looking back at the crowd of people. It sounded like Wade was still pounding on Todd. Good. It would help if there was blood.

"Jesse, your face. It's cut. Let me take care of you." I pulled his hand hard. "Please."

"Okay, okay." His breath calmed slightly, and he leaned toward me. "I just . . . no one should ever touch you like that, Cara."

"I know, baby, I know." I brushed his hair from his bruised forehead gently, like I still loved him. "Give me your keys. I'll turn on the light so I can see the damage."

Jesse reached into his pocket. "I guess I'm a lover, not a fighter," he said with a small laugh, pulling his hand away from his nose. The white sleeve of his jacket was covered in blood. I didn't laugh with him, but he didn't notice. I couldn't pretend anymore.

"Have you seen Anna tonight? I haven't talked to her yet," I said. I sounded like I was reciting lines.

"No," he lied. I felt my skin crawl.

"Oh. I guess I'll just have to find her myself." Jesse didn't notice the threat in my words. He was too busy ministering to his wounds with the sleeve of his shirt, like he was the hero in the story. I touched my neck, undoing the clasp of the locket my dad had given me. I let it slip into the puddle while Jesse dabbed his nose.

"Oh no!" I cried, kneeling suddenly. "I think I lost my necklace! Oh, Jesse! It's the one my dad just gave me. It fell into the water. Can you see it? I'll turn on the headlights."

I stepped into the driver's seat and watched as he leaned forward, placing his hands and knees on the ground beside the puddle. His face was just inches from the water. His back lined up perfectly with the front tire of his small truck. He was making it easy for me. All I needed was a little pressure.

"It must have fallen to the bottom. Please find it, Jesse!" I said. He lay down on the dry ground beside the puddle, reaching a hand inside the murky water. I started the truck.

CHAPTER TWENTY-SEVEN

September 2016

I wake up before Anna's bedroom starts to turn gray with the light of dawn. I have to go get my car before Rick and Maggie get out of bed. My head pounds with each movement as I pull on the same clothes I wore to work yesterday. My stomach cramps as I catch a whiff of gin on my blouse. My mouth feels like I've swallowed paste. The streets are empty and pink by the time I get to our house. As I pull away, I wonder if the sound of the garage door opening and closing woke Rick. I hope Maggie slept through it.

I'm an hour out of Fraser City when my hangover hits with full force. A pounding mixture of poison and shame makes my hands shake. I left Rick. I pull over. I need gas. I need to call work. Then my father. I take out my phone and leave a quick message to tell Larry I won't be in today as I fill the tank. After I hang up, I stare at my father's name on the screen for long seconds before the click of the gas pump startles me into action.

"Dad?"

"Hello, Cara."

"I'm . . . driving there. To Rapid Falls."

"Oh."

His silence makes me want to hang up, turn around, undo things, but I can't. I have to come back.

"Is that okay?"

"Anna will be here."

"I know."

He hesitates again, but I pretend not to notice.

"I'll see you in two hours."

His sigh fills the line, as if something heavy has crushed his chest. "Okay."

I buy a coffee. The smell makes me nauseated, but I need to find a way to clear my mind. My lips feel chapped; I imagine Brian's mouth on mine. Remorse fills my body with a low-lying dread. As I get closer to Rapid Falls, I keep imagining steering my car over the sheer cliffs, jerking suddenly to the right and hurtling myself into oblivion. Being alone feels dangerous, but the thought of being with other people feels worse. I wonder what Rick is telling Maggie right now. It's Thursday. I should be leaving for work, kissing her three times on the lips and winking as I whirl out the door. I have never been missing in the morning before.

I press the gas, and the BMW hums back onto the highway. A few trees have begun to change. It is colder here than in the city; fall comes earlier. I catch a glimpse of a deer in the forest, and it makes me think of Maggie mewing on the phone yesterday afternoon. I shake my head. *Don't be stupid. Baby deer don't make sounds. Their silence protects them.*

I blink hard, trying to follow the jumbled thought. Anna and I found a baby deer once. No, it was just me. My mother asked me to grab a handful of tomatoes for our salad when I noticed the quivering caramel-colored fur. It was lying under our lilac bush in the back of the garden. I was so young that at first I was scared, thinking it might hurt me. Then I figured out what it was. Bambi. It was folded in on itself, trembling, small and low in the undergrowth of the bush. I reached out to touch its heaving sides and was surprised by the coarseness of its fur. I wanted to tell Anna, so I turned to run the twenty steps back to the house.

When I got there, my mom and Anna were crying. Anna was in her arms, and my dad was yelling. Anna always cried—she was only four—so I wasn't scared about that. But my mom's face was all red, and her lip was bleeding as she yelled. I closed the distance between us, trying to make sense of what was going on. Tears were running down my dad's face and that made my stomach flip. He never cried. He reached out to me and I ran, calling at my mother's back as she opened the car door. She turned and looked at me. Anna was wailing, ripping at her shirt, and my mom's eyes were pleading. Then they hardened, and she turned on her heel as if she had made a decision about me. Everything felt wrong. I screamed as I realized what was happening. I ran toward the car, but it was too late. My mother drove away.

I turned to my dad, but he was gone. I raced back through the garden and fell onto the small deer. My sobs were so loud that I made it shake with fear as I ran my hands through its brown fur. I thought it was the lilacs and the crying that was making my throat burn. I was only five. I didn't know what the beginning of strep throat felt like. I didn't know that the infection would move from my throat to the rest of the body. Neither did my father, who ignored me for days while the red rash bloomed across my chest. It was Mrs. Turner who noticed when she came to check on us. She told me to keep a wet towel pressed against my eyes while we drove to the hospital. She told me it was to cool my fever, but now I realize she didn't want me to see the welts that had spread across my face and body. I thought my mom would meet us at the doctor, but she never came.

My light blouse feels wet with sweat when I pass the sign marking the outskirts of Rapid Falls. I can't go into my dad's house yet. I need more time. It all started here. With Anna. I take the route to the diving rocks. The road is rougher than I remember, as if no one uses it

206

anymore. My legs are stiff when I get out of the car and start to walk down the narrow path. I have to turn around when I start to stumble in my heels; I will never make it down the steep slope. I can hear the river in my ears as I walk back. I remember when it used to lull me to sleep. Now it just seems like a dull roar.

I get back into the car and head toward the center of town. There is a new traffic light at the intersection where Anna stalled my dad's old Cadillac when she first learned to drive. It's red when I pull up despite the fact that there is no other traffic. A new grocery store has been built on the highway by the Rapid Falls Inn, leaving Mr. Johnson's store, where Jesse once worked, abandoned and derelict. A new playground stands empty and forlorn. Rapid Falls seems sadder than I remember it. But it feels like there's an anger here too, simmering below the surface, as if the town resents its own failings. I can see it in the peeling paint of the church where they held Jesse's funeral and in the overgrown, weedy lawns in the park. I can feel it as I drive over the river, which looks black and furious.

I pass the turnoff to my dad's place and keep going up the dusty roads that I've visited more times than I can count. I'm driving to the Field. The back end of my car scrapes the rocks that erupt out of the overgrown road. Branches rake my windows, like fingernails scratching down an arm, pleading for mercy. I park at the top of the hill and look at the Field for the first time ever in broad daylight. It would be a lovely meadow if it wasn't so fouled by the things that happen here. Plastic six-pack rings and crushed cans mar the grass every few feet. Brown broken glass glints ominously in the places where footsteps have crushed any chance of something growing. I look at the woods. Jesse seemed so happy that night. I wonder if I ever made him feel like that. I wonder what he had been planning to do with the ring. As I step toward the green trees, rage fills me. I realize that I have never stopped feeling it. For years I had it under control. Now, as Anna threatens to ruin my perfect life, it is rising again.

After three years in prison, Anna came out broken by the weight of her guilt over what she had done to us. I walked away from the accident almost unscathed as far as anyone could tell. It had felt like enough back then—a punishment for each of them to fit their crimes. Death for one, destruction for the other. I thought that they had destroyed me. But they didn't. I thought it was over. But it's not. My survival proves that I did the right thing and that I would know how to do it again. As I stand in the Field, sunlight breaks through the overcast sky and shines directly on me. It feels like confirmation. I am calm. I'm ready to go home now.

I take the back way home, even though the metal of my car screams in protest at the sharp rocks scraping its undercarriage. As I cross the bridge over the river, I close my eyes and will it to keep its secrets. Everything, including Jesse, stayed at the bottom of the river. If Jesse's body had been found, things might have been different. It's a strange kind of luck to never have to answer the questions that should have been asked. I don't want it to change now. I drive up to my childhood home. When I walk in the door, it's like walking into a distorted version of my past. My dad has made some changes; the cupboards are a different color and the linoleum has been replaced with laminate. Surfaces are piled high with old mail and empty cans and bottles. The kitchen table is buried under boxes of fishing gear, books, and magazines.

"Hello," my dad says. He closes the fridge and passes me a beer. My hands feel clammy at the thought of drinking again, but I take it anyway.

"Anna is in the attic," he says.

"Okay." I open the can and drink. My pulsing headache lessens.

"She said she wanted to go and look through some of those old boxes. Needed a little time to sort things out, she said." He rocks back on his heels.

"What is she looking for?" I distract myself from my panic by looking at the tangle of golf clubs wedged in the corner of the kitchen behind an old rolled carpet and a couple of pairs of boots. I need to know, but I can't appear too eager.

My dad looks at me and opens his mouth to say something. Then he closes it. We stand in silence for a moment.

"It's good to see her," my dad says. He offers no similar sentiment for me.

"Yeah. It's good of you to have her," I say, forcing down the urge to gulp my beer at his indestructible favoritism, even after all these years, even after everything she's done. "She doesn't have anywhere else to go," I say.

My dad nods again, though he doesn't seem to be listening anymore. I take a deep drink as I realize that I don't have anywhere to go either. Anna and I have both burned bridges. The only place she has left to go now is Rapid Falls. Just like me.

"You hungry?" my dad asks. I shake my head. Judging from the contents of the shelves, my dad lives on hot dogs and canned beans. My stomach twinges at the thought. I take another swig of beer to calm it down. The can is almost empty.

"How is Rick? Good?" My dad is awkward, as if he's stuck in an elevator with a person he doesn't like.

"Yep. He's doing great," I lie. Or maybe it's the truth. I don't even really know. Maybe he's glad to get rid of me.

"Maggie?"

"Good." I struggle to think of an anecdote before I remember that my dad doesn't care about my daughter.

He shrugs. "Want to sit down?"

"Sure," I say. We walk to the living room, where heaps of old newspapers and more empty cans litter the coffee table. Silence. We have run out of things to say. My dad clears his throat.

"It's really nice of you to let her stay here," I say again.

"She's always welcome," he says. I finish my beer. It helps me not to think too deeply about what my dad is really trying to tell me.

My dad looks uncomfortable as he pushes an issue of the *Rapid Falls Times* toward me. "They did an article in the paper last week about the twenty-year reunion for your class. Looking for volunteers to get it organized, I guess."

I nod, willing my face not to show revulsion at the idea of attending the event. "Huh."

"Must be hard to come back here, have it all stirred up again."

"It feels like a lifetime ago to me." I sigh, trying to indicate boredom.

My dad looks at me. "I guess it would. I guess there's a lot you'd like to forget."

"It was a long time ago," I repeat.

He pauses. "Ran into Wade the other day. You keep in touch with him?"

"Uh, sort of." If you count liking each other's posts on social media.

"He's doing good. Married one of the Smith girls. They've got a couple of kids now. Asked about you." My dad finishes his beer. "Another?"

"Sure."

He opens a camping cooler beside his armchair and pulls out two more. The beer is lukewarm, but I don't care. I'm just happy to have another drink in my hand.

My dad fiddles with the pull tab on the can. "Been thinking a lot about those days," he says without looking at me. *Me too,* I think.

"Pretty tough time," my dad continues. I nod, sip my beer, and lean in. This is the most my dad has said about any of it in years.

"You know, when Anna started asking about all that stuff, I looked through a few boxes. Found these."

He reaches beside him to the top of a teetering pile of magazines and grabs an envelope full of photos. I open the orange flap and pull out the glossy paper. The photos are of Jesse, Anna, and me the afternoon before prom. I nearly drop them. My dad plucks the one off the top and holds it up to me. It's a candid shot that my mom must have snapped when we weren't paying attention. I am fussing with the hem of my dress. Jesse is looking at Anna and smiling like his world is about to begin.

"I remember your mom taking these."

I nod. I can't stop looking at Jesse's eyes.

"I saw them once. Just the two of them. Anna was filming that movie." He frowns. "They looked close. Really close." He meets my eyes and holds them. His are surprisingly clear and unmistakably searching.

"We were all friends, Dad."

He shakes his head. "Maybe. Sometimes I think I should have said something."

"Something about what?"

I jump when I hear the door to the attic creak open. I hear footsteps, and Anna walks into the living room. She is wearing a denim jacket that's a size too big, like she got it secondhand, but the style suits her. Her hair is clean and her skin is clear. Her eyes look brighter than I've seen in years. As she approaches us, I see my dad slip the photos back into the envelope, out of sight.

"Anna." My dad steps toward her with his arms outstretched, and they hug. I shrug my shoulders to try to get rid of the crawling sensation on my neck.

"Hi, Cara."

I nod at her. "Hi." She has a strange look on her face. I wonder if she's waiting for me to hug her too.

"Did you find what you were looking for?" my dad says.

"Not all of it. But it's okay. There was some stuff . . . I really needed to figure out." Anna has tears in her eyes, but I ignore them.

"Like what?" I say. She looks over at me with an unreadable expression.

"Oh, you know. Just high school stuff, I guess." Anna smiles just like the goofy sister who's grinned at me a thousand times before. But it looks like a mask.

My dad cracks open another beer, and the sound ricochets. "Maybe there's no point in looking back, Anna."

"You could be right, Dad. But I'm an alcoholic, remember. It's kind of what we do."

I laugh weakly, and my dad sets his beer on the table. "Yeah, right."

"Hey, Anna," I say. Something feels off.

"Yeah?"

"What were you looking for?" *And what did you find?* I want to say.

"Oh, nothing really."

"Want a soda or something? I stocked up on Coke this morning." My dad walks to the fridge. I return to my seat, trying to figure out how to get her to answer my question.

Anna nods. "Thanks, Dad." When he returns, he casually puts his arm over Anna's shoulders. He looks happy. They both do.

"I could really use some fresh air after being in a car so long. How was your drive, Anna?" I say. I need to get her alone.

"Good. It's good to be here. I wasn't sure it would be, but I'm glad to be back." Anna trails off and takes a sip of her Coke. I notice my dad has put his beer down on a low shelf. I place mine on the table, in her direct view.

"It's good to have you here." My dad speaks only to Anna.

"What do you say, Anna? Want to go for a walk?" This time I am more direct.

"Sure, Cara. Maybe in a little while?"

All of a sudden, I feel cooped up like I need to escape, but I try to stay calm.

"No rush." I force myself to smile in what I hope is a nonchalant way. "Yeah, let's hang out for a bit. Catch up with Dad."

"Great," she says.

Silence descends. The TV's dark screen feels conspicuous. When I last lived here, it was the most talkative member of our family. I thought the quiet had been suffocating before Anna pleaded guilty. But after she went to jail, it grew even worse. I left to escape it, but now I'm right here in it again. Anna is preoccupied, I can tell. She taps her foot so fast it almost looks like a tremor. Her hands reach up to her face, and she wipes the slate. Something is definitely wrong.

"Maybe we can go fishing while we are here. You still got some rods, Dad?" I try to fill the silence.

My dad seems just as lost in thought as Anna. He turns to me in confusion. "Sorry, what was that?" There are only three of us in the room, and he still doesn't notice me.

"Fishing? You guys up for it?" I say, feigning excitement.

"Oh. Sure."

"You know what? Let's go now," Anna says suddenly.

My dad looks back and forth between us. His mouth twitches before he speaks. "Sometimes, Anna, it's best to just let sleeping dogs lie."

"What if you can't?" I can hear the tears in her voice even though I keep my eyes focused on my hands. They are acting like I'm not here. Like I don't exist. It makes me want to scream, but I tear a hangnail off my finger with my teeth instead. It doesn't matter how much I do for either of them. My dad will always love my sister best.

"Just be careful. I love you, Anna."

"I love you too."

I clear my throat, but he doesn't speak again.

Anna calls goodbye, and I turn back to see my dad standing at the liquor cabinet, a half-empty bottle of whiskey in his hand, as if beer isn't enough to keep the dogs sleeping today.

CHAPTER
TWENTY-EIGHT

June 1997

Jesse was heavy, heavier than anything I had ever tried to lift. I could drag him only a couple of inches before I felt something in my lower back pull tight. The muddy water from his head and shoulders was all over me. I had turned off the headlights right after I reversed the truck off his body, but the moon was bright. I could see his torso had made an impression in the soft mud during the minutes he had been pinned down like an animal forced to lap water. I was not strong enough. I couldn't move him alone. My plan was failing. Panic painted black spots in front of my eyes. I breathed deeply, willing myself to be calm. I let Jesse's body fall back to the ground.

I looked around quickly. Everyone was still at the fire. *He needs to sleep it off,* I practiced saying. Tire marks marred the white leather on the back of Jesse's jacket. I cursed and peeled it off his body, pulling his flopping wrists out of the cuffs. I shoved the jacket in my backpack, on top of my crumpled prom dress. I carried the pack with me as I stepped deliberately over Jesse and trampled the soft mud where he had lain. I didn't want to leave any evidence.

I plunged my hand into the puddle, feeling for the chain of the locket. When I pulled it out, it was smeared with mud that still felt warm from the weight of Jesse's body. I dropped the locket into the backpack on top of the clothes. I would deal with it later. First I needed to find Wade. Then Anna. I grabbed the bottle of painkillers from the outside pocket of the pack, then crammed the bag back behind the seat. I crushed the pills against the dashboard with the bottom of the vial. My hands were shaking so much that I spilled more powder on the floor of the cab than I got into the small mouth of the wine cooler. I hoped there would be enough. I dropped the empty vial behind the seat as well.

Jesse always kept a gallon of water in the truck, for emergencies. I grabbed it and washed the powder and the mud off my hands as best as I could, swiping water over my face. I used my dress to dry off. My stomach dropped when I looked down to see a deep black stain on my shirt where Jesse's head had rested when I tried to lift him. I climbed back into the cab so I could check on my cleaning efforts in the dim light of the interior. I pulled down the vanity mirror on the passenger side. My face was flushed and my eyes were wild. I realized I was breathing heavily. *Calm down,* I told myself, as I clicked the dome light to the off position. That way, it wouldn't turn on automatically when the door opened. I put the cooler on a stump close to the front of the truck. Then I walked back to the fire, trying to focus on inhaling and exhaling.

I passed another fight, and I stopped to scan for Wade. I wondered if the violence was the result of a casual insult or a real grudge, but then I realized it didn't matter. You set something in motion when you wronged someone. You could count on what was going to happen if you made someone angry enough to hurt you.

Wade was standing at the edge of the crowd, sipping at a beer, looking wobbly and disoriented. The front of his shirt was stained with blood. I could barely believe my luck.

"Hey, Wade."

"Cara! You and Jesse disappeared . . . Where were you? I kicked Todd Carter's ass." Wade could barely focus on me as he took another swig of his beer. Half of it landed on his chin and dribbled down to his collar. Even in the half light of the moon, I could see that it was not the first time Wade had miscalculated the location of his mouth.

"Well . . ." I let the word dangle in the air and looked at Wade with suggestively raised eyebrows. "We just needed a little alone time."

Wade snorted. "Oh, I get it. I get it. Good for you."

"Yeah. Jesse's pretty drunk, though, Wade. He totally passed out in the mud afterward. I can't get him up. Can you give me a hand?"

"He passed out? What a lightweight." Wade spat unintentionally as he laughed. He wiped his mouth sloppily with his sleeve.

"I know. He's wasted." I laughed too.

Wade threw his beer can. "Loser," he slurred affectionately. "Okay, let's go." He stumbled across the uneven ground like a punch-drunk boxer, weaving from side to side. He nearly ran into a parked car. When we got to the spot where Jesse was lying, face tilted to the side, Wade prodded him with his shoe, and I tried not to scream as my nerves rattled.

"Wake up, loser," Wade half yelled. Jesse's body looked somewhat normal, I was relieved to see. I moved to stand near his head.

"Can you grab his legs?" I said as I reached for his shoulders.

"The head's the heaviest part, Cara," Wade said, shoving me aside as he grabbed Jesse under his arms and turned him over, hoisting him under the armpits. His face was staring right at me. His eyes were open. The moonlight made them glint, and I shuddered.

"Grab his feet!" Wade yelled, out of breath. I rushed over and grabbed them clumsily, lifting him toward the open passenger door. "Drop his legs and open the door."

I followed Wade's directions.

"Hop in," he said, and I obediently jumped into the cab as he pushed Jesse's body up onto the passenger's seat.

"Doesn't this thing have an interior light?" Wade asked. "It would be a lot easier if I could see."

I looked up at it, pretending to be confused. "It must have burned out."

"Jesus Christ," Wade grunted, pushing Jesse over. "He's out cold." Wade stepped back and wiped mud on his jeans, and I slid over Jesse and shut the door quickly so Wade wouldn't see his empty stare. Jesse's head lolled to the side and hit the window. His skin looked bluish. He didn't look passed out. He looked dead.

"Yeah," I said, stepping behind Wade to direct his gaze away from the truck. "Maybe I should get him to the hospital. His nose was smashed up when he came back here. It got all over my shirt. Probably yours too." I was taking a huge gamble, but I knew it was what I was supposed to say.

Wade looked down at his shirt. "Cara, I saw the punch he took. It wasn't that hard. I think Jesse just had too much whiskey. My nose bled more than his widdle one." He said the last sentence in a baby voice, designed to mock Jesse, as if he could hear it.

"You're probably right. He just needs to sleep it off." I was relieved that it didn't sound rehearsed. Adrenaline coursed through my body. It focused my mind. I felt sharp. I felt ready. Wade turned back toward the fire, and I followed with the doctored wine cooler in my hand. I needed to find Anna.

We walked back to the party, nodding at people beginning to stream away from the tight circle of spectators. Anna was standing by the fire next to Sandy. They both looked tired, sober people surrounded by a sea of drunks. I needed to finish this. We walked over to her, and Wade slung his arm around Anna's shoulder.

"Little Piper! How's your night?" Wade said.

"Amazing." She smiled, pretending she was having as much fun as she thought we were.

"How are you feeling, Cara?" Anna asked.

"Great. Jesse is completely passed out," I said with what I hoped sounded like gleeful abandon. "We just put him in the truck to sleep it off."

She looked at me with concern. "Is he okay? Was he in that fight earlier?"

I took too long to answer as I tried to contain my rage at her thoughts for Jesse. "Yeah, he's okay. Just wasted. I brought you a wine cooler."

She looked at it dubiously. "I'm pretty tired. If Jesse is passed out, maybe we should just go home."

"Anna, it's my graduation night. I just want to stay a little longer. Have a drink with me!"

"What will Jesse say when he finds out we left him crashed in the truck?"

"He'll never know," I said. It was the truest statement I'd ever made. I felt sick at her familiarity, her assumptions about the man who was supposed to have loved only me.

"Wade, you up for another drink?"

"Sure."

"See! Come on!"

Anna hesitated.

"Don't worry about Jesse. He and I had a private celebration. He's never felt better," I lied, watching Anna's face closely. A flicker of disgust crumpled her forehead, and I dug my nails into my hands to stop myself from tearing at her face.

"Okay, fine, I'll have a drink."

I handed her the wine cooler, watching carefully as she raised it to her mouth.

"Bottoms up!" I held the bottom of the bottle. Her eyes widened, but she still managed to finish the contents in one go.

"Cara! Slow down," Anna said. Her voice sounded froggy and she coughed, trying to clear her throat.

"One more? For the road?"

Anna shook her head but took the can when Wade passed her another drink. I looked around. The music was still blaring, but I could hear truck engines revving as people began to drive home. The party was beginning to die. Wade, Anna, and I sat in silence as we finished our drinks. Anna barely touched hers, and I watched her carefully, hoping that what I had given her was enough. Wade was too drunk to talk. I was too angry. Anna swayed slightly beside me. The stars were beginning to fade. We had to go. She took a step backward and stumbled a little on a bottle behind her.

"Should we call it a night?" I asked.

She grinned. "Lead the way."

"Happy graduation, ladies," Wade slurred as we hugged him. He was slumped forward on a tailgate, the bottle of whiskey hanging loosely in his hand. He waved at the last of his farmer friends still at the fire.

"You going to catch a ride down with them?" I said.

Wade nodded cheerfully and slammed my body with one last hug. Choruses of goodbyes followed us, and Anna smiled happily, waving at everyone like she was the star of the show. Fury crept up my spine. We walked to the driver's side of the truck, and I pushed ahead of her to block her view as I climbed into the middle seat. She seemed wobbly, drugged, but I couldn't take the chance. From this angle, I was relieved to see that Jesse looked convincingly passed out.

"The keys are in the ignition," I said.

"Why isn't the interior light coming on?" Anna asked.

"I don't know. Let's just go." My leg touched Jesse's. I did my best to ignore it. Anna turned the key and the truck roared to life. I shoved a tape into the stereo and turned it up loud. We didn't talk, just let the music flow over us as she navigated around the rocks and craters of the Field, steering toward the back road. Everything in me turned black with hate as I sat sandwiched tightly between Anna and the body of the person I used to love. The back road felt rougher than usual;

tree branches whipped the windshield. Jagged boulders loomed as if admonishing me. Jesse's head rolled, and I squeezed down my disgust and leaned hard against him to lessen the movement.

We got to the main road, and Anna turned her head toward me as she lowered the volume.

"Did you have a good night?" she asked. I could tell the pills were really hitting her now. Her smile looked messy.

"Best ever," I said, pretending to hug Jesse's arm.

"Until my graduation." Anna smirked. She always needed to one-up me. She always wanted what I had.

The sky was lightening. I congratulated myself for getting us away in time. Once the darkness lifted, I wouldn't be able to hide what I had done to Jesse. The night felt like it had lasted a lifetime; I needed only a few minutes more, and then nothing that I did would matter. We would all be lost to a legend of Rapid Falls. It was romantic, in a way. I unwrapped myself from Jesse's stiffening body as the truck hummed on the smooth pavement.

The town was deserted; we were the only vehicle on the road as we passed the ice-cream stand and the lake where we went swimming in the summer. We sailed past the turn to our old elementary school and the police station. Anna was beginning to weave across the road's dividing yellow line as we approached the river. There was a small joint between the pavement of the road and the concrete surface of the bridge, and the truck bumped slightly as the wheels rolled over it. Anna looked at me and smiled again.

"Almost home," she said. She waited for a response. I could have told her that it was dangerous to take your eyes off the wheel. She was driving faster than she should, and she had only one hand resting lightly on the top of the steering wheel. She was too out of it to see my left hand reaching for the bottom of it. I jerked it hard to the right, as hard as I could. Then I waited for the shock of the water.

CHAPTER TWENTY-NINE

September 2016

Anna and I don't talk much on the way to the falls. As I drive, it almost feels as if nothing has changed in the last twenty years. Anna breaks the silence. "I'm glad you asked me up here. I think—"

She stops talking and I don't prompt her. Unspoken words fill the car with expectation, as if the next thing she says will make everything right. But I know it won't. It's too late for that. She looks at me helplessly, and for an instant, her face looks young again. Scared. Fragile. Hurt. "I have a lot to say to you."

I nod as I make the turn into the parking lot for the waterfall. I haven't been up here for decades. The last time, I was with Wade, asking him for something he was more than willing to give but probably shouldn't have been. I should call him. He was a good friend to me, better than he ever knew. We pull into a parking spot. I'm discouraged to see at least half a dozen vehicles. A family is standing by a new chain-link fence that's been built at the edge of the cliff, and a few couples are sitting down at the picnic tables. I get out of the car quickly and start walking down the trail. As I expected, Anna scrambles to follow.

"Let's go past the lookout," I say. Tourists never go that far. The warning signs scare them. Most people don't want to go past the point where the guardrail ends. Anna inhales sharply, like someone preparing themselves to do something they don't want to do.

"Sure." She brushes past me, jostling my arm as she goes by. We pass the picnickers. A few nod in greeting, and I return the friendly gesture. Anna doesn't respond. Her hands are wedged deep in her pockets; her forehead is creased with a frown.

"They seem happy," I say. I'm surprised to hear the note of envy in my voice.

"They're not from around here," Anna says. I laugh, but Anna doesn't. It wasn't a joke. We kick rocks as we shuffle along the path, stopping briefly at the designated lookout. There are a few people taking photos, positioning themselves with the majestic roar of water behind them as a backdrop. We walk gingerly through their photo shoot, earning a small hello from the father and a distracted nod from the mother. The kids ignore us.

The path veers away from the cliff's edge, and we fall into silence as the woods close around us. It's cooler in here, and the light is refracted by the fingers of the cedar trees. I've always liked walking in the woods. I have been surrounded by pavement and concrete for so long that I forgot how peaceful the forest can be. I let Anna get ahead as the trail turns back toward the falls. This part is why the signs were posted. The trail is just inches from the fifty-foot drop to the river and its rocky bank. Anna slows and I match her pace. It's pretty here, more so because every step matters.

"There's a spot up ahead where we can sit down," she says. I nod, trying not to remember when the two of us were here with Jesse, when Anna was finishing her film-school application, but it's too late. I clench my fists hard and release them, trying to dissolve the bubbling anger that is flowing through my body. Anna and Jesse had been laughing at me the whole time. I thought Jesse had invited Anna out of pity, but it was me who wasn't welcome. He had already chosen her. We follow the trail for another few minutes until the waterfall rushing out of the rocks is clearly visible again and the trail ends. We can hear the pounding of the water, hurtling down relentlessly, its journey determined by the inevitable force of gravity. The trees crowd the edge of the cliff here, and we stop and stand inches from the edge. It's the best view of Rapid Falls you can get. And the most dangerous. I can never look at Rapid Falls without remembering the dark world underneath the surface of the water downstream. Jesse's grave. The place where I'd thought Anna and I would die. As our car had fallen into the water, I hadn't known if either of us would make it out. I hadn't cared. I'd never expected to get out of the water that morning. I had no idea that my instincts would take over. I still don't know why I swam so hard to save myself. And her.

"I forgot how beautiful it is," Anna says with a wistfulness in her voice.

"Yeah," I reply. She frowns like I just disagreed with her. We sit down on the warm ground, scooting back to rest on the trees behind us. I wish I had a drink. The afternoon beer with my dad is starting to wear off, and I feel nervous not knowing when I'll have another. I wonder if Anna really believes that she will never have a drink again. She grabs a stick and draws in the dirt, nudging rocks down into the groove she's made. She pushes one too hard and it rolls toward the edge. I watch it fall.

"You know, when we were growing up . . . I thought you were perfect." She is staring at the falls. "Everything you did. I was so jealous of you. You were always Mom and Dad's favorite."

My mouth is dry. "You thought I was their favorite?"

"I didn't have to think it. It was true. Look at where we are now. Mom won't even talk to me. I was always second in their eyes. I wanted to be like you so badly."

My gaze is drawn to the arc of water plummeting its way to the ground. The waterfall is relentless. It pounds through granite, eroding the strength of the rocks, drop by drop.

"I know you did." I can't keep the bitterness out of my voice.

"I came back here today because of that feeling. I need to work through . . . what happened. Dr. Hinkley thought it would help." Her mouth twitches lightly, like she's embarrassed. "I haven't come back to Rapid Falls since the accident. Dad invited me back here so many times, but I just couldn't bear it. I thought it would tear me apart, to be reminded of . . . everything. Now I realize that staying away was worse. There was so much left unsaid."

"What do you want to say?" I force myself not to ask her about the invitations from our father, the secret conversations that she kept from me. I dig what's left of my nails into my palms instead.

Anna is working up to something. What had she been looking for in the attic? What had she found? The divers never recovered my backpack. I always wondered how I'd explain it when the police brought it to me with questions. But they never did.

Anna takes a breath and screws up her eyes, rubbing them deeply as if trying to pull something out of her mind. "Therapy is complicated." She pauses. "At least for me. There's so much I don't remember. I'm trying to work through the twelve steps. I got through the first four while I was in rehab. This time, I want to do it right. I want this to be my last time, you know? No more secrets." She winces and then turns to me, finally looking me in the face. "No more secrets, right, Cara?" There is a threat in Anna's eyes. I nod, though adrenaline prickles my hands. "I got hung up on the fifth step, and I couldn't figure out why. It was only a few days ago that I realized what the problem was. I needed you." She pulls a folded piece of paper from her back pocket. "Number five is that I have to admit to God, to myself, and to another human being the exact nature of my wrongs."

I do my best to meet her gaze, but she stops, seeing something in my face.

"Why are you smiling? Is this stupid to you?" Her voice is flat, but there is anger.

I realize I am smirking and force my face into an expression of concern. Relief has caught me off guard. I was worried that Anna was going to do something real, but she just needs me to go through the same old rehabilitation ritual. She has started and stopped the twelve steps more times that I can count.

"No, no," I lie. "It's just a lot to take in."

"I know. It's a lot." Anna sighs. I convinced her. "Dad has been so helpful. I thought it would be easier with you. But it's never easy with you."

"What do you mean?" I feel a flicker of anger. "I gave you so much."

Anna shakes her head slowly. "You have given me more than you know." She pauses and looks down. "Oh my God. This is so hard." She looks at the falls again, as if trying to gather strength. It seems to work When she turns back to me, her gaze doesn't waver. "You know what a mess I am, what a disaster I've made of my life. I've stolen, Cara. I took fifty dollars from your wallet when you weren't looking a few months ago. Your husband hates me; he thinks I'm disgusting. Your daughter is scared of me . . . She told me the last time I saw her that I smell weird." She stops and stands up, like she can't bear to admit the next thing while she's sitting so close to me. Her back is to me, and her feet are less than a handbreadth from the edge of the cliff. The implication is clear. She would rather put herself in danger than sit beside me.

"I took Jesse away from you."

My hands flare like they've been submerged in freezing water again.

"The night of the accident, I only had one wine cooler, maybe two. I know that. But I took that painkiller from you. And I was so tired." She pauses. "I will never forgive myself for what happened on the bridge. For what I did to you. And to him."

The words of forgiveness I am supposed to say catch in my throat. They feel so sharp that it hurts.

"But that's not the whole story. I took him away from you a long time before that."

My stomach feels frozen solid. I meet her eyes without a word.

"I loved Jesse," she says.

I say nothing. I feel the churning of the falls as if it were driving the blood inside my body.

"And he . . ." Tears begin to fill her eyes, which still look angry. "He loved me, Cara. We loved each other. He was going to tell you. He was going to break up with you."

I stand up so quickly that Anna jumps. "You are a liar. What is wrong with you?"

"I'm not lying." She swallows hard. "It started as a joke, sort of. I was so angry at you, for what you said to Ross. You made him break up with me, and you didn't even care. You always took things from me. You never wanted me to have anything good. So I started flirting with Jesse. Just to piss you off. Then . . . it turned real. Neither of us meant for it to go so far, behind your back. We both felt terrible, but it seemed worse to tell you right before graduation and prom. We didn't want to ruin it for you."

"Anna. Stop this." My voice contains more fury than I've ever allowed myself to show to her. To anyone. Her words make no sense. They wanted to protect me until prom only to destroy it all later? The logic is so adolescent that I realize it must be true.

She reaches into her pocket and pulls out something shiny. It's a ring. The ring that Cindy used to twist on her finger and tell me one day would be mine. The ring I had been waiting for Jesse to give me. Rage kicks in, and I grab Anna by the shoulders. The whites of her eyes are huge, like a dog hysterical in a thunderstorm, but she keeps talking.

"He gave it to me that morning when we went for a run. He said he couldn't wait any longer. He wanted me to marry him. I didn't want to show you until after graduation was over. I kept it in my jewelry box, and I never ever thought I'd want to see it again after he died. I left it at Dad's all this time. I couldn't bear to hold it again. But now I'm ready to close the circle. To tell you the truth."

I see red streaks as I struggle to comprehend her words. My fingers dig into her shoulders, and she winces.

"It was in the attic. The whole time. In a dusty box. I went looking for Jesse's graduation jacket too. I had a dream that it was here. That I could wear it one last time and say goodbye. I got obsessed with it, but it was so stupid. I remember now. Jesse was wearing it . . . that night." She shakes her head. "I need to tell Cindy. I need to tell Mom and Dad. I want his death to be honest. I'm telling you first, though, Cara. I owe you that. I'm so sorry." Fury flows down my arms and makes me hold her even tighter. She tenses, sensing how close she is to the edge. My biceps start shaking.

"Cara, I'm sorry," she says.

I try to imagine living a life that is no longer mine, where history is rewritten and Anna becomes the girl that Jesse died loving. Everyone in Rapid Falls would know that Jesse chose her, that he made a fool of us both. No. I cannot let Anna humiliate me. I cannot be less than her. I cannot face Rick and get him back if I feel so undone. My life is built around being the perfect wife, the perfect mother, and the perfect sister. I cannot be the person I have created if people know that Anna was the best all along.

"I can't help but think what could have happened for us. How happy we could have been." She is still talking. She has to stop. "Jesse loved me, Cara. But it was so long ago. We both need to let him go." She looks at me with pity, and the blood rushing in my ears becomes louder than Rapid Falls could ever be, but I pretend that her words have given me comfort.

"I'm so sorry," I say. It's true. I release her shoulders, feeling relief waft off her like cheap perfume. We are both breathing hard.

"You have nothing to be sorry about, Cara. It was love. We couldn't help it."

"Oh, Anna. I forgive you," I lie.

She reaches up to wipe the slate, relieved of her burden of dishonesty, like I knew she would. Her eyes are covered for only a second, but it's more than long enough for me to shove her, as hard as I can. Rapid Falls is a dangerous place. People die here. Like that girl my dad knew. Sometimes they fall. Sometimes they jump. Sometimes they get pushed.

"Help!" I scream, hoping someone is still within earshot. She was troubled. I was trying to help her. That's what good sisters do.

CHAPTER
THIRTY

September 2016

Rick looks almost impossibly handsome in his simple black suit. His blond hair is shining, and his eyes are clear and bright despite the tears of the past few days. I hope my fitted black dress makes me look as polished and perfect as he looks. I want everyone in Rapid Falls to know that he belongs to me and that we belong together. I want them to know that I made it. That I'm a success. That I left this place behind and I'm not coming back.

"Do I look okay?" I say. So many people are going to see me today. There is so much at stake. He walks behind me, meeting my eyes in the full-length mirror. He puts his arms around my waist and crouches slightly to rest his chin on my shoulder. He gives me a sad smile. It seems to contain a kind of peace that I don't think I will ever find.

"You look perfect," he says.

I had called him the moment I got back from Rapid Falls.

"Cara?" His voice had contained a multitude of angry questions.

"Anna is dead. She . . . killed herself." The words felt strange, even though I had said the same thing to the police officers who had driven me home.

"Oh my God. Are you okay? How did it happen?" There was no anger, only worry. Anna had absolved me. Finally she had paid me what she owed.

The tears that caught in my throat as I answered were honest, even if the words were not. "I'm . . . not okay. Not at all. She jumped right in front of me, Rick."

"Oh my God." His sigh pushed through the phone. "This is awful. I thought . . . I thought she was getting better. She seemed okay in rehab. Like she wanted to move forward."

"I should have known, Rick. I should have seen the signs. Last time she tried to kill herself . . ." I paused. It was important that I shift his thinking about Anna's recent behavior. "The psychiatrist at the hospital told me that sometimes people seem to get better right before they finally succeed, like they want to leave everyone around them with the best possible memories of them. As we drove up to the falls, she kept talking about how much she loved us both. I should have figured out she was trying to . . . be forgiven. It's all my fault."

Even over the phone, I could hear the ferocity in my husband's words. "Don't you dare blame yourself, Cara. You did everything you could for her. Everything."

I let his words hang in the air to allow them their full meaning.

"Thanks, Rick. I'm just so tired. Maybe I'm still in shock."

"We are on our way, Cara. I just need to pack a few things. We'll be there soon. I love you."

"I love you too."

Within hours, he had arrived with my mother and Maggie in tow. Immediately he began planning the service, working with the local minister to put it together as quickly and quietly as possible. He really is an incredible husband. I don't deserve him.

As we drive to the church, I let Rick handle the endless toddler patter from Maggie about the birds flying by and the color of the river. I can't let myself be distracted. Rick, my mother, and I have told everyone how despondent and destructive Anna had been in the last few months. We have spent hours talking to the friends and neighbors who have streamed into my dad's house over the past three days. This incident has inspired a lot more visitors than the last Piper family tragedy.

"I wish I could say I was surprised," I heard my mom admit to Sheila Black the day before, as I walked into the living room with fresh coffee for both of them. Her eyes were full of faraway sadness. "She was never the same . . . after the accident." I walked over to my mom and took her hand as Sheila nodded, her eyes full of sympathy and satisfaction, cataloguing every word for retelling.

I smiled sadly at Sheila. "Anna struggled for years. I don't think she ever really accepted what happened that night." People needed to know how troubled Anna was. I was sure Sheila Black would help spread the word.

Rick joined us, taking the warm cup of coffee I offered to him. "This wasn't her first attempt, you know. I guess it was just a matter of time."

I looked at him gratefully. He could not be a better partner.

Sheila nodded, right on cue. "You have all been through so much."

My mom reached over to hold my hand. "Cara carried the heaviest load. She tried so hard with her sister. I think she's the reason that Anna lasted as long as she did."

Rick laid his hand on my leg as he murmured agreement. I closed my eyes, as if overcome with grief. Really I could barely contain the joy I felt at finally being recognized for who I really was: the perfect daughter, wife, and mother. The one who no one would ever leave behind.

My dad is different. The afternoon that Anna died, I returned to his house with two police officers. I asked the older officer to be the one to deliver the news to him. I told them I was too shaken up. My dad nodded unemotionally as the officer spoke. It was clear he was drunk, and I wondered if he was fully comprehending what they were telling him. After they left, he didn't say a word to me, just turned his back and walked up to his bedroom. Once Rick and the others arrived, we tried to get him to join us for meals, but he refused. My mom began bringing plates up to his room, which he left untouched.

Rick offered my dad a ride to the funeral, but he refused that too, saying he'd drive himself.

Rick turns to me and speaks softly so Maggie can't hear. "I hope your dad is okay to drive. Anna's death seems to be hitting him so hard."

"Yes," I agree. "He's taking it very badly." I'm struck by the number of cars in the church parking lot. We are forced to drive past and angle into a spot on the road about three hundred feet from the church. After all these years, there can be only a handful of people in attendance who actually knew Anna. The rest are here for the show.

"Can you walk?" I say to Maggie.

"Walk, balk, talk, gawk," Maggie replies.

Rick smiles in spite of himself. "Let's take that as a yes."

I smile back, but it disappears quickly as I walk to the back seat to release Maggie from her seat belt. I clasp Maggie's hand in one of mine and reach for my husband's with the other. I need to be physically connected to them right now. Maggie pulls hard at my arm like a puppy fighting against its leash as we make our way to the church.

"You ready?" Rick says quietly as we approach the steps.

"No," I say.

"Me neither."

There are no pallbearers holding the door this time. My mom, Rick, and I agreed that we didn't want a complicated service. We need to bury her and move on. As soon as we get inside, a big man walks toward me with arms open. It's Wade, a grayer and doughier version than the one I remember, and he sweeps me into his arms. His kindness nearly undoes me, but I fight my tears as he releases me. Wade shakes hands with Rick just before Maggie sprints away, forcing Rick to weave through the crowd to follow.

"Helluva thing, Cara," Wade says, nodding to a couple who have just entered. They look vaguely familiar to me, but I don't have the energy to try to figure out who they are. "I ran into your dad the other day. He said Anna was getting better."

"Yeah," I say, letting tears come to my eyes again. "They say sometimes that can happen right before . . ." Wade grimaces. "Sometimes they try to make everyone think it's okay. So no one suspects."

"Jesus," he says. We stand in silence in a crowd full of conversation. He smiles gently. "Maybe she felt better because she knew she was on her way to something good? Maybe she knew that her troubles were finally over." Only Wade could find a bright side to suicide.

"I hope you're right." I look through the small groups of people to spot Rick.

"I'll let you sit down. I just wanted to give you my condolences." Wade pats my arm and turns away.

"Thank you." I walk toward Rick, who's holding Maggie in his arms. I scoop her onto my hip and grab Rick's hand. We are united as we walk up the aisle to the first row. My mother is already there, and she turns toward us. A slight hush falls in the pews as we walk. Not like the one that Anna faced. It feels like the people in this church believe in us and are grateful that the Piper family has finally found peace.

No one has asked too many questions, at least not to my face. Sergeant Murphy must be retired by now. I didn't recognize the officers who came to the scene. They were sympathetic as they spoke to me, just like the visitors who came by the house with their too-sweet banana bread and too-solemn faces. They all seem spooked by Anna's suicide, especially since they think of her as a murderer. Maybe they wonder about why she did what she did at Rapid Falls, but they have enough respect not to ask me for too many details. I know this story will be told again and again in this town. They will shudder as they speak of the Piper sisters and how it came to an end, but I realize suddenly that I don't care what they think of me anymore.

We sit down beside my mom and do our best to keep Maggie occupied. Rick eventually relents to her requests and gives her his phone, which he loaded with toddler-friendly games just for this purpose. I hear the crowd's buzz quiet again. I turn to look down the aisle, and I see my father. He walks, his face carved in a mask of grief and his shoulders stooped with the weight of misery. I nod, but he doesn't respond. It seems like it's taking everything he has to walk forward, trapped in the gaze of so many people. He reaches the front and slides into the pew beside me.

"Hi, Dad," I say. He looks at me blankly as if his mind has shut down, as if he has nothing left to give.

The service is simple and short. Rick asked the minister to use a few traditional mourning verses from the Bible and to close with a short hymn. No one from our family wanted to speak. As the minister brings the service to a close, I hear the shuffle of bodies as people ready themselves to leave the church. The minister asks the congregation to respect our family's wishes for privacy and says coffee and baked goods will be served in the Sunday school room in the basement. Rick picked up a huge assortment of pastries from the local bakery and dropped them off early this morning. There won't be a burial. The police had to bring a helicopter in to find her body. The ring was never recovered. It must have fallen from her hand into the river. Rick, my mom, and I had decided that cremation was the best option.

"I'm hungry!" Maggie announces.

"We'll take her," my mom says as she and Rick stand. "We'll give you a minute." They shuffle out of the opposite side of the pew. My dad doesn't move.

I nod at them and turn to my dad. He is still staring at the front of the church even though the minister has left and the lectern is empty. The room empties around us and the conversations disappear. His sadness pushes into me, and I open myself to it. It feels like penance. He breaks the silence with one quiet word.

"Triage," he says.

"What?"

He is still staring at the space where her coffin should be.

"What do you mean, Dad?"

He doesn't respond and I don't ask again. I don't want to know. My steps echo in the emptiness as I walk slowly back down the aisle. As I reach the doors, I turn back. He has not moved an inch. He is still facing the front of the church, hands clasped in his lap, like Anna's only true mourner.

EPILOGUE

September 2017

A year after the funeral, my cell phone vibrated in the middle of a meeting with Larry. It had been so long since my dad and I had spoken that, at first, I assumed he had dialed me by accident. Larry nodded when I let him know that it was my father and I had to take the call. I had told Larry almost everything about my sister when I returned to work. Now that Anna was dead, I spoke about her much more often than I ever had when she was alive. My dad was calling to ask if I could come back to Rapid Falls. He wanted me to be there when he spread his third of Anna's ashes. My mom, Dad, and I had divided them. I agreed, feeling touched, and told him that I would bring mine as well.

The trees on the roadside are painted with dots of orange and red as I drive through the early fall sunshine. I feel grateful for the warmth. Rapid Falls is far enough north for September to be a month of uncertainty. Sometimes it's lovely, and sometimes it's harsher than anyone could anticipate. When I arrive at my dad's house, he is already outside.

"Hi, Dad."

"Let's walk down to the river," he says. He has a small box in one hand, which I assume holds the ashes, and a silver flask in the other. He looks older and thinner than he did at the funeral. I realize suddenly that he has become an old man. I follow him. The fallen leaves on the trail crunch under our feet as we walk down the path that Anna and I used so often as kids. It is overgrown now. My dad must not come down here much anymore. I look around at the layers of fallen branches and dried ferns that make up the dying undergrowth, thinking of the baby deer that didn't survive my touch. I know now that a mother will leave a fawn behind if she detects that taint of human scent.

My dad sits down on a gray log a few feet from the eroding edge of the bank. There is enough space for us both on it, but I stay standing. Some people might think the river is a strange place to lay Anna to rest, but I understand his decision. This river is a part of us all. It was the landscape of our lives for many years. It isn't good or bad; it drowns, it saves, and it never stops.

"I saw her, you know," my dad says suddenly. My stomach lurches and I take a deep breath. He couldn't have seen her. Anna and I had been alone. "Her red hair was so bright. I called out. She was so close. She turned so quickly that she stumbled. I was trying to help."

It takes me a long moment to realize he is talking about the girl at Rapids Falls, not Anna. The girl who died on his class trip. My dad continues, "I knew she was too close to the edge. She was writing in her book. She wasn't paying attention to where she was walking. She fell so fast."

"I know, Dad." I have heard this story before.

"There wasn't anything I could do to help her. I tried and I made it worse."

"There wasn't anything I could do either." My voice is hard. He looks up and our eyes lock. There is no love in his, but that doesn't surprise me anymore. My father hasn't loved me for a long time.

"I thought then that I could change it, but I know now that no one can change the course of events. You think you know who needs saving and how to help. You guess who is in the most danger and how to make it better. Sometimes you're wrong." He turns back to the water in front of us. The river is high. It looks as calm as a lake, but we both know there are strong currents under the water that trap logs under the surface. We can't see them now; no one ever can, but every so often, the rocks shift and the logs shoot to the surface, smashing through boats. We used to call them deadheads.

"I thought I was doing the right thing, every time. I called to her, and she fell. I moved that boy, and he died. I looked the other way, and Jesse drowned. I kept your secret, and I lost Anna. I thought I could make it better, that I knew how to make it all right. I made the calls, and they were all wrong."

His face is dark with sorrow. "Turns out, I don't know a goddamn thing. When she came here that day, I knew Anna was ready to ask questions she shouldn't ask. I should have told her to leave it all alone." He clears his throat. "Some things are best left in the past." His voice changes on the last word, and he faces me again. His eyes are damning.

I want to scream at him to stop talking, but I dig my fingernails into my arm instead. They are long now. I haven't bitten them in months.

"You know, after the accident, it took about a week to haul Jesse's truck out of the water. They had to call in someone from Nicola to help them tow it to the police station. Allen looked it over for evidence, but I got the feeling he wasn't searching too hard. He'd pretty much made up his mind about what happened by then. He asked me if I wanted to take a look and see if there was anything of yours or Anna's that you might want back. The backpack was wedged deep behind the seat." His voice was gruff but steady again. "I was trying to help. I wanted to see if there was anything you or Cindy would want back.

"When I opened it, the mildew had already started. God, it stunk. I was just going to throw it all away, but then I saw the jacket and knew Cindy would want it. I pulled it out to let it dry. There was a mark on the back, Cara."

I stare at the river, as if looking at it hard enough will burn every detail in my mind. I know now this is the last time I will ever return to Rapid Falls. My dad swallows like I do when I'm trying not to throw up.

"I've been a mechanic for a long time, Cara. I know what a tire mark looks like." My shoulders stiffen at the words. "I thought, well, maybe it was on the ground at the Field and someone ran over it by accident. But this one was even and deep. It could only have been made if that white leather was stretched tight over something. Like someone's back."

An acrid smell of rubber and leather fills my nostrils and takes my words away.

"I couldn't sleep for weeks. I didn't want what I was thinking to be true. But then I found the ring, Cara. In Anna's room. I should have told Anna and your mother. I should have told the police. Instead I burned the jacket and put that jewelry box in the attic. I thought that would end it. I didn't think she'd come back for it."

I hope he can't see my hands shaking.

"I saw the way Jesse looked at Anna, Cara. And I saw the way she looked at him back. Sometimes you see things and you wish so hard they aren't true. I thought it would fizzle out, that you and Jesse would leave Rapid Falls and it would all be over. I didn't want to confront a kid about breaking my daughter's heart. I've never been good at fixing things when I tried, so I thought I could ignore it. I thought I could make it go away. But the truth is always there, even if you make yourself not believe it."

I keep staring at the water as I hear him unscrew the cap of the flask and take a long drink. I can't look at this river without feeling cold, even when the sun is on my shoulders.

He has waited so long to say these words. Maybe he thought he would never have to say them at all. He starts speaking again, but his voice is so quiet I can barely hear him over the whisper of the river.

"The whole town had turned against her. I needed to keep one of you out of prison. I thought it would be enough to save her. I couldn't prove what you did, and I knew just saying it out loud would tear us all apart. Especially Anna. I thought she could survive prison better than she could survive knowing what you did to him. And to her. I thought you would let it go. After you took Jesse away from her." My dad reaches into the pocket of his light jacket. "I was wrong. I've always been wrong."

He sounds so tired.

"I can't prove anything, Cara. But proof isn't the same as knowing. I can't imagine you'd ever want to come back here." He stands up.

"I found another thing when I went through that backpack. You can take this so you don't forget."

He stands beside me and slips something cold and small into my hand. I close my palm around it without looking down. He opens the lid of Anna's urn, and in one sweeping arc he spills her remains into the river. Her ashes lift in the air and fall like gray rain. I stare at the water as my dad turns back up the trail. I wait until I can't hear his footsteps anymore before I open my hand.

It is the locket my dad gave me on the day of the prom. I pop it open, and my eyes scan the words cut into the metal. JUNE 24, 1997. The date of my graduation. The anniversary of Jesse's death. Underneath, there is a new line of writing. The etching is messy, done by an unpracticed hand.

SEPTEMBER 15, 2016. The date of Anna's death. The locket seems to burn in my palm, so I hurl it straight into the icy river. It barely breaks the surface of the water before it sinks. I open the lid of my box and send Anna's ashes into the water right behind it. It's over. I turn my back on the river and walk up the steep trail.

ACKNOWLEDGMENTS

This book contains nearly 76,000 words, and it took almost that many people to get them to a place where they could be read. Now it's time to say thank you.

Rapid Falls is about a family, and it could not have been created without the love and support of my own. Ben, thank you for always picking me up when I fall. Your love has made my dreams come true. Morgan, you kept telling me that this fantasy could be real, and it gave me the will to make it so. I will always need you and always love you, and two out of three ain't bad. Marc Hollin, my admiration for your incredible intellect and impressive wit knows no bounds. Since the moment we met, I've been trying to impress you; I hope this book does that. Kim Slater, you are fearless and fierce, and I'm so grateful that you help me find those qualities in myself, thankful for all that we've shared together, and excited for everything else to come. Viceroy Nash, you told me not to stop trying, and because of you, I didn't. Eve and Thompson, my incredible children, you are the biggest reason that this became a real live book and not just one on my computer. You gave me the courage to show you that you can be whatever you want to be when you grow up.

To my grandmother, Joan Jacobsen. Thank you for all the love and licorice, and thank you for always being my biggest fan. Some days, knowing you might hold this book in your hands was the only thing that kept me going. I hope Grandpa Dale would be proud. To my grandparents, Helen and Myron Smith. Thank you for your kindness and the belief that I could write. Thank you to my father, Deryl Cowie; you showed me the force and beauty of a river and taught me how to love and respect the forest. For my mother, Ava Perraton: you gave me the knowledge that books are magical and contain worlds beyond my own. Darlene Cowie, you shared the inside secrets of a librarian and kept me working hard at improving my punctuation. Chris Cowie, you inspired my wicked sense of humor. Carla Wilson, you showed me how to make darkness beautiful. Dale and Linda Jacobsen, your enthusiasm and belief that this book could actually be published stopped me from giving up. Linda and Ulrich Hollin, your unending kindness and support made me believe in myself and have helped me through some of my hardest moments. Jeff and Joanne Greenberg, thank you for your insight and encouragement. Jasper and Emmerich Hollin, thanks for being such awesome and amazing nephew dudes. Natasha Matieshyn, Griffin, Siryn, and Phoenix Cowie, thank you for your strength and the joy and happiness you bring to my life. Lucas Cowie, thank you for your stories.

Thank you to the amazing editors of Lake Union and Amazon Publishing. Thank you, Alison Dasho, managing editor extraordinaire, and my very own Diana Barry, for believing in me and my work, for the fantastic book recommendations, and for always getting my jokes. Shannon O'Neill, I couldn't have asked for a more gifted developmental editor. Your skill and intelligence prompted me to answer questions that I didn't know to ask.

Signing with Fuse Literary made me feel like the newest member of the Avengers. Thank you, Gordon Warnock, skilled agent and fount of knowledge, for your wisdom, your guidance, and your astonishing sense of timing. Your messages stop my mind from spinning before my thoughts start to change my center of gravity.

Thank you to one of my most valued readers. Mallory Windsor, you told me that you were my first fan. Those words, and the hundreds of others that you have sent to me, compelled me to keep trying and fight through the dark days of rejection. This book would not have been published if it were not for you.

Stella Harvey, celebrated author and force for all things literary in Whistler, your mentorship, encouragement, and unflagging support are a gift beyond measure. You are a model for me as a woman and a writer. I admire you so much. Lynn Duncan and Kilmeny Denny at Tidewater, thank you for seeing something worthwhile in my manuscript. Your expert eyes and valuable critiques made my work better and helped quiet my doubts.

To my dedicated, brave, and stunningly patient beta readers and friends: Christine Lee, your love of wonderful books and your excitement for what I do have made my work better. Heather Davies, I've always been so proud to know you and love you. Your willingness to put up with the roughest of my drafts and give me exactly the tools I need to improve it has deepened my love and appreciation for you and our wonderful friendship. Given Davies, you lend me a perspective that is unique and invaluable. I've never heard your thoughts on my work without knowing they will change it for the better. Jan and Jenne Pratschke, somehow you find space for me in the madness of your world, and the gift of your time is something I will never undervalue. I can't wait until you take my books around the world on your sailboat. Seth Hollingsworth, there are so many lines from your critiques that I repeated in my head like mantras. You gave me hope, and I can't wait to blurb your first book.

For my fantastic friends who believed in me—thank you always for the awesome and encouraging messages, texts, and visits: Tasha Sargent, Kate Rose, Jon Bennett, Megan Hetherington, Justin Ford, Nicole Chomechko, Chris Berry, Anne-Marie Belanger, Kate Leslie, Paul Johnston, Alex Merrick, Nicholas Scapillati, Kas Shield, Alison

West, Grant Matzen, Bridget Ku, Dennis Ku, Orissa Forest, and Dennis Van Dine. Thanks to Nicole and James Thomson, for giving me the space to write.

Finally, thank you to the incredible and supportive network of Lake Union authors. The bench is deep, and everyone has already taught me so much. I am deeply grateful for the work and support of you all and the incredible kindness of Emily Carpenter, Kerry Lonsdale, Catherine McKenzie, Barbara Claypole White, Barbara Davis, Jenn Sy, and Dina Silver. I am so grateful and excited to be part of this team.

READER GROUP QUESTIONS FOR
RAPID FALLS

1. Duality plays a huge part in the narrative: hiding one's true self (in Cara's case) or being out of touch with one's true self (in Anna's case). How does the structure of the novel work to enhance the theme of duality? Are there any characters who present themselves truthfully throughout?

2. Many people are hurt deeply by their sisters and their partners, yet few resort to extreme measures, as Cara did. What drives Cara's decisions, both as an adolescent and an adult? Is her primary motivation love or fear?

3. Why is Cara so desperate to leave Rapid Falls as a teenager? How do her adult circumstances (a husband from a wealthy family, a comfortable standard of living, an influential career) contrast with her childhood circumstances? Would she have been as ambitious if she'd been raised in a bigger city or in a family with better financial circumstances? Would she have been as ambitious if her sister hadn't been applying to film school? What draws Cara to a life of politics?

4. Is Anna a sympathetic character? Her sister frames her for murder and the town shuns her; she also makes self-destructive and selfish decisions. Can her shortcomings be explained away by the unjust label she was given in her teen years?

5. Why do you think Cara works so hard to prevent her sister from successfully committing suicide in her first few attempts? Is there some small part of Cara that feels guilty for what she did? Is she keeping her sister close to ensure that the truth never comes out? Or does she believe the life that Anna is living as a result of her addiction to be punishment for her crimes?

6. Jesse is an attractive boy who is well known in the small town of Rapid Falls and well liked by Cara and Anna's parents. What makes him compelling enough that Cara would be willing to kill for him and Anna willing to betray her sister? Is it his own qualities that inspire the Piper sisters to hurt each other? Or is he a symbol of something else for them?

7. How does the town of Rapid Falls contribute to the tone of the novel? Is it significant that residents must cross a bridge to enter and leave the town? How does that kind of isolation affect the older people in town? How does it affect the teenagers? Is Cara's perception of the town trustworthy, or does it seem clouded by her state of mind?

8. What does Rick see in Cara—why did he fall in love with her? If he ever learned the truth about her past, do you think he could forgive her? Can you?

9. What do you think would happen if Cara and Rick ever have a second child? How will Cara's experiences with sibling rivalry and jealousy manifest in her parenting?

10. How did Cara and Anna's parents' actions in the girls' early childhood and following the accident contribute to the way that both Cara and Anna coped with the consequences? What could they have done differently?

11. Do you think that Cara is bothered by her father's confrontation at the book's end? She works so hard to keep up the facade of the forgiving, generous, and caretaking sister. Will it eat away at her to know that her father sees her true self? Or can she dismiss his knowledge because he's essentially given up on being a part of her life?

12. "Even though the river was calmer here, just a few curls of white water over rocks, every time my feet touched the road on the other side, I felt like I had narrowly escaped something. Years later, my high school biology teacher explained vertigo as a sensation caused by an inner ear vibration, but my ears never felt strange when I walked across the bridge. I didn't think I was going to fall. I was worried I was going to jump." Cara justifies her actions as a result of external circumstances and blames her sister for Jesse's death, both publicly and privately, as if his death was inevitable once the two of them hurt her. How are the river and Rapid Falls used as metaphors for the rush of time? How does Cara's perception of herself skew the way she describes the world around her?

ABOUT THE AUTHOR

Photo © 201/ Benjamin Greenberg

Amber Cowie is a graduate of the University of Victoria and was short-listed for the 2017 Whistler Book Award. She is a mother of two, wife of one, and a debut novelist who enjoys skiing, running, and creating stories that make her browser search history highly suspicious. Amber lives in the mountains in a small West Coast town, but you can find her online at www.ambercowie.com.